MAGDALENA

OF

HY BRASIL

A

BLOODLINE OF MARY MAGDALENE

BETTYE JOHNSON

Books by **BETTYE JOHNSON**

Secrets of the Magdalene Scrolls ~ Book 1

Mary Magdalene, Her Legacy   Book 2

Awakening the Genie Within

A Christmas Awakening

An Uncommon Education ~ a Memoir

What the Blank Do We Know About the Bible?

Italian Edition
I SEGRETI RIVELATI NEI ROTOLI DI MARIA MADDALENA

MAGDALENA

OF

HY BRASIL

BOOK 3

A

BLOODLINE OF MARY MAGDALENE

BETTYE JOHNSON

Copyright © Bettye Johnson 2013

This book is a work of fiction. All characters, dialogue and incidents are taken from the author's imagination.

All rights reserved. Printed in the United States of America. No part of this publication may be reproduced or transmitted in any form or by any means, electronic or mechanical including photocopying, recording, or by any information storage and retrieval system without the written permission of Bettye Johnson.

The scanning, uploading and distribution of this book via the Internet or via any other means without permission of the publisher is illegal and punishable by law. Please purchase only authorized electronic editions, and do not participate in or encourage electronic piracy of copyright materials. Your support of the author's rights is appreciated.

Cover art © Kenneth Brown

First Edition

ISBN: 978-1492393764

Dedication

To the women of the world

And

All the Magdalenas

ABOUT THE ANCIENT MAP OF HY BRASIL

The island of Hy Brasil is labeled a myth by numerous naysayers. However, according to others, Hy Brasil could be possibly real. One can find a facsimile of the map on Internet. Actually it appears to be two islands with perhaps a schism or river between the two. One may have a vision of wings of a butterfly in the Atlantic Ocean. To the right is ancient Ireland.

    The island was shown on a Venetian map by Andrea Blanco in 1436 A.D. A Catalan map circa 1480 A.D. named it as two islands – "Illa de Brasil" with one being southwest of Ireland and the second south of Greenland. In 1497 John Cabot reported he had found the island and alleged it had been discovered in the past by men from Bristol. In the 1500's during a voyage, Pedro Alvarez Cabral, a noted navigator alleged he reached the island. In the 1600's Captain John Nisbet along with his crew were in ocean waters off of the west coast of Ireland and their ship became covered in fog. When the fog lifted, they saw an island and with a small crew a small boat was lowered and they rowed to the island. After spending a day there, they returned with a gift of gold and silver. How valid this is, I can only say it is possible. History records Pliny the Elder (23-79 A.D.) alleging the Tuatha De Dannan left Ireland when they were defeated by the Milesians. Perhaps they went to Hy Brasil. This book is a work of fiction based on the possibility there was and is actually an island of Hy Brasil surrounded by mists.

LANGUAGE OF HY BRASIL

Afore = Before
Alrite = all right
Ans = a year
Aye = Yes
Be = was, were, is
Eats = food
Ere = were
'Erefore = before or therefore
Hold = a Castle and land of High Ranking Officials
Magentheld = a ruler of a country with title of Queen or King
Me = my
Nae = No or Not
Naow = Now
Sarma = an island off of Scotland
Tay = tea
Tis = it is
Tyme = time
Yere = you are or your
Yew = you

France

2013

Prologue,
A Disturbing Dream

Dreams are today's answers to tomorrow's questions. ~ Edgar Cayce

Slowly, her consciousness began returning to her. Where had she been? She could hear Peter breathing next to her and usually she snuggled up to him. This morning her dream left her with a sense of sadness and a sense of anger - or was it a dream? She lay there remembering being in another place and in another time. The name Magdalena kept running through her mind. *Who was Magdalena? What connection does she have with the Magdalene?* As she lay there, she recalled that it did not appear to be the period of time when Mary Magdalene lived. Peter rolled over and pulled her to him. He was about to kiss her when she broke into tears. "Hey, what is this all about?" He held her until her sobs stopped.

"Oh Peter! I had a most peculiar dream and I'm not sure if I was in another world or this world. I, I am filled with a mixture of anger and sadness."

"Care to tell me about it?"

"I think I was observing something from a long time ago – in another time. It is hard to keep it in my focus; however, I remember being in an old castle with a woman sitting on a bed with an old man."

"Magdalena? Not Magdalene?"

"It definitely was a Magdalena and she had long red hair and her skin tone was a light brown. Everything seemed to be centuries in the past."

Peter kissed her with a long yearning kiss and the two began their lovemaking climaxing it with each knowing that their love was deep and real.

Ellen sighed. "You always know just what I need to fulfill me. You are truly my dear wonderful love."

Peter leaned over her with his elbow resting on the bed and his hand on the side of his head. "My sweet love, I think this is mutual." He glanced at the clock and at that moment, the alarm went off. He reached over her and turned it off. "Well, my love we timed that pretty well. Let's shower and then make sure the children are up. As I recall, I think today is my day to drive the twins to school."

Peter with the twins Magda and Joseph left for school where he would drop them off while little Eleanor had gone with Yvonne to the Nursery for play and games. Ellen sighed as Marie came in to clear the breakfast table. "You are sad Madame?"

Ellen managed a smile and replied that she had not slept well and would now go for a walk. Marie watched Ellen leave and thought to herself that something was troubling *Mme.* Ellen. She shook her head and began taking the used dishes off to the kitchen.

Purposefully she turned and began walking to the small lake. Her thoughts were churning and she felt confused. When she reached the lake, she walked out on to the small pier and sat down on the bench placed there.

Silently she watched the ducks, geese and swans as they began swimming towards her. She knew that they were spoiled and looking for a handout. A container of grain was nearby to feed the wildfowl and she went to it. Taking a scoop out, she filled it and walked to the lawn where she scattered it for them to come and feed. Within moments, there was a scramble with hissing and squawking. Briefly, she felt her mind lift, and it came to her that it was truly a joy to watch them eat and their antics.

She returned to the bench and stared out over the rippling of the water. A small breeze was ruffling her hair. At any other time, she would have been laughing and feeling lighthearted.

Today, she felt depressed over her dream. *Oh god*, she thought, *please, no more scrolls.* Memories of the time when she and Jill had discovered unknown scrolls written by Mary Magdalene in a cave located in the Pyrenees began flooding her mind. It had been difficult to get them translated with adversaries determined to stop them. She had been kidnapped and dear Peter managed to find her. Briefly, a smile came on her face as she remembered her torrid romance with Peter ending with marriage. In addition, Jill had fallen in love with Sebastian who was responsible for the translations and their relationship had also ended in marriage.

Ellen sighed as more memories came. It seemed, as though their lives were in what one could say is a period of normalcy. She and Peter now had the Twins – Joseph and Magda along with the youngest, a girl Eleanor. Jill and Sebastian now had a boy named Arthur one year younger than the twins and a little girl named Aimée, a year younger than Eleanor. Then there was the second episode of having a mysterious stranger drop a valise of scrolls in front of her while she was walking in the forest with more turbulence, kidnapping, injuries and the loss of a life. Nevertheless, they had continued with the translations of the new scrolls, which had been written by Sarah, the daughter of Mary Magdalene and Jesus.

The thought came to her that perhaps this dream was a prelude of what was entering their lives. Giving another sigh, she told herself *what will be, will be.* With a start, she got up and remembered she had promised Eleanor she would read to her. In addition, there was her job of seeing that everything at the chateau and the grounds ran smoothly. She stood for a moment and said a prayer to her Holy Spirit to fill her with the strength she would need in the days ahead.

Little did she realize what lay before her in the following weeks.

ΩΩΩ

~ HY BRASIL ~
400 A.D.

THE RETURN

The Journey is another beginning.
~ Anonymous

The mist lay heavy upon the water. The oarsmen dipped their oars softly into the silent water while steering the small boat as it quietly moved toward the shore. The mist held all sound in abeyance. There was only silence.

Along with the oarsmen, two figures shrouded in dark cloaks sat immobile in the boat while the mist swirled and danced softly about them. One could wonder how the oarsmen could direct the boat to its destination. There was no compass or instrument to indicate the direction. There was only a knowingness developed over a passage of many years.

Finally, the boat with its two passengers touched land and with a muted grunt, one of the oarsmen swiftly jumped out and drew the boat further ashore. The pair of cloaked figures stood up and began to alight upon the shore. For a brief moment, the mist parted and the light of the early morning sky revealed one of the figures to be a slight woman with wisps of red hair curling out from her hooded cloak. Her brilliant green eyes landed briefly on the figure of the man walking next to her. He was stooped with age – but agile nonetheless.

As the woman and the man began a swift ascent to higher ground, the mist swirled in and around the tall stately trees that abound the well-trodden path. During the brief moments of sunlight, the early morning dew danced in a myriad of rainbow colors upon the leaves of the trees, bushes and plants.

Pausing a moment, the woman inhaled the air of the early morning and turned to face the east. Stretching her arms out wide, she slowly brought her hands to her forehead and bowed low to greet the Isness of all life.

With a pensive look on his face, the man waited for her to resume her walk. Within moments, they emerged into a clearing where a company of six guardsmen were waiting with two horses. Without a word, the woman and the man mounted the steeds and began to canter, which soon turned into a gallop as the group sped to their destination.

The rutted road twisted and turned over small hills and valleys. Smoke curled out of chimneys of the small farmhouses they passed. The sounds of cocks could be heard crowing and there rose a cacophony of sound as though all creation was coming awake. The thunder of the hooves caused some to pause in their early morning routines and with a shrug of shoulders turned back to their tasks.

The morning sun had risen while the mist lay silently upon the river channel from whence they had come. The woman appeared neither right nor left but looked straight ahead. This was deceptive because she used her soft eyes to take in all the scenery and life as she passed.

The nearer the group traveled to their destination, the more houses and activities were seen. At last, the large mansion loomed before them. Its stone structure was imposing. In other realms, it would be called a castle. This was the home of the King, Lord of the Realm also known as the Magentheld.

Green banners flapped in the wind as they hung from the ramparts above the gate leading into the courtyard. Looking up as she passed under the banners, the woman paid a silent homage to the standing Black Lion with a golden serpent wrapped around its body while its head rose above the head of the Lion.

She was home. She was home in the place of her birth. Bringing her horse to a quick stop, she slid down from the steed and handed the reins to a young page who solemnly looked at her with wonder as he led the horse away.

Waiting for no one, the woman walked quickly up the steps to a terrace and into the large double doors emblazoned with the same insignia as the banners. Silently the doors opened as though some unseen hand had opened them.

She entered the large foyer and looking neither to the right nor to the left. The woman mounted the circular stairway leading to the floor above. Passing portraits of the ancestry of the Magentheld, she turned to the right and entered a long hallway leading to the quarters of the King also titled Magentheld.

The guardsmen standing watch at the door to the King's quarters quickly opened the door for her. She paused a moment before entering. As she stepped into the room, she adjusted her eyes to the darkness. The drapes had been pulled closed and the only light came from dimly lit lamps placed around the room. .

The quarters of the Magentheld consisted of one extremely large room serving as his bedroom and sitting room combined. At the north end of the room stood a large imposing bed placed upon a dais. Two women attendants were attending the figure in the bed.

The woman observed a man standing in the shadows as she approached the bed.

The great Magentheld lay in the great bed. The stench of sickness permeated the air. The low ceiling of the room acted as an enhancement of the sick and fetid air. Its original purpose was for keeping the room warmer in the winter and cooler in warm weather.

Stepping into the room, the woman advanced to the sick man's bed. The King opened his piercing eyes of blue – the blue of melting snow waters tumbling down from the great mountains to form ice blue pools.

"Ah, Magdalena," he sighed. "Yew came."

"Did you think I would nae come?" Magdalena did not move and stood waiting for the reason of her coming.

"Yew knows I be dying. It is tyme fer yew to come home."

"Come home! Naow that you be dying, yew think yew can undo all the years that 'ave passed since yew sent me away?" She laughed derisively.

"Enough girl! Yew knows much, but nae enough and is so little tyme." With that, he went into a spasm of coughing. Waving his attendants away, he fixed his great eyes on Magdalena. "Come closer Magdalena." In addition, to the attendants he told them to leave the room.

Magdalena stepped to his side and as he motioned for her to sit on the bed, she sat down beside him.

"Yere pretty like yere mother. It does nae hurt to tell yew naow that she be the love of my life. Love as I could know it. But enough. Yew must listen carefully and remember all I be telling yew."

Nodding her head as a yes, Magdalena sat with hands clasped on her lap and looked deeply into her father's eyes.

"I'm be dying. I've called yew home as yew be the next ruler – the Queen Magentheld."

Gasping with shock, she half rose while uttering, "Oh nae! I cannae. I be a woman! Nae woman ever be ruler of this land!"

"It tis yere destiny girl. Naow listen to me. It be written long ago that one day a great ruler would come. A woman. This woman be to lead her people into a new kingdom. A kingdom of the mind. Yew be that woman."

With utter disbelief, Magdalena laughed. "Me? Yew sent me away 'erefore I be ten ans of wisdom. I 'ave made a life of me own with the Druidesses. I be a healer and a teacher."

"Girl, when yew 'ere borne, yere mother and I both received a vision. We both knew yere destiny to be my successor. We each received the vision separately – that Yew be the chosen one. Yew 'ave been prepared over many lifetimes fer this. Be still and listen to yere inner knowing."

Taking a deep breath, she closed her eyes and sat quietly. Turning her eyes to the within, she allowed memories to surface. Memories she had stifled and ignored all her life. She felt as though she was catapulted into a deep abyss while spinning faster and faster. She expected to hit a hard wall. Instead, her momentum slowed and with her inner eyes, she saw she was in a large temple. In front of her were thirteen columns with thirteen podiums in front of them. Standing behind each podium was a radiant being. Without speaking, each gave her a picture of her previous preparation for this lifetime along with her agreement.

She knew she had been in this temple many times before. The soaring crystal columns rising up to the vaulted ceiling sparkling with the colors of the rainbow, and the floor with its white marble tiles inlaid with gold symbols seemed to be a place of forever. She did not want to leave this radiant energy, however she felt a tug and knew she must return.

Slowly she opened her eyes and looked at her father. "Yew saw," he said. With eyes full of wonderment, she nodded a yes. "This be why yere mother decided to leave this plane when she did. I knew it be tyme fer yew be educated as the future Magentheld and why yew be sent to the Druidesses fer yere further training.

"Yew saw," he again said. With eyes full of wonderment, she nodded a yes. He repeated in his raspy voice. "This be why yere mother chose to leave this plane when she did. I knew it be tyme fer yew be educated as the future Magentheld and why yew be sent to the Druidesses fer yere further training."

"Father, who else knows?"

He smiled when he heard her use the word *father* for the first time since before her ten years of wisdom, the Magentheld replied, "The Holy One and our Lady of the Druidesses."

"Aye. It all begins to make sense. Of course they know." Magdalena spoke more to herself than to her father. Feeling a pull of energy, she looked off to a corner of the room near her father's bed and noted a man standing in the shadows. With a start, Magdalena stood and with her hands clasped she bowed her head. "Greetings Lord Cyran, the Holy One."

Cyran, the Holy One returned her greeting and stepped out from the shadows. His unlined face was framed with a flowing white beard and a mane of white hair, which fell over his shoulders. Peeking out from white bushy eyebrows were piercing black eyes. His countenance was one of strength combined with gentleness.

"I be most happy to see yew again Magdalena. I knew yew to come at yere father's request. Tis naow the prophecy must be fulfilled. Yew 'ave been trained well. Heed what yere father tells yew."

"Thank yew, my Lord Cyran," murmured Magdalena as she once again sank onto her father's bed. Now she took both of his hands in hers and gazed into his icy blue eyes. It seemed as if they were locked into the gaze for an eternity. She felt a powerful surge of emotion well up inside her.

"Magdalena, yere brothers both fell at the last battle with the Skagerraks. They passed on valiantly. Each 'aving played their part in this game of life. They never be meant to rule, but only to hold yere place fer yew. This we honor. Naow the jackals be hounding at our very gates." He closed his eyes for a moment as a spasm of pain wracked his body. When the spasm passed, he continued, "They know I be a dying and with no apparent heirs feel this realm ripe fer the taking.

"Naow listen up girl. There be a few men yew can count on as it tis seen. Kanen, Keeper of the Treasury and Oris, General of the Right Flank, Bosenio, the Arms Keeper as well as Rath, the Trainer of Guardsmen and Hyreck the Historian. They be about all yew can trust. Yew will 'ave to use all yere faculties and yere knowingness. Yew cannae rely or trust Brannon of the Left Flank. He speaks from both sides of his mouth. Yew 'ave the gifts. Use them well."

Cyran signaled to her to follow him. Upon leaving the room, he asked the attendants to remain in the room and issued orders for them to send word to him and to Magdalena immediately when the Magentheld wakened. The attendants bowed and agreed to follow his orders.

Magdalena and Cyran walked to the end of the long hallway and out onto a balcony. "Methinks the very walls 'ave ears," spoke Cyran. "There be much in the wind. There be rumors and there be rumors. Naow is the tyme to strike afore the true state of yere father becomes known abroad."

Nodding in agreement, she replied, "Aye, the very airways vibrate with uncertainty. What be it I am to do?"

"Milady, I pledge to thee my loyalty. I can only be a counselor and an ear fer yew. I 'ave sent fer all generals, captains, lords and ladies to attend a general meeting this night. Yere father will appear to be much improved and will grace them all with his presence. Yew be alert. Watch and observe while betraying no emotion."

"I thank yew my Lord and I understand. Naow, I be off to find my quarters and to contemplate all that has been revealed to me. I 'ave much to contemplate."

Walking purposefully, she went to her deceased mother's quarters. Instinctively she knew they were prepared for her. She paused a moment before reaching out to open the massive door. A woman had completed a floral arrangement and curtsied when she saw Magdalena. "Is alrite M'Lady?"

Seemingly taking in the room with one glance, Magdalene nodded and asked, "How do I call yew?"

"I be known by Mireen," she shyly replied while looking down at the richly woven carpet of roses on a sky blue background. "May I fetch some tay and eats fer yew?"

Magdalena smiled and told her it would be very nice. When the serving woman left, she walked around touching various objects while thinking, *Aye, it be left exactly as it be when her mother lived in it.* She could almost smell the scent of her mother. Her scent always reminded her of roses – red roses.

When the serving woman left, she walked around again touching various objects. *Aye, it be left exactly as it had been when her mother lived in it.*

Walking past a large standing mirror, she stopped with a start. Except for looking into the great pool of water, she had never seen herself as an adult in a mirror. She gasped! It was as though she was looking at her mother with the same green eyes, the red hair with one long braid hanging down the back and wisps of curling hair framing her delicate face. The nose was not too pointed, nor too blunt. The lips were shaped like a small pink bow. She took off her cloak and noticed her breasts thrust from her bodice. Not overly big, nor overly small. With a smile, she curtsied as the figure in the mirror curtsied with her. She took her long skirt in her hands and twirled as the skirt rippled about her. With a sigh, she stopped and thought of the vanity of the flesh. Ah, she had been warned over-and-over of its intoxicating enchantment.

At that moment there was a knock on the door and she knew it was Mireen. She gave the order to enter. Mireen carried in a large tray of tea made from herbs grown in the garden carrying an aroma of a bit of mint to it. On the tray was a steaming bowl of grain cooked in fresh milk and accompanied by a plate of fresh baked bread along with a pot of honey. Mireen deftly went about placing the meal on a small round table and curtsied when she had completed the preparation.

Magdalena sat down and realized she felt very hungry and began eating with a zeal that won the approval of Mireen.

"Me Lady, will yew be wanting me to run the bath?"

"Aye Mireen. That be splendid and I do thank yew."

Magdalena smiled as she remembered the sunken tub in the room next to the bed quarters. Running water! She had never experienced running water in pipes since she left before her tenth year. The Druidesses believed in austerity. Or, could it be living simply without distractions?

Once she finished her breakfast, she disrobed and stepped down into the steaming water. *Ah, it felt so good. I must remember*, she told herself, *nae to get overly enamored with the senses of the flesh. But, it be delightful!* It was very different from the cold-water baths at the commune of the Druidesses!

When she completed washing herself, she stepped up and out of the bath, and allowed Mireen to rub her briskly with a soft cloth and then to array her in a soft robe of midnight blue. She felt glad the robe had not been her mother's and it felt new. For this, she felt grateful.

When she walked into the bed quarters, she noticed Mireen had turned the covers of the bed down. Once her head touched the pillow, she barely remembered Mireen covering her and leaving.

🏛🏛🏛

REMEMBERING

*Can calm despair and wild unrest be tenants
of a single breast. Or sorrow such a changeling be?*
~ *Alfred Tennyson*

She woke with a sense of dread. For one who was almost ten ans, this was not usual. Somehow, she knew that on this day her life would be changing. Snuggling down into the bedcovers, she closed her eyes and tried to think of a happy thought. Her mother always told her when she was feeling sad or lonely to change her thought to a happy one. This time it did not seem to be working to alleviate her concerns.

With a flash of insight, she knew something was amiss with her mother, beautiful Golornia, wife of the Magentheld of the Realm of Hy Brasil. Oh! Her mother must be giving birth to the new babe! It be much too soon! Leaping out of her bed, Magdalena began running out of her room and down the long hall to her mother's bed quarters.

A guardsman stood outside the door looking most solemn. As Magdalena started to pass him and open the door, he blocked her way. "Out of my way! I will see me mother!" she screamed in a loud voice.

Before the guardsman could explain, the great door opened and the midwife of the manse keep poked her face out to see what the commotion be. When she saw it was Magdalena,, her face softened from one of sternness. She turned to the guardsman and told him to allow the young mistress to enter. The atmosphere felt ominous and she paused. When she entered the room, she noticed her father was present along with Cyran, the Holy One. The Birthing Woman motioned her to come to her mother's bedside. Something was very wrong!

Golornia lay pale against the bedcovers. Her red hair now in a long braid and wisps of curls framed her face. Slowly, she opened her pure green eyes and managed to give her daughter a wan smile. Speaking barely above a whisper, her mother told her to lean down as she had something important to tell her.

Magdalena leaned over her mother and took her mother's feverish hands into hers. "Aye Mother. I be listening."

"Me darlin' it will all unfold. Allow it to. Promise me you will do whatever is asked of yew. It be important!"

With tears streaming down her face, Magdalena muttered "Aye, me promise." With a sigh, Golornia took her last breath. Her father and the others in the room allowed Magdalena to cry until there were no more tears. Her father gathered her up in his great arms and carried her to her room where he laid her on her bed. He was followed by old Remenia who had taken care of her since birth.

"Let her sleep and when the arrangements 'ave been made; bring her to the burial ceremonies."

"Yas me Lord Magentheld," she answered as she curtsied.

The Magentheld left the room. Magdalena slept and was not aware it would be the last intimate touch she received from her father.

The burial ceremonies were a blur to the young Magdalena. Immediately after the ceremonies, she along with Remenia were packed up and sent away to the Commune of the Druidesses. There was no farewell from her father.

The journey by carriage, by ferry and again by carriage took seven days. Each time Magdalena asked why they were going, Remenia replied it would all unfold and reminded Magdalena she promised her mother she do whatever was asked of her. At one time, Magdalena became so exasperated that she shouted, "Aye! I know I promised, but I did nae promise I nae ask why!"

Her outbursts and pleas were to no avail, as Remenia remained tightlipped. This was most unusual for the old maidservant as she always before laughed and played with Magdalena. Her behavior was not her usual manner. Magdalena sunk into a deep despair. The journey carried them to the far reaches of the realm passing through great forests to the very foot of the great mountains. It was here where a small group of Druidesses met them.

Magdalena was informed that Remenia could not go with her. With great sobbing and grief, she and Remenia parted never to see one another in this lifetime. When questioned, the Druidesses only told her she was to study and live with them until the time when she would be summoned. Until then, she would be completely in their charge.

Before Magdalena's escort party traveled out of sight, one of the Druidesses gave her a pair of soft leather boots and told to put them on, as she would be walking the rest of the journey with them. Magdalena gasped in sheer horror! She was about to open her mouth and refuse when she looked into the eyes of the Druidess. She knew there to be no choice but to comply.

INTO THE UNKNOWN

There are things known and things unknown and in between are the doors.
~ Jim Morrison

The journey through mountains covered two days and they followed the course of a river climbing upwards. There was no idle chatter among the Druidesses. They only spoke to Magdalena to give her instructions. One or another seemed to sense when she was thirsty and offered her a bladder skin of cool water. A small slight Druidess became in charge of Magdalena. "I be called Moiree. Yew may call me this. Come, I be showing yew how to make yere bed fer the night. There be a chill in the air."

Magdalena was aghast. She expected a nice warm inn with a soft bed. Moiree's look stilled any rebuttal she wanted to make. In silence, Magdalena followed her.

Moiree instructed her on locating a tree with a fork in it. Next, they located a long limb propping it up in the fork of the tree, and then securely attached it with long reeds growing along the banks of the river. Other smaller branches be gathered and propped against the limb pole so as to make a small shelter. Moiree instructed her to gather as many leaves and bits of moss she could find to make a soft place to sleep on. Magdalena only nodded and began her task of gathering while her mind churned with fear, anger and dismay. At last she completed her shelter under the guidance of Moiree.

By now, a small fire was made with a steaming soup bubbling in a reed basket one of the women had quickly woven and soaked in water before placing it on the fire. A third woman who Magdalena learned was called Leeta, gathered roots and greens, which were placed in the bubbling water.

Later she recalled it to be a memorable meal. Magdalena was famished and ate with a great appetite. She asked for a second helping. The three women smiled at her for the first time and told her it was the time for evening vespers and to observe as she was not ready to participate.

With arms outstretched, the three women closed their eyes and faced the setting sun. They began chanting.

Ohm, Ohm, Ohm,
Ohm, Ohm, Ohm, Ohm
Oh Great Isness,
Beloved Mysterious One,
I be filled with gratitude for this day.
This night fill me with wisdom and knowing.
Blessed One, I accept.
Ohm, Ohm, Ohm.

They repeated this three times and then each brought their hands to their forehead and bowed slowly and deeply. Magdalena felt enthralled with the sincerity and feeling each gave to this ritual.

Moiree told Magdalena to wrap her cloak around her and go into her shelter headfirst. She was surprised at the warmth and coziness of it. She fell into a deep sleep before she could contemplate the questions swirling inside her head.

Once they cleaned the area and turned it back into nature. Magdalena and the Druidesses again began climbing. Magdalena protested inwardly the toll it was taking for her to keep up with the women. She noted there were tall stacks of big rocks along the path they were taking. Towards the evening Magdalena could hear the roar of a waterfall long before they reached it. The Druidess who appeared to be in charge announced they were staying the night at the base of the falls.

  Again, the same procedure for creating a bed, the gathering of food for the meal and finally partaking of the evening meal gave Magdalena a respite. Before they completed the meal, Magdalena asked what the big tall stacks of rocks were and was told they were cairns for markers to follow the trail.

She woke briefly thinking she heard her mother call to her; however, all she heard was the water from the falls. The drone of the waterfall became a comforting sound to her exhausted body and she became lulled into a dreamless sleep until she became aware of a shaking of her feet. Moiree called her to come out of her shelter, as they must be on with their journey.

  By the time Magdalena managed to get herself out of the shelter, the three Druidesses were facing the East and making their greeting while facing the rising sun. They began to chant.

Ohm, Ohm, Ohm,
Ohm, Ohm, Ohm, Ohm,
Oh Great Isness – Unknowable One,
Create this day full of Joy, Awareness,
With opportunities fer wisdom.
I accept.
Ohm, Ohm, Ohm.

  Bowing deeply with their hands brought to foreheads, the women now turned to Magdalena.

Evanah, the third Druidess who appeared to be in charge was tall and rather gangly. Her number of years were hard to determine. She had not spoken to Magdalena since the group who brought her had departed. She informed her there would be no stopping until they reached the Commune.

Magdalena swallowed hard while choking back her tears. Leeta gave her a small packet of dried fruits and nuts, telling her to eat along the way slowly as this had to sustain her until they arrived at the Commune. She was also provided with another bladder skin of water.

Moiree again quickly showed her how to dismantle the shelter and to return the limbs, leaves and twigs to their natural habitat. By the time she completed the task, it was difficult to see where anyone had spent the night there.

The climb around the waterfall was steep and the path narrow. Even in the soft leather boots, Magdalena's feet were protesting. She knew there were blisters. She gritted her teeth refusing to cry,. She managed to keep up with the agile women. Moiree once told her to think of something else and the pain would not be so bad. Magdalena was surprised Moiree knew. It was almost as though she read her thoughts.

The path became steeper and once they reached the crest, she looked down and viewed the river flowing in a deep gorge. It looked to be an abyss. The air felt cool even though it was in the midst of the season of ripening. The flowers bloomed in riotous color in the meadow in front of them. Beyond she saw a grove of tall trees. Evanah cupped her hands and let out a loud yodel. The sound echoed and immediately came an answering yodel. She turned to Magdalena with a smile. "We be almost home."

Home. Magdalena felt tears well up in her eyes. A wave of bitterness flowed through her while she silently followed the trio of women. For the first time, she saw goats with small kids nursing at their udders.

Soon they approached a cluster of small buildings in odd shapes built of stones. This was the Commune of the Druidesses known as Argania. Thus began Magdalena's twelve years sojourn away from the home she had once known.

⛫⛫⛫

Magdalena of Hy Brasil

~ FRANCE ~
2013

The Gift

A gift consists not in what is done or given, but in the intention of the giver or doer.
~ Lucius Annaeus Seneca

A few days had passed after Ellen's vivid dream. She was sitting at her computer in the sanctum, the name for her office. When the Magdalene Scrolls were first being translated, this room had been given the name and it was off-limits to the staff as well as the children. Today she was reviewing the expenditures for the upkeep of the chateau.

There was a knock on the door followed by the voice of Marie. "Madame, a package has been left for you at the gate. Shall I send Jacques to get it for you?"

"A package? I haven't ordered anything for delivery here. Please call the gate and ask Guy to scan the package."

"*Oui Mme.*"

Ellen was perplexed and thankful Peter had a scanner placed in the guardhouse from their challenges in not only having the Magdalene Scrolls translated, but the Sarah Legacy Scrolls as well. He said this was necessary for their safety.

Sighing, she stood up knowing she was not in the mood to dealing with expenditures. Even though they had an accountant, she wanted to review them herself. She buzzed Marie and told her she would meet her in the solarium. She then called Peter and told him about the unexpected package and he said he would be right over. He had purchased the chateau next to theirs and used it for his businesses and for housing employees who lived on the grounds.

She had just entered the solarium when Jacques knocked before he entered. "*Merci* Jacques. The package must be okay since you have brought it here."

He held out the box, which was almost the size of a shoebox. He smiled at her and said that it was his pleasure. "*Mme.* I, I do not think it is a bomb. It, it is something that I feel is unusual for you to open."

"In what way do you think it is unusual?"

"*Mme.* Ellen, I request that *M.* Peter be here and I will return to explain."

After he left, she looked at the box and wished that Peter would get here soon. *What did Jacques mean by 'it is something I feel is unusual'?* Gingerly, she picked up the box, and holding it, she knew that whatever was in it was not too heavy and she speculated as to what it could be. *No,* she thought, *I will wait for Peter.* She walked over to the window and looked out at the garden. She watched Jacques as he worked to put the garden beds and plants to bed for the winter. Yes, it was fall.

She jumped as Peter quietly came in and placed his armed around her. "Oh my god! You scared the livin' bejeesus out of me!"

He turned her around and bent down kissing her with passion. He caressed her hair and said, "You always turn me on." They both laughed. "Now, what is this about a package?"

"Following the routine, Guy scanned it and reported it appeared to be okay. When Jacques brought it in he did not think it was a bomb, but he thought it was unusual and for you to be here. I have not opened it, as I wanted you here. I know I did not order this nor anything. Is this something you ordered for me?" She picked up the box and handed it to Peter.

After he took the box, he said, "It wasn't me my love. I think first I will make a call to Jacques." Peter picked up the house phone and rang Jacques. When Jacques answered, Peter asked him to explain what he saw in the package. Ellen stood by feeling a bit of impatience while the two talked. When Peter hung up, he looked at her with a perplexed look on his face. "I have an idea we won't get any fingerprints off of this wrapping, however there could be some on the box. Let's go into the sanctum and get a pair of gloves."

Ellen agreed and the two went to the sanctum. She already knew what the drill was from previous experience and took out a pair of thin rubber gloves along with a cutting knife. She watched as Peter carefully slit the wrapping off. There was a plain brown cardboard box and he cut the tape. Looking at her, he said, "Now, since it is addressed to you, you have the honor of opening it."

Ellen nodded and slowly pulled the top off. Inside was some cotton and when she unwrapped it, she let out another, "Oh my gawd!" Peter gave a long whistle. What they saw was a dagger with the hilt in the shape of a standing black lion with a gold serpent wrapped around the body. The head of the serpent rested on the head of the lion whose eyes were amber stones. The serpent's eyes were green stones. "Do you think these gems are real?"

"Um, they look real. I also think the black lion is made of onyx. It looks to be quite old. Here, look at the hilt and notice that it does look like there has been some wear. Look at the blade. I'm not sure if it is steel. There is something etched on it. Here, take a look."

Ellen held the dagger and looked at the blade. "These markings are strange. Could they be hieroglyphics?"

"Perhaps. I would like to send this off for testing."

"Of course. I cannot imagine who would send something like this to me."

Peter smiled and carefully lifted the rest of the cotton out of the box and saw a piece of paper. He carefully picked it up and handed it to her.

"What the?" Ellen unfolded the paper and saw the printed words:

WELCOME TO THE GAME.

"Peter! What is this? Someone playing a joke on me?"

"Sweetheart, I cannot imagine this being a practical joke. Let's put this back in the box. I think it best we call Alain and hear what he has to say. We both know he has access to people who can perhaps ferret this thing out."

Ellen nodded in agreement. She began stripping the gloves from her hands while Peter placed everything back in the box. "You're right. I understand he is back in Paris."

Peter smiled as he removed his gloves. "Your brother is quite a world traveler since he connected with Louise Bianchi."

Ellen smiled. "Somehow I don't think they will marry. Jennifer was his true love and when she left, he was devastated."

"In the meantime, I am going to photograph this along with the packaging." Peter went on to say, "Sweetheart you do pick some interesting adventures and along with the fact that you are beautiful, perhaps that is what attracted me to you in the first place."

She smiled and reached up pulling him down to kiss him. "Ah, I always knew I wanted a Prince Charming and you fit the bill."

"Careful my love. I just might take you right here and now. However, I will postpone it until another time. I have an appointment with Tony Bradshaw regarding the new computer prototype. Will you call Alain?"

"Of course I will and in the meantime, don't forget that you promised Eleanor a story sometime this afternoon."

"I have that on my list and it is hard to believe that she has reached the ripe young age of three."

"I agree, and this year she will be four." Ellen gave him another kiss. "Now go to your appointment with a light heart. I think I will contemplate this."

"Okay sweetheart. I'm off."

Ellen looked at the dagger and somehow it looked familiar, but she could not place it. She had not taken her gloves off, so she picked it up and looked to look at the markings. She puzzled over what she would call the inscriptions. *Were they actually hieroglyphs? Damn! It means we have to find someone who can decipher them. Oh well, I'll call Alain and see if he is available.*

Michele, Alain's secretary answered the phone and when she heard Ellen's voice she connected her to Alain. "My dear sister, what a pleasure to hear your voice again. And, how are you and your family?"

Ellen smiled and replied that they were all well. They talked briefly about Alain's latest trip before she told him about the unexpected gift. For a moment, there was silence. Then he chuckled. "You do seem to attract the most unusual events. Why don't you and Peter meet me here in my office tomorrow? I will schedule you in with Michele."

Ellen agreed and the two continued to speak of the family and his travels before he connected her with Michele. An appointment was set for 2 p.m. the following day. After she hung up, she called Peter's office and spoke with him and Peter said he would clear his calendar.

She placed the box with the dagger in the safe and sat down to contemplate. Her mind was swirling with questions. Why was she chosen? What was the purpose of sending it to her? What were the markings on the blade revealing? Her mind was churning with questions. Finally, she realized that this was not giving her any answers so she left the room and decided to take Eleanor for a walk.

Ellen enjoyed taking her daughter for a walk because she was inquisitive about almost everything. She wanted to know the names of the various plants and trees and she was adept at retaining the information. Today she insisted they go to the lake, as she wanted to watch the birds and wildfowl. Ellen also knew Eleanor wanted to feed them.

"Momma, why do ducks fly funnier than geese?

"If you look carefully at the ducks, you will notice that they are smaller than the geese and therefore, it is possible that they do not have the ability to fly as gracefully."

"Oh. Is that why ducks quack and geese honk?"

"Umm. Ducks are created different from geese and their quacking makes them special so others like them are able to communicate with them. It is the same thing with geese. They honk as a way to communicate with other geese."

"Oh. And chickens squawk and cluck as their way of talking." Eleanor felt proud of herself for being able to connect the sounds of the fowls.

"Yes, you are learning and I am very proud of you. I think it is time to go back to the chateau as your father will be there soon to read you story."

"Yesss!" Eleanor began almost skipping. Her older brother and sister were attempting to teach her and she was proud of herself.

ΩΩΩ

The Quest Begins

Life is just a journey. ~ **Princess Diana**

The following day, Ellen and Peter left mid-morning in order to do some shopping at the *Au Printemps* and *Galleries Lafayette,* as both were located on *Boulevard Haussmann.* She and Peter had agreed with Alain to meet him for lunch at *Carré des Feuillants* before going to his office. The restaurant had been renovated from an old 17th century convent. The shopping did not take too long and they arrived at the restaurant within moments of Alain.

Ellen noted how handsome her brother was with a tinge of grey in his dark hair. Actually, he was her half-brother, but that was another story. With kisses and hugs, the threesome was led to one of the small dining rooms. They chose one that overlooked a flowering courtyard and a glass-enclosed kitchen. The décor was now done in tones of black, beige and off-white. Ellen ordered the scallops with a truffled celery mousseline while Peter and Alain ordered the braised veal with mushroom cannelloni.

Their talk began with Alain sharing his latest trip, which was to China. He had become the legal advisor to Louise Bianchi's businesses now that Maurice had died. He seemed to thrive on the challenges presented. He admitted that he was happier now that he did not have to appear in court as often or have as many clients.

Peter shared that he was creating a prototype for the latest quantum computer and of course, he was happy with his family and children.

After Ellen shared her news of the children, Jill and Sebastian as well as others who she thought he would want to know about. Alain suggested they go to his office and discuss the business at hand.

When they arrived at Alain's office on *Avenue Hoche* near the *Arc de Triomphe*, Michele ushered them in and Alain had arrived moments before. Once seated, Ellen brought the box out from her large bag and placed it on Alain's desk. He looked at her quizzically. "My dear sister, what mystery are you bringing to me this time?"

The three laughed and she began relating her dream and then the arrival of this gift. She and Peter had discussed the circumstances and wondered if the two were connected. She then brought out several pairs of gloves and handed a pair to Alain. This time, he raised his eyebrows. "I know," Ellen said. "When you see the gift you will understand." She put on her pair of gloves and opened the box. When she showed the dagger to Alain, he let out a slow whistle.

"*Mon dieu! Il est beau!*" Alain put on his pair of gloves and asked if he could look at it. Ellen smiled and handed it to him. He gingerly took it from her and began examining it. "This is quite old. In fact, I would think it is an ancient relic."

Ellen nodded. "We think so too. Peter suggested that you might have someone in your repertoire of acquaintances that could possibly identify it and estimate its age."

Alain smiled. "I have a person in mind that can do it and if not, she will locate someone who will. Will you leave it here with me?"

"Yes. Peter and I were sure you knew of someone. I know you have your sources so I won't ask who."

"Thank you. After the two of you leave, I will make some calls. I am also going to photograph this for my own records. Did you find any fingerprints?"

Peter stood up to leave saying, "Everything was clean as a whistle. Somehow, you always seem to come through knowing some source and I am grateful for this."

Ellen also stood up to leave. Alain came around from his desk and embraced her. "I am delighted that I have a sister who has mysteries always coming forth. I will be in touch."

Once they were in their car driving back to the chateau, the two discussed their meeting. Peter grinned and spoke. "My beautiful wife and love, you do seem to have opportunities that come to you that I could never imagine." She laughed. "I would have never imagined a gift such as a dagger from some past. However, who sent it? Why me?

"Now that is the sixty-four dollar question and I have an idea that we are all in for a surprise of great magnitude."

ΩΩΩ

~ HY BRASIL ~
400 A.D

DEATH AND THE CROWN

Uneasy lays the head that wears a crown.
~ **William Shakespeare**

A gentle tapping on the door wakened Magdalena from her slumber. With a start, she sat up and it took her a moment to realize she was in the castle of her father, the King – the Magentheld. "Enter," she commanded.

Mireen entered carrying a large tray ladened with fresh fruit, a steaming bowl of barley soup along with a glass of mead. Placing it on the small round table, she pulled the chair out for Magdalena to sit on.

"And how be my father, the Magentheld?" asked Magdalena as she seated herself.

"He be holding his own tis said," replied Mireen as she took away the cover of the soup bowl. "He requests yere presence in the Great Hall within the hour. All the lords and ladies of the realm be fillin' the place now."

Magdalena narrowed her eyes as she contemplated the coming meeting. She knew it could well be explosive. What did her father mean by *kingdom of the mind,* and was she up to it? A knowing feeling answered her to allow it to unfold.

All too soon, Mireen was at her side with a beautiful silk garment of a deep blue tinged with a hint of rose. Its high waist fit snugly under her breasts and the soft round neck was cut low enough to reveal the shape of her lovely neck. The rounded neckline and the bodice were encrusted with pearls and gold threads creating a design woven into a lion with the entwined serpent. The beauty made Magdalena gasp in appreciation. It went well with her darkened skin.

With Mireen's assistance, she put the gown on. It fit perfectly. Stepping back, Mireen clasped her hands in glee while saying, "Oh me lady! Thee be indeed wondrous! Naow yere father requested that yew wear this ringlet and this neckpiece he called a torque."

Magdalena looked at the golden tiara and knew it had to be her mother's. She allowed Mireen to brush her hair while seated at the dressing table. Her shining red hair cascaded around her shoulders. Even she had to admit that she made a lovely picture as she gazed at herself in the gilded frame mirror. With pride and a small flourish, Mireen placed the tiara on top of her head.

Next she placed the golden torque around Magdalena's neck. Magdalena remembered seeing it on her mother at state affairs. The etchings around its outer rim were designs she wanted to understand and her mother had told her she would know later.

At that moment, there was a knock on the door. Mireen opened the door to a small company of guardsmen who were to accompany Magdalena to the Great Hall. Nodding her head to acknowledge them, Magdalena swept regally out of the room and followed the six guardsmen down the long flight of stairs. The moment she stepped off the bottom step, a fanfare of horns blared forth to announce her arrival. With her heart pounding, she paused momentarily, giving thanks to her God within asking she be filled with clarity of mind and strength for whatever was to be unfolded.

The two massive doors swung open and she walked slowly into the Great Hall. The Hall was filled to capacity with all the Lords and Ladies of Realm seated along the walls length-wise in rows seating six.people and facing the aisle.

Everyone swiveled their heads to see who was arriving. Immediately there was a ripple of audible gasps as the appearance of Magdalena created a surprise and her beauty breathtaking. She looked almost the image of her deceased mother. As a body, they stood up to pay homage to this mysterious personage.

Magdalena looked neither to the right nor to the left. She used her soft vision, which gave her the capacity to see in a 360-degree sweep. Her brain and her mind were registering it all. After what felt like an eternity, she arrived at the gold throne where her father was seated. She brought her two hands together up to her forehead while giving a deep bow. Before she could kneel, her father managed to stand and offered his hand to her. Taking the proffered hand, the father and daughter turned to face the people.

The deep silence could be said to be almost deafening. It appeared as though each person was afraid to breathe. With the strength he could muster, Sarenhild, the Magentheld spoke. "My beloved people, I know yew be surprised I be still alive and able to meet with yew this fine day." He paused to note the guilty looks on many of the faces.

"My people and my friends, I 'ave made a decision to enact a very old law. It be my right and tis my duty to do so. The woman at my side be my beloved daughter Magdalena. She be away since the death of my wife Golornia. She be with the Druidesses who trained her well fer these twelve ans."

Magdalena stood by her father with an impassive face. Inside, her thoughts and emotions were anything but calm. With effort, she brought them under control and carefully listened to everything her father said, and at the same moment observing the large audience.

The Magentheld paused a moment. It seemed as though he knew Magdalena needed a pause to bring her concentration under control. Continuing, he went on to say, "Under the Corif Law, it be written that if I 'ave no male sons to follow me, I may choose either a male or a female from my blood lineage to inherit the Office of Magentheld. It be my decision; my choice and the law that my daughter Magdalena be naow the first Magentheld Queen of the Realm of Hy Brasil."

Turning to Magdalena, Sarenhild reached up and removed the crown from his head as Cyran the Holy One stepped forward and removed her tiara. The Magentheld waited a moment and began speaking. "With the powers vested in me by the authority of the Corif Law, I pass my crown of Magentheld to yew Magdalena, daughter of my loins and yere deceased mother Golornia." After placing the massive crown on her head, he took her hands and kissed each one before kissing her on each cheek.

At this moment, Magdalena became very aware of the enormous power entrusted to her. There was a stunned silence from the lords and ladies. Cyran stepped forward and handed Magdalena a staff encrusted with precious jewels. The head of the staff was the standing black lion encircled with the gold snake. The standing lion had been created from black onyx with amber for the eyes. The gold serpent had green stones as eyes and was tall as Magdalena.

Cyran spoke, "I give my blessings to the new Magentheld. May her rule be just, compassionate and strong."

By the time the Holy One completed his blessing, the entire Great Hall began roaring with seemingly acceptance. Drums began rolling sending a message to each Hold of the realm.

With a smile, Magdalena acknowledged the tribute of her people. She was also aware of an undercurrent of distrust. She knew her future would be shaky until she proved her worth. Moreover, by the grace of God, this she would do!

Speaking with assurance, she told the audience after the cheering had quieted down, "I accept this trust and this Office of Magentheld to rule fairly. I be honored to follow the footsteps of me illustrious father. The hour be late. I meet with my father's Council tomorrow morning at the hour called nine. Please feast, dance and be merry. This audience be over."

She walked down the long corridor between the lords and ladies, smiling and nodding from side to side while carrying the massive staff as if it were a feather. The Crown of Magentheld sat heavy on her head. There were seven stars encrusted with jewels. The center star being the largest with the other six graduating to small sizes. The center star was encrusted with pearls. The other stars encrusted with rubies, diamonds, emeralds and lapis lazuli set in gold. The effect was stunning.

Once out of the Great Hall, she walked purposefully to her father's quarters. She knew he had been taken out of the Great Hall by a side entrance as he was too weak to walk down the long room.

When she entered the room, she set the staff down and removed the crown to begin assisting the attendants in getting her father undressed and into bed. He was too weak to protest. She immediately ordered a pot of hot water to be brought along with a drinking cup. She sent one of the attendants to her quarters and gave orders for him to return with her small leather medicinal pouch that she carried with her most times.

Sarenhild lay back on the pillows. His eyes were closed and his breathing labored. When Magdalena took his wrist to check his pulse, he opened his eyes. "Do nae attempt to save me. Tis me destiny. Do nae give me any of yere draughts or herbs. Let me go in peace."

With tears slowly rolling down her cheeks, she nodded saying she would comply with his wishes. Before she could speak, her father continued. "I 'ave sent fer Cyran and my trusted ones."

A serving woman reentered the room with the pouch and hot water. Following her were Cyran, Kanen, Oris, Bosenio, Rath and Hyreck. They gathered on the opposite side of the massive bed from where Magdalena sat on the bed waiting for Sarenhild to speak. His voice was labored and weak.

Sarenhild asked for the serving women and Peppo, his personal attendant of many years to come forward. "I thank yew fer the many good years of service. Master Kanen be giving yew a stipend after my death. Yew may either stay or yew be free to go." Pausing, Sarenhild seemed to be reaching for an inner strength. "All of you! Let it be known that I died of me own free will. It be my destiny. Naow I ask each of yew in my presence to swear allegiance to my daughter the new Magentheld."

With that, the Trusted Ones and the serving attendants kneeled and each swore their allegiance to Magdalena She rose from the side of the bed and stood before them. "I accept yere loyalty."

Sighing, Sarenhild gave a long breath and passed into another realm. Cyran stepped forward and closed the eyes. The serving women began sobbing and Peppo had great tears rolling down his face. Magdalena stood transfixed. A scent of roses permeated her senses.

Her first order as Queen and Magentheld was to order the body prepared for review and burial. "I be speaking with yew in the morn. Fer naow, I desire to be alone with me thoughts." She swept out of Sarenhild's room and returned to her quarters.

Mireen was there to help her undress and then departed.

Magdalena walked to the window and looked out at the great full moon. *What is to be, will be. I call forth wisdom, strength and love fer all people. Oh God I Am, let me be an anchor fer my people*.

Mireen had darkened the room and Magdalena climbed into bed falling into a dream state. It was the beginning of a new era.

AWAKENING TO A NEW REALITY

Every new sovereign brings her own ministers. ~
Anonymous

For a moment, she felt disoriented. Where was she? Slowly she opened her eyes waiting for them to adjust to the darkness of the early morning. "Arise Magdalena. Our Lady be awaiting yew." Through the fog of waking up, she knew it was the voice of Leeta.

Startled, Magdalena realized she was sleeping on a pallet of rushes, grasses covered with a deerskin. Holding back a sob, she could only nod. Her heart lay heavy in her chest and she felt betrayed and alone. Momentarily, she allowed a feeling of anger to well up inside of her.

Following Leeta's instructions, she washed her face from a small bowl of water placed on the stump of a tree. Leeta led the way to the outside pit and told her that this was where she would pee and relieve herself. With horror, she followed Leeta across the compound to the Lady's abode. While walking, her eyes observed the various ways the small stone huts were erected so to become part of nature's architectural plan. Some were round. Others were square or rectangular. Another was domed shaped with one in the shape of a pyramid. The stones used were a puzzlement to Magdalena. They were not in the shape of the familiar stones of the castle or of the stones and reeds of the farm folk nearby. In addition to the stone huts, some appeared to be living trees and growing. However, the trees did not grow in a natural upward way, but horizontal in the contour of the geometric pattern selected. They were most unusual.

Leeta stopped in front of a stone domed hut. After knocking three times, a strong melodious voice commanded, "Enter." The door was much lower than the normal doors Magdalena had been accustomed to. Leeta stooped to enter and Magdalena followed bending her head to avoid hitting the top of the arched door. This act made her acutely aware she indeed had been brought to a strange place.

Standing as they entered was the Lady of the Druidesses. She appeared regal in her bearing and only a little taller than Magdalena. Her dancing green eyes were set back in a beautifully shaped face. She had an ageless appearance.. Her blue-black hair had been pulled back in a long braid and she wore a headband of midnight blue emblazoned with various symbols. Her robe had been made of coarse homespun material, which was dyed midnight blue. Magdalena fixed her gaze on the blue five-pointed star painted on the center of her forehead below the headband.

She felt the Lady could read her every thought and appeared to be amused at Magdalena's assessment. She felt herself blushing and not knowing what to say, remained silent.

The Lady spoke in a soft tone of voice. "Welcome young Magdalena. We be expecting yew. Yew will be here fer yere next step in yere education. After you be indoctrinated into our ways, yew be moving into teachings to expand yere mind. Discipline be a way of life here. We expect yew to comply. Leeta be yere first teacher. She be instructing yew in our ways and the laws of our compound. Naow, we go to greet this day."Without waiting for an answer, the Lady bent her head and swept through the door. Leeta motioned for Magdalena to follow with Leeta coming behind her.

They walked a short distance to an open area where others were assembled and with the arrival of the Lady, they all turned towards the East. Raising their arms outstretched and up, they began chanting the *Ohm* in a beautiful harmonic. She felt herself caught up in the exaltation of the chanting and joined in. The great sun rose magnificently above the crest of mountains and sent its rays out piercing the early morning darkness. For her, it would be an experience always etched in her mind.

When the ritual had been completed, Leeta motioned for Magdalena to follow her. On the way, Leeta told her they were now going to the eating hall to join the others. After the morning meal, Magdalena would be given a tour of the great cooking room.

Entering into a long rectangular stone building, Magdalena was struck by the simplicity of it. There were long wooden plank tables with long benches. On each of the tables she observed several urns full of flowers. Leeta noticed her observation and quickly explained that during their seasons, various flowering plants were cut and brought into the great hall. After the flowers were enjoyed and blessed, the flowers would be used for medicinal purposes or dyes. Everything in nature had a purpose and utilized here for its potential. Magdalena could only nod.

Leeta led her to a long table near the center of the eating hall. She could feel all eyes on her as she sat in her place. Her heart began beating rapidly and she felt everyone must hear it. Slowly she met the eyes of the young women sitting across from her. Her gaze was met with a smile and she began to relax. Turning to her right and then to her left, she acknowledge the smiles of the other women. She began to relax until her attention became riveted on the serving person for her table. It was the Lady!

The Lady smiled, saying every woman took turns in serving meals regardless of her exalted station. Service to others became part of the training.

No one picked up her spoon to eat the porridge until it had been served to everyone. Magdalena followed suit. When the last woman was served, everyone cupped their hands around their bowls giving thanks in blessing the food to nourish their bodies.

While eating, she managed to notice the many other women. Some were almost her age while others were older, and as far as she could tell, they were of all ages. Some looked ageless. Their clothing was consisted of loose robes tied with belts of various colors. Some wore robes of midnight blue. Others wore robes of a natural white. There also were green robes and yellow robes. The young women closest to Magdalena's age wore the natural white robe. Some of the women who were older wore the midnight blue robes and had five-pointed stars in the color of blue on their foreheads. It appeared the skin had been dyed.

When the meal ended, each woman passed her bowl to the left along with their spoons. These were stacked neatly and the Lady returned to collect them. Leeta indicated Magdalena to follow her.

They walked to the cooking area where Magdalena observed the cleaning of their bowls, spoons and cooking pots. "After I be showing yew around, yew be given instructions. Soon yew be part of the serving ones." Magdalena nodded she understood. She was enthralled by the singing and the joyous countenance of each cook, cook's helper and the serving ones.

As they walked out, she silently asked herself if she would ever sing again or be happy. Leeta must have picked up on her thoughts. "Little one, yew will indeed be happy here. Once yere so r row passes, yew begin to see the wonders of our commune and the teachings."

Swallowing her tears, Magdalena only nodded. Later she wondered how Leeta knew what she had been thinking. Did she have second sight? Would she, Magdalena have it too?

They spent the rest of the morning and day visiting each area of the commune. Magdalena was amazed at the wide diversity of activities. There were herbalists and healers they visited first. She felt in awe of the many jars of herbs, ointments and tinctures. Upon leaving the dispensary, Leeta introduced her to the food-gathering house where the Druidesses were bringing in large baskets from the gardens. These in turn were sorted by another group of women. She was introduced to a massive Druidess named Jorene, meaning the 'joyful one', and she began shouting directions to the scurrying young neophytes. She laughed and she sang. Her height and breadth was awesome.

The stable enchanted Magdalena. There were young kids frolicking as they were being weaned from their mother goats. The mothers' udders were heavy with milk. A group of the novices were being instructed in the art of milking. Leeta whispered, "You too, soon be learning this art." Next they moved on to the fenced-in area filled with sheep. Leeta told her it soon be the time to move them to the meadows.

Leaving the stable, the two entered the area for chickens, ducks, and to Magdalena's amazement peacocks. She had heard of them, but never seen them alive. When they left, Leeta told her there was more, but she felt this being enough for one day. It was now time to go to the clothing house. There she was given her white garment with the novice's belt together with other essentials she had to care for. She learned she now would be living in a six novice house with one of the advanced Druidesses.

While walking to the sleeping house, Leeta introduced her to the bathing area and the pit for relieving oneself. Everything appeared spotless and immaculate.

Arriving at her sleeping house, Magdalena realized she was feeling fatigue. Leeta did not allow her to rest. She showed her the bed mat and the pegs to hang her clothing. There also was a small chest to hold her essentials. She quickly changed into the white garment and tied the black belt she had been given around her waist. For a moment a great feeling of sadness almost overwhelmed her when she thought of all her beautiful clothes and her comfortable bed at the castle.

Before she could give in to her sorrow, Leeta urged her to make haste because it was now time for the evening meal followed by the ritual of the closing of the day. The evening meal ritual was similar to the morning meal. Another Druidess clothed in a yellow robe and a multi-colored belt was serving. Around her neck hung a medallion of a triangle encrusted with lapis lazuli and gold. There were so many questions she wanted to ask; however, she already had been informed by Leeta the rule was no speaking during meals because everyone needed to enjoy the food and be attentive. The serving One brought out a huge tureen of savory stew full of vegetables, herbs and chunks of lamb. This was followed with loaves of fresh baked bread.

When they left the eating hall, she and Leeta walked with the other Druidesses and novices to the large amphitheatre carved out of a high tor. The craggy rocks were shaped into seating benches. The unusual outdoor amphitheatre faced east and at this time of day the sun was beginning its descent for the night. They all turned facing west with their faces uplifted along with their arms outstretched. The Ohming began echoing throughout the valley behind them. The sound reverberated repeatedly. When the last word had been spoken, there was a hush and the words were echoed back to them.

Magdalena felt mesmerized by the entire ritual. Leeta nudged her and in silence they made their way back to her sleeping hut. The other young novices began arriving at the same time. Leeta introduced her to each one. Every young novice gave her the greeting of hands to the forehead and bowing low. She returned the greeting she already observed throughout the long day.

Leeta waited until the senior Druidess arrived. She wore a green robe with a dark crimson belt and she was introduced as Doretha. Leeta's parting words were that she would come for her in the morning. Swallowing hard, Magdalena nodded in agreement.

Doretha began instructing her in the rules of the sleeping house. There would be no talking after the lamps were extinguished. There would be a period of one-half hour beforehand and instructed her as to where she was to wash, relieve herself or bathe. During this time, she would be allowed to talk with the other novices. Doretha called a young novice named Callan to meet Magdalena.

"Callan, yew be to assist our new young novice in her preparation fer the night." Doretha turned her attention to another young novice who asked a question.

Callan was very eager to assist the new young novice. She chattered incessantly and said she had only been there for six months. At first, she had a horrid time until she learned to change her attitude. Her father died and her mother already had six other children. Out of need, she had been given to the Druidesses. By the time they completed their absolutions, Magdalena realized she had not spoken one word – only nodding.

Callan asked about Magdalena's background when the lighting lamps were extinguished. Magdalena did not reply. She crept into her bed pallet. The enormity of the day engulfed her and the tears began to flow. She attempted to stifle her sobs with her rough blanket stuffed into her mouth. Soon she felt the strong arms of Doretha enfold her while holding her tightly against her bosom. Doretha continued to hold her until she fell asleep. She began to dream a dream.

Magdalena of Hy Brasil

~ France ~
2013

A Dream ~ Again

In forming a bridge between body and mind, dreams may be used as a springboard from which man can leap to new realms of experience lying outside his normal state of consciousness. ~ Ann Faraday

She felt herself gently being shaken awake. When she became aware, she found she was clutching the sheet in her mouth and she was silently crying. Peter whispered into her ear, "Remember the dream. Tell me what you are seeing." Ellen relaxed and began recounting this disturbing dream. The two had agreed that if she had a dream similar to her first one that somehow Peter would wake up and turn on a tape recorder.

He tried not to disturb her while the recording was on and his heart was beating fast. *Was this a breakthrough?* He wondered? They had discussed a number of times why she had been the one to find the Magdalene scrolls and was also given the Sarah scrolls. Now, the dagger had come into their lives.

Ellen's voice stopped and he realized her breathing was normal and that she had fallen into a deep sleep. Slowly he eased himself out of bed and after going to the bathroom, went into their sitting room where he had his own computer. He looked at the clock and it was 5 a.m. and hopefully, she would sleep until at least seven.

He played the recording back and began transcribing it. This was a major piece of the game and he surmised, *It had to be*. He stopped and began reading what Ellen had said.

"There's a little girl. She's crying and stuffing an old something in her mouth to stifle the sound.

"She's, she's in an ancient hut with other girls. It is night. She feels lost. She feels abandoned – betrayed. She misses her mother.

"Images coming. She's an adult. She's dressed – dressed like a queen. Has a crown on and holding a – a staff." Ellen groaned. "It's, it's" – and her voice trailed off. This is when Peter removed the recorder, as she was now asleep.

He sat there and contemplated if there was a staff that had a black lion with a golden serpent entwined around it. He got up and walked to the window looking out at the early morning sun coming up. *There has to be a connection*, he thought.

He turned as he heard the door open. It was Ellen. Quickly, he went to her and lifted her up to his level. There was a vast difference between their heights. "My darling, my darling," he murmured and kissed her long and passionately.

Ellen leaned back in his arms. "I think you had better take me back to bed. I want you."

After their passionate lovemaking, she lay in his arms. "Peter, you recorded my dream – I think."

"I did indeed and received a revelation. However, before I let you listen to it; tell me if you remember anything?"

"There is something nagging at my consciousness, but it is elusive. I think it would be better if I listened to what you heard me say."

"Okay. Let's go into the other room where I left the recorder."

The two put on robes and went into the sitting room where Peter turned on the recorder. Ellen listened and then asked him to repeat it. This time, she almost shouted it. "I remember now! The staff! It was the staff she carried that had the standing black lion entwined with the gold serpent."

Peter reached over and kissed her. "Sweetheart, I think we made a breakthrough. Somehow, it seems you have reached back in time through your dreams."

She gave him a rueful smile. "It seems that way. But, why me? What is my connection with the little girl and the queen?"

Peter took her hand and held it. "Perhaps this is a clue as to what the game is all about. I think we are on some kind of treasure hunt with the treasure being an unknown at this time."

"Well, my beautiful husband, I agree. Now it is time for us to shower, and get ready for our three little tornados. Or, are they tornados?"

Peter smiled. "Perhaps tornados is too strong, but they are live wires and we are so fortunate in having them,"

After breakfast and the twins were off to school, Ellen played and read to Eleanor for an hour. Yvonne came in to take Eleanor to the playground while Ellen turned her attention to her dream. She went on-line to search the meaning of the black lion and came up with a definition that it meant "power." The serpent's meaning was "knowledge," or "wisdom." *This makes sense, she mused to herself. Now as pieces of the puzzle, we have also at that moment in an ancient time, a little girl, and a queen along with symbols.* The phone rang. It was Alain with his news.

"Hello my sister. I may have something from my source. The dagger could possibly be Egyptian and my source is working to determine the age of it because it appears to be a bronze blade. Possibly, and I am saying this as a potential that it could be from around 1350 b.c. It seems your gift is indeed ancient."

Ellen was silent for a moment. "Alain, I had another dream early this morning. She then told him of her dream and that she had seen the lion and serpent as the head of a royal staff."

Alain let out a low whistle. "You do have opportunities for adventure. The markings on the blade appear to be hieroglyphics and I have a lead on someone who perhaps could decipher them. I will call you when I hear more from my source. In the meantime, tell me about my nieces and nephew."

She laughed. "Joseph and Magda are doing well in school. Eleanor is doing her best to keep up with them. Why not come for the weekend? Sebastian and Jill with their children will be here."

"I would enjoy that. I will clear my calendar and let you know an approximate time."

She called Marie on the house phone and asked her to have a room prepared for *M*. Delacroix. Marie replied that she was delighted and asked Ellen if she had the menus for the meals ready for her. Ellen responded that she would have them ready within the hour. *Oh, gawd, I forgot about the meals.* She pulled up her menu list from her computer and set about creating meals while their guests were there.

After she completed the menus for the weekend, she printed a copy and went to the kitchen to give the list to Marie. The two went over the menu, when Cerise came into the kitchen. Cerise, a niece of Marie, had been there for a year as an assistant to Marie and her job was primarily to keep the chateau clean. *"Excusez-moi Mme,* Ellen. I do not want to intrude."

Ellen smiled. "I'm glad you are here as I am discussing with Marie the preparations for our guests this weekend." She then gave her instructions for which rooms would be assigned to the guests. "It would be best if Arthur slept in Joseph's room, and Eleanor and Aimée share the same room. I will have Yvonne keep an eye on them during the night and perhaps you will assist Yvonne during their stay here."

Cerise smiled. "*Merci Mme*. I am most happy to do so."

The morning came when the guests were to arrive. The twins and Eleanor were excited about the arrival of their favorite friends Arthur and Aimée. While they were eating breakfast with their parents, Magda complained that she really did not have a friend her age. "Joseph and Arthur do their boy things and Aimée and Eleanor are too young for me. I just know it will be a boring week-end for me."

Peter laughed at his daughter. "My dear sweet girl, you do have a dilemma. You can either play with the boys some of the time and Eleanor and Aimée at other times. There is another alternative for you."

"All right Papa. What is that?"

"You can play by yourself and either read, write or draw."

Magda was about to reply with a retort when she looked at her mother and changed what she was about to say. "Well, I will take your suggestions under advisement."

Peter and Ellen began laughing. Joseph joined in and soon the cloud had lifted and plans were discussed.

It was mid-morning when Sebastian, Jill and their children arrived. The twins had kept watch, and when the gatekeeper called to say that he had just opened the gate for them, two tornados burst through the door just as Sebastian drove up. Eleanor was running behind with a "Me too. Me too."

Ellen and Peter followed and soon they were all hugging, talking and laughing. Jacques came out and began removing the luggage to take up to the bedrooms. Yvonne called for the children to follow her to the playground. She pretended she was the Pied Piper and there was much giggling as the children followed her.

Peter and Sebastian turned and began walking into the château.

Jill and Ellen stood looking deeply into one another's eyes. There was a deep bond between the two women who had been friends since their university days. They had shared the tribulations and the joys of the *Magdalene Scrolls* and the *Sarah Scrolls.* Ellen spoke first. "I have missed you and I will say that you look wonderful."

Jill chuckled. "Well, I can say the same that I have also missed you. However, I am sensing something amiss with you."

Ellen swallowed hard and managed a smile. "You have come just in time to help me understand a most unusual event. But, we will talk about that after lunch."

Jill asked, "Are you into another set of scrolls?"

"Oh gawd no!" Ellen replied.

Yvonne and Cerise had taken the children to the lake for a picnic lunch; therefore, the adults were able to enjoy their meal, which Marie served with great delight. Jill was the first to speak, "I thought Alain would be here. Is he still coming?"

Peter answered her. "He will be here later. I received a call from him this morning and something came up to delay him."

Jill noticed a shadow in his eyes and chose not to pursue why Alain was delayed. Instead, she nodded and continued eating.

Ellen suggested that they go to the sanctum after they completed their meal. This raised the eyebrows of both Sebastian and Jill. "*Eh bien.* You have uncovered another secret I think."

They all laughed and Ellen answered him. "Sebastian you are astute as always. However, I think that first we should have coffee and dessert. Marie has made a beautiful torte. Now, Peter and I want to hear about your latest adventures."

Jill nodded to Sebastian. He cleared his throat as Marie cleared the luncheon dishes and left to bring in the coffee and torte. "We are thinking seriously of moving to Canada because I have been offered a teaching position at the *Université du Québec* in the European History Network. I have until January before I have to make a decision. There is much to consider." He looked at Jill and she smiled.

"It is a hard decision to make." Jill took a deep breath and continued. "I love France and it has been my second home country. We, we have you – our friends, and it will be heart wrenching to be so far away. I, I know this is a wonderful opportunity."

Ellen reached over and took Jill's hand. "My beloved friend, you must do what you feel is right in your heart. And, we are only a phone call away. Yes, I will miss you; however, I am happy that you have until January to make your decision. Whatever it is, I promise to support you in whatever decision you make."

Peter said that he also supported them and in the meantime, perhaps they should adjourn and go to the sanctum.

Jill laughed and said, "This must be something big if we are going to enter the sanctum."

Sebastian shook his head. "*Mon dieu!* Are there more scrolls?"

Ellen and Peter laughed and he suggested they will learn about their latest gift.

The foursome entered the sanctum and Jill asked, "Do we need to put on gloves for this?"

Ellen chuckled. "No, not for this one. I have a tale to tell you – a strange tale." She began with her first dream and how it led up to a gift. "I received an unusual gift from an unknown person or persons, and we have loaned it to Alain for verification of its age. In the meantime, we do have photographs that we will let you see."

Peter handed copies of the dagger to Sebastian and to Jill. They looked at them and Jill burst out, "My god! This is a dagger! Why would an unknown person give you this?"

Sebastian was silent for a moment as he studied his photo. "Eh, it appears to be quite old. I see markings on the blade. Are you having them deciphered?"

Ellen answered his question. "We have met with Alain and he has someone who may be able to tell us what the markings are and the dagger's age. He will be here later and perhaps he will have information.

Sebastian appeared lost in thought and then he looked up. "It could be Egyptian, but I am not an authority. This is a mystery and I wonder what it portends."

Jill also said she wanted to know. "There is something about you my friend that attracts exciting things such as scrolls. Now it is a dagger. I'm waiting for its unfoldment."

It was late afternoon when Alain arrived. The five children ran out to greet him when he drove through the gate and stopped in front on the château. Five little voices screamed, "*Oncle* Alain, *Oncle* Alain! He's here!" He laughed and hugged each one of them. From his jacket pocket, he pulled out a treat he had brought for them. At that moment, Yvonne spoke up and suggested they allow *M.* Alain to greet their parents and perhaps later they could spend time with him. Alain gave her a smile and said *"Je vous remercie."*

Before he could open the door into the chateau, Jacques opened it and greeted him while taking his overnight case to the bedroom. Alain thanked him and turned to greet Ellen. "Ah, my sister it is wonderful to see you.'

The two embraced and Ellen stepped back and looked at him. His face was haggard and drawn with sadness. "Alain, what has happened? You look so sad."

He gave her a weak smile and suggested they go to the sanctum. At that moment, Peter arrived and the two men embraced. He looked first at Ellen and then back to Alain. Ellen told him that Alain wanted them to go to the sanctum.

Once they were inside, Alain spoke first. "Forgive me. I am in shock. I, I have some bad news and it involves the dagger you brought to me."

Ellen asked, "Has it disappeared?"

He shook his head and replied, "No. It is even worse. I told you that I had someone I trusted who could possibly date the dagger and perhaps have the markings on the blade deciphered. I am devastated as *Madame* Gillet was found this morning in her shop bludgeoned to death. The police contacted me as she had listed my law office in her address book."

Peter asked, "Is she the person you took the dagger to?"

"*Ah oui*. However, all is not lost as she brought it to me late yesterday evening and I have brought it back to you safely."

Ellen fought back the tears. "Do, do you think this murder is connected to the dagger?"

"Possibly. She gave me a written copy of what she had learned about it. It appears that she has dated it to approximately 1350 B.C. and theorized that it belonged to an Egyptian Pharaoh. I brought my briefcase with me and I have the dagger and her findings inside." He opened his briefcase and handed her papers from *Mme*. Gillet.

Ellen stood there dumbfounded. "I, I hope to god that her death is not connected to this, however my gut feeling is that it is." She turned to Peter and handed the findings to him. "I can't read this. Please, you do it."

"Sweetheart, I know you are seldom wrong about your gut feelings." He opened the papers and gave a low whistle. "She had dated this to around 1350 b.c. in the New Kingdom of pharaohs. She goes on to say that because the pommel of the lion encircled by a gold serpent would in all likelihood belong to a pharaoh or a member of the pharaoh's family. As for the encryption on the blade, she had not bee n able to have it deciphered."

"Holy shit! Why would it be me to get this? How could I be connected to something as ancient as this?"

Alain shook his head. "It is a mystery. When she returned the dagger, she told me that she had a photocopy of it blown up and was now seeking someone who could possibly translate this. Since her untimely death, perhaps we should bring Sebastian in on this."

Ellen took a deep breath. "Yes, let's do it. We have already told them and they have seen pictures of it. But what is the game?"

ΩΩΩ

~ HY BRASIL ~
400 A.D.

THE COUNCIL MEETING

A rock pile ceases to be a rock pile the moment a single woman contemplates it, bearing within her the image of a cathedral.~ Antoine de Saint Exupéry

Magdalena woke just before the rising of the sun, as was her custom. She quickly dressed in her usual robe of midnight blue and went to the set of windows facing the east. Opening the curtains, she unlatched the window and breathed in the early morning air. Her nostrils flared as the scents of the castle permeated her senses. Gone was the freshness of the mountain air along with the purity of the trees and plants.

She raised her hands up to her forehead and bowed to her god to begin her early morning greeting. Not wanting to awaken the household, she silently mouthed the ohms knowing she was sending out the energy of this ancient sound. This was followed by her morning prayer.

Oh Great Isness, Unknowable One.
I call forth this day
Strength and Clarity of Mind.
Fill me with power
Fill me with knowingness.
Create within me the awareness and passion to fulfill my mission.
I accept. It be so.

Just as she completed the 'It be so,' she heard a knock on the door. She knew it would be Mireen bringing her early morning cup of tea and gruel. Mireen curtsied as she entered. With a broad smile, she placed the tray on the small table.

She smiled back to Mireen. The enormity of her new role again was becoming her reality. She allowed her mind to expand and to ebb and flow. It was a method for emptying the mind taught by the Druidesses. One by one, she focused on each of her father's Trusted Ones as well as Brannon.

Bringing the image of each of them to the front of her mind, she allowed herself to feel each one. This could be called *tuning in.* She knew without a doubt the weakest of them was Rath, the Trainer of the Guardsman. Brannon would be a formidable foe. He had a devious mind and was filled with jealousy. She knew there were others. As she continued, she knew she was fully prepared to meet each of them on their own level of mind. When she completed her tuning in, she finished her breakfast.

While Magdalena was contemplating, Mireen laid a stunning robe of red on the bed. She felt tempted to turn it away when she realized she would have to play a role in the beginning. She remembered it being traditional to wear red when there was a death and to pay homage to her father. It would be expected she do so. Sighing, she knew it to be a great test to be in the midst of opulence and trivial rituals after 12 years of being away. It was difficult to allow Mireen to dress her and to brush her hair.

After Mireen deemed her ready, she sent Mireen to ask Cyran to meet her in the gardens. She used this respite to call forth communication with her Druid sister Callan. Magdalena stilled her mind to bring up the image of Callan and when they made the mind-to-mind connection, she directed Callan to come to the castle as soon as possible because she wanted Callan to be her secretary and assistant. Callan agreed.

Magdalena found Cyran waiting when she arrived. After their greeting, she suggested they walk to an open area. "I almost sense each of the plants 'ave ears."

Cyran laughed and agreed. Without hesitation, he gave her a report on the progress of her father's passing ceremonies. He would not be buried until three full days passed. Since most of the lords and ladies were already here, it also allowed others to come from the far reaches of the realm. The Lady of the Druidesses would be arriving with a sizeable contingent of Druidesses. This was only fitting since Magdalena lived and studied with them for 12 years. She and Cyran both smiled, as they knew the Druidesses were adept in the art of teleporting themselves.

Cyran turned the conversation to the coming meeting. "Yew be needed to use the power of yere mind and be alert fer the treachery of Brannon. His cohorts are Thran, Gareth, Wens and Morfred. Yew will 'ave to seek out their weaknesses. Yew 'ave the mind training and be quite capable."

Nodding in agreement, Magdalena then asked Cyran to be with her during the meeting this morn. She described the perceptions she received earlier this morn.

Cyran gave her a look of appreciation. He told her that she was quiet perceptive and must always trust her knowingness and insights. "Twill soon be a viper's nest around here. No one dares make a move until Sarenhild be laid to rest. Be at peace Magdalena, and know the vipers well 'erefore yew make a move."

Magdalena entered the meeting alone and was quick to notice the attendance. They stood with alacrity except for Brannon. His posture screamed with resentment and she felt his inner turmoil. She said nothing nor did she sit until he stood up. She felt his hatred and anger.

The table of the council was large enough to seat thirteen. Hewn from an extremely large oak tree 6 feet in diameter, it set upon a large pedestal. This morning there were only seven in attendance. She greeted each one individually and requested a scribe to be sent for. She wanted this meeting recorded. She noted the surprise and a note of appreciation from them all except Brannon. Once the scribe arrived and sat in place to record the meeting with his papyrus and quill, Magdalene asked Cyran to give his report on the burial ceremony of Sarenhild.

After Cyran ended his report of the burial, Magdalena asked Kanen, Keeper of the Treasury to report on the status of the kingdom's finances of the realm, which did not include Sarenhild's personal wealth.

Clearing his voice, Kanen began his recital in a rather monotonous voice. He was of medium stature with balding brown hair worn to his shoulders. His well-manicured beard had been cut to a point and he enjoyed stroking it whenever he wanted to make a point. She knew she had been correct in her earlier assessment. She knew he could be trusted and a shrewd man. His appearance of being vain was all for show. Beneath his appearance lay a deep river of knowledge and reverence for the god within.

Following Kanen's report, Magdalene asked for Oris, General of the Right Flank to give his assessment of the unrest in the realm. Oris bowed with a genuine smile towards Magdalena. He was of a tall stature. His dark, almost black hair was in stark contrast to her red hair. Flashing green eyes exuded strength and wisdom. His tanned skin showed none of the swarthiness that was common of the black headed people. A muscular body rippled under his tunic of scarlet. As he spoke, his voice carried a melodious lilt to it.

He reported it appeared the Skagerraks[1] were gaining a foothold in the northeast part of the realm. It had been two years since the Skagerraks managed to come in through the mists surrounding Hy Brasil. The weakest point of intrusion appeared to be the area of Thuster. Their method of intrusion being of small raids on outlying villages, and the kidnapping of women and children. The burning of granaries had been reported. He recommended a regiment of his top fighting men to be sent to Thuster to quell the unrest because the Skagerraks were stirring up the populace with false propaganda.

Magdalena acknowledged his report and indicated that she would make no comment until she heard from Brannon. He stood and said, "My Lady Magentheld, I be most honored to be of yere advisory." Before he could say more, Magdalena intervened.

"General Brannon, perhaps yew be nae acquainted with court etiquette. Yew will address me nae as My Lady Magentheld. Yew will address me as Your Majesty the Queen or Lady Magentheld."

Brannon's face turned red with anger. He replied in a sardonic tone of voice, "Forgive me Yere Majesty the Queen fer my blunder." She nodded and told him to carry on. He continued saying that he suggests perhaps Oris overemphasized the severity of the Skagerrak incursions. He stated his reports are said to be very small infractions, but if she desired, he too would be sending a regiment to the Thuster area to quell any disturbance.

---

[1] From the areas of the southeast coast of Norway, the southwest coast f Sweden and the Jutland peninsula of Denmark.

Brannon continued to speak and she felt signals to be alert for here was a master of deception. She realized he reminded her of a weasel. His eyes were quite small and narrow. It was difficult to distinguish his brown eyes. His mustache drooped on both sides and his thinning mottled brown hair pulled back to make it look fuller. The longer she allowed him to talk, the more his left eye twitched. She knew he was nervous and with his fawning manner, he thought he was doing a beautiful downplay of the seriousness of the incursions.

She knew Brannon had a lust for power and at the core of his personality he was dishonest and cruel. She recognized somehow this man must be replaced.

Following Brannon's lengthy dissertation, she asked Rath, the Trainer of the Guardsmen to give a status report of the Guardsmen training. When he began speaking, she became aware he was nervous; however, she knew him to be loyal but weak. There must be a way to strengthen his loyalty. Loyal in the moment, but not to be trusted.

She was grateful for the training she received with the Druidesses. At one point in their training, the young novices had been sent out to villages with the objective to observe the people. They had been taught techniques of the mind to render them invisible. During the training trips, she learned very well to read the energy fields around each person and to assess their personality traits by the way they walked, their posture, their speech and the tone of voice. She excelled in this training. She could tell when a person needed to relieve themselves or were hungry. She finally developed the technique of reading other people's thoughts.

Boseno, the Armskeeper gave a very concise report of the status of weaponry. He was alert and she felt a great depth to him. She knew her father chose well when he named this man to be Armskeeper.

She did not ask Cyran for a report as Historian because she knew he would tell her whatever history she wanted to know.

Thanking each of the men for their excellent reports, she told them she would be taking it all under advisement and be meeting with them again the following day at the same hour. She stood wishing them a pleasant day and walked regally out of the room. She understood Cyran's signal that he wished to meet with her. Using her mental telepathy, she told him to meet her in the great library.

When she entered the library, she was struck with nostalgia. It had been her favorite place when she was a child. The many scrolls, bound papyruses had been her friends. She mastered the art of reading by the time she became three years. The air smelled musty and she knew it was little used in the past few years. She made a mental note to have her staff give this an airing and a cleaning.

With her mental powers, she scanned the room and detected there were no listening spies. No one expected her to use the library as a meeting place with Cyran. At this moment, Cyran made his appearance. After they exchanged greetings, Magdalena suggested they sit at the reading table. He paused a moment while he also mentally scanned the room for spies, and arrived at the same conclusion as Magdalena as he took a seat.

"Yere Majesty, yew did quite well this morn. I could tell yew be assessing quite rightly. Tis Brannon we must watch and cultivate."

"Holy One, yew 'ave no need to address me as 'Yere Majesty.' I prefer 'M'Lady'. I recognize I 'ave much to learn and I will use the tools of the mind I 'ave learned. What be yere assessment of the Skagerrak incursions?"

He paused before speaking and then replied, "It be my feeling the raids will become more numerous naow that Sarenhild has passed. They will assume this because the new Magentheld be a woman and they deem she be weak. It be possible Brannon will strike a bargain with them."

"What do yew advise?"

"At the moment, I suggest sending some of our trained Druidesses to the northern reaches to ferret out how the wind blows."

Magdalena laughed and agreed. "Oh Holy One, this be brilliant! Who would ever suspect women be our news gatherers! Will yew ask our Lady Alinor to initiate this mission immediately?"

"Tis as good as done," replied Cyran. "Naow I suggest yew meet with the lords and ladies fer the evening meal this night. It be understandable yew need nae tarry. 'Owever, an appearance be quite appropriate."

She nodded in agreement and thanked Cyran for his great advice and support. "What be coming from the village?"

"Ah tis said they be a bit surprised. There 'ave been nae murmurings of yew being the new Magentheld. Yere peoples of the village loved yere mother and since yew be from her loins they accept."

She smiled and replied, "I remember my mother loved them. I will invite them to come to the burial site fer Sarenhild. Who be the head Druid in the village?

He smiled. "It be the Druidess jurist Muirno. She be wise and she be fair."

"I will meet with her after the burial." She stood up and they agreed to meet after the first greeting of the morn in the gardens. Thus she spent the remainder of the day with the Chief Steward. Together they toured the castle and she met all of the staff. This she insisted because she knew she must assess each and every one for his or her degree of loyalty.

Once she was satisfied, she returned to her quarters where she found Mireen waiting for her and the bath water already drawn.

"M'Lady, t'was a great deed yew did to meet with staff this day. I, I be overwhelmed. Never 'erefore has any Magentheld done this," Mireen said with tears in her eyes.

"Mireen, I be nae just any Magentheld. I be the Queen. A new wind has blown here and there be many changes abroad. This must be so to bring new life to old ways. Thus, Hy Brasil will grow and prosper." Magdalena smiled because she knew she had a trusted ally in Mireen.

When she stepped into the sunken bath, Magdalena silently reminded herself that she must not be lulled into the comforts of the body. She spent too many years training her mind and body to respond to the responsibility she was destined for. She used her time in the bath to contemplate and assess all she learned this day. There was treachery among the staff and these she would gradually weed out. She thought, *When Callan arrives, I be turning this task over to her.*

Mireen interrupted her contemplation by offering a large fluffy cloth to dry her. She already had placed another red gown for her to wear on the bed. It was encrusted with pearls and threads of gold. It was indeed fitting for a ruler such as a Queen. After Magdalena slipped the gown on, she caught sight of herself in the full-length mirror. This was a view of herself she did not know and was not comfortable with; however, she allowed Mireen to place a pair of shining gold slippers on her feet. She thought it was amazing that everything was the right size and fit. In a flash, she knew the Lady Alinor had ben responsible for this.

Had she known what would be in store for her, she might have rebelled. Mireen brushed her hair and arranged it to flow over her shoulders. Last, she placed the Crown of Hy Brasil on Magdalena's head. Mentally, Magdalena created an attitude of lightness and the heaviness of the crown disappeared.

Magdalena carried herself regally as she walked into the large eating hall. Cyran was there, waiting to escort her to the head table. The configuration of the long tables consisted of one long horizontal table with three lateral shorter tables coming out from one side of the main table. Somehow, the energy of the tables did not feel right to her and she silently resolved to change this while thinking it needed a better geometric configuration.

Cyran was seated on her right and on her left were Kanen and his lady. She smiled inwardly when she noticed Brannon sitting next to Cyran. Oris sat next to Kanen's lady and apparently he either had no lady or else, she was unable to come. To Brannon's left were Bosenio and his lady followed by lords and ladies of lesser rank. Seated next to Oris was Rath with his lady followed by lords and ladies of lesser rank. The bells rang and the serving people began placing platters of wild boar, goose, venison and other meats on the table. This was followed by mounds of millet in silver bowls, along with yams and other roots. Great loaves of bread accompanied the meal. Other serving people kept the silver goblets flowing with wine. She ate sparingly and only pretended to sip the wine because she knew she had to keep alert. Lastly, the fresh fruits and cheeses arrived. These were more to her liking.

The talking reached a crescendo as the wine mellowed and loosened the tongues. It reminded her of a cacophony of geese. She received a whisper from Cyran that it would be a good time for her to welcome all first and then call in the minstrels and bards.

Magdalena stood with a smile on her face. The great hall became very quiet. "I welcome each and all of yew to this great gathering. I honor yere presence. The ceremonies fer the burial of Sarenhild take place the day following the morrow." Her voice carried a powerful melodious tone and she knew she be captivating her audience, as be her intent.

"It be my desire yew complete this meal with the singing of the bards and minstrels. They be singing the praises of Sarenhild. The wine continues to flow until the hour named eleven. I bless yew and I thank yew. Naow I depart." Without a backward glance, Magdalena swept out of the dining hall and on to her quarters. Cyran and the others remained behind. There was much to learn and assess from the mood and loosened tongues of those remaining.

When she arrived at her quarters, she allowed Mireen to help her take off the crown and gown. After putting her night robe on, she told Mireen she wanted to be alone now. Mireen curtsied and left the room.

Magdalena heaved a big sigh and walked to the great window and opened it. She wanted to feel the cold night air. It was invigorating to her and she relished the coldness. After taking a few deep breaths, she began her night greeting to the Isness within.

Oh Isness, creator of all.
Mysterious One.
Fill my night with dreams divine.
Come forth knowledge and wisdom I gain.

Let me never forget from whence I come.

As she lay in the great bed, she drifted into a trance-like state. She knew she was tapping into her deeper mind.

⛩⛩⛩

Magdalena of Hy Brasil

~ France ~
2013

The Meaning

"Understanding is the first step to acceptance, and only with acceptance can there be recovery."
~ Joanne Kathleen Rowling

Alain returned to Paris early the following day due to a call he received from a friend in the investigative unit of French National Police regarding the murder of *Mme*. Gillet. Before he left, he met with Ellen, Peter, Sebastian and Jill. "I have been invited to discuss with *détective de la police Reynaud* about my connection to *Mme*. Gillet as my name was written in her appointment book for the evening before her murder. I am to meet with him at two this afternoon.

Ellen felt tears welling up and choked them back. "We understand. Please keep us informed. Oh drat! I'm sorry I dragged you into this!"

"Ah my sister, I would not have it any other way. However, her murder may not have anything to do with the dagger. In the meantime, I urge each of you to be alert and notify me if anything unusual happens."

"This we will do." And Peter hugged him.

After Alain had left, Ellen picked up the photo of the dagger. "What is the meaning of this? What is its purpose? And why have I been selected to receive this ancient dagger?"

"Sweetheart, somehow together we will learn the meaning of this. I remember your dreams are connected because you saw the queen holding a staff with the head of a black lion and a serpent entwined around it."

"Sometimes during the day, I have flashes of the little girl and at other times a woman who is a queen."

"Hmmm. You haven't told me about these flashes. Are you writing them down in your journal?"

Ellen leaned against him. "Yes. I will share them with you after the children are bedded down."

He bent down and gave her a long passionate kiss. "Hey, big guy if you keep this up, I may ask you to take me here."

"That's a possibility." He kissed her again and at that moment, a small voice was heard from outside the door into the sanctum.

"Papa, Eleanor won't give me back my crayons and she is running around giggling."

"Okay Magda. Walk away from her and act as if it does not matter. Your mother and I will be out in a moment."

"Well, if you say so."

Ellen was trying not to laugh. "One of the children seems to know when to interrupt us. I think we can save our love-making until after they are asleep."

Peter shook his head. "You're right. But I will have you tonight."

Jill and Ellen were walking in the woods. The two women had not had an opportunity to have a heart-to-heart talk since Jill and her family arrived. "Ellen, you look a little bit frazzled. Is everything okay with you?

"As far as the family and my relationship with Peter it is terrific. I am frazzled because of the dagger I received. I have feelings that this isn't a gift out of gratitude or love."

"It is an awesome piece and must be extremely old. It does have the appearance of being an ancient Egyptian artifact, and as you told me, it could have belonged to a Pharaoh."

"Umm, it does. I feel dreadful about *Mme.* Gillet being murdered and I pray that it has nothing to do with the dagger."

"Ellen, have you ever considered that there is a purpose – or a reason why you fell into the cave and found the cache of Magdalene Scrolls, and then having the Sarah scrolls almost fall into your lap? Could they have anything to do with the gift of the dagger?"

"I've tried not to think about it or connect the dots. There was so much that happened in connection with them. But, now a dagger. What worries me is the slip of paper in the package."

"Well, I am wondering too. Since I am connected with you and participated, I am also curious about the message of "Welcome to the Game." What game is this? Is this something out of the past?

"I would think it is from a past life." Ellen sighed and kicked a few leaves that were falling from the trees. "Tell me Jill, are you sure you want to go to Canada?"

"Well, it is an opportunity for Sebastian. Yes, I think I am looking forward to a change. Oh, life has been okay in Toulouse, but I miss you and you family. I also think Sebastian needs a change. However, it won't be until after the first of the year."

Ellen swallowed the lump in her throat and hugged Jill. "Dear friend, I am truly happy for you. And, I know we will only be a phone call away. I say let's walk to the stream and really talk. Peter had a bench placed there and we can be by the water, even though it may be a trickle now that it is Fall."

"I'm with you. Lead on. I would enjoy a long talk and I know it wouldn't' happen if we were back at the château."

Walking quickly, the women came to the stream and the bench, and sat down. Jill was the first to talk. "Perhaps this is silly of me, but I want to reminisce about our trip last year. We needed that vacation alone without husbands and children. It was great that Peter assumed responsibility for our children while we were gone and Sebastian away at a conference. "

"It was fun and I agree with you. Of course, Peter had help and he actually enjoyed it. Thanks to your suggestion that we attempted to follow the clues that the Magdalene and Sarah gave in their scrolls."

"Yes, and even though I had been to *Rennes-le Château* for a number of times, this time I saw it with a new perspective. I chuckle when I think that few people realize that the statues flanking the altar are Mary Magdalene and Jesus holding infants representing Sarah and James."

Ellen smiled. "That may be true; however what if the statues represent Joseph and Mary with each holding a twin. You know, Jesus had a twin named Thomas."

"Ouch! You got me on that one. I think you are correct."

"I know there are numerous mysteries about the area. I don't think I told you this, but after our trip I came across a book written by Patrice Chaplin with the title *City of Secrets*. As a teenager, she and another girl were traveling – umm, I have to backtrack. They were both from England and stopped in *Girona, Spain* where Patrice fell in love with a local man. She stayed while the other went on. What I want to say is that while there, she learned that *Abbé Saunière* often went there to visit. During this time in *Girona*, there was a Magdalene Tower, or *Tour de Magdala*. He went there from time to time as he became part of group steeped in the history of the *Cabbala*, an ancient Jewish secret organization."

Jill looked at her with surprise. "Oh my god! And you forgot to mention this to me? No, don't answer. I know we became busy after our trip. However, do go on. This is fascinating."

"The man Patrice fell in love with was a member of this organization, if I remember correctly, and it was through his connections that she learned about this. According to her, *Saunière* created an identical Magdala Tower in *Rennes-le-Château* on a ley line that connected the two towers. *Mary Magdalene* has become resurrected from the lies and omissions surrounding her."

"I agree and isn't it interesting that the Cabbalist group there knew about her and created a tower in her honor? I know I will get the book and read it and then we can have an in-depth discussion."

"That would be great. I'm sorry that I didn't mention this before."

"Tell me Ellen, what do you think was the highlight of our trip?"

"I think it was when we went to the *Isles of Scilly* to see if we could find information about the isles being once part of *Cornwall*."

"I have to agree with you. The natives do not like them being called *Scilly Isles*, although I will say that the people were friendly. We really did not get any concrete information about the islands once being one big one attached to the coast of *Cornwall*."

The two women paused and watched and listened to the gurgling water flowing over the rocks.

Ellen was the first to speak. "I know that the people laughed at us for the most part, although others thought it might be possible."

"Yes, I remember and I also remember that you had very strong feelings about once being there. Do you think this could be connected to the dreams you told me about?"

Ellen took a deep breath. "I didn't think so at first, however I am now having second thoughts. Perhaps there is a connection, and I really don't know what to do or perhaps to accept that it is possible. However, from time to time I have visions of an island surrounded by mists."

There was a moment of silence and a small breeze came up ruffling the shallow water and fallen leaves were moving down as if they were tiny boats. Jill broke the silence. "I have read that the past, present and future times are all happening simultaneously. What do you think?"

"I had not thought much about it before, however now I am thinking it may be a possibility. Perhaps it is true that the past, present and future are all happening now, but am I having dreams about another past timeline? It is a bit frightening."

"Why I brought this up is because of the feelings you had when we went to the *Isles of Scilly* that you had been there before."

"Yes, I had feelings that I had been there before and that it had been *Lyonesse* before it sank. And yes, there had to be either a big earthquake or a tsunami that had to inundate it." Ellen sighed. "Let's walk back towards the chalet. Talking to you has eased my concerns. We do make a good pair."

ΩΩΩ

Sebastian

"The oldest and strongest emotion of mankind is fear." ~ H.P. Lovecraft

Jill and Sebastian had chosen to remain for a few more days as the symbols on the dagger intrigued him. After the weekend, he made an appointment with a well-known authority on Egyptian symbols who lived in Paris and whose name was Andre Lefevre.

The morning after Jill and Ellen had their heart-to-heart talk in the forest; Sebastian announced he had made an appointment with *M.* Lefevre today, which was a Tuesday. He was excited because he thought perhaps this could be a breakthrough regarding the symbols on the dagger. The appointment was for 11 a.m. and after the appointment, he was going to the Sorbonne to meet with an old friend for lunch.

Jacques had brought the car around to the front for Sebastian and with a kiss to Jill and their two children he left in a cheerful frame of mind. Jill looked down at their children, "No, Papa will return after his appointment and his *le déjeuner* with *M.* Predeaux who teaches at the Sorbonne. Come, it is time for play."

It was around noon when Marie came to Jill and told her the office of *M.* Lefevre was on *le téléphone* wanting to know if *M.* Sebastian was late for his appointment. Jill looked startled and took the phone and began speaking to *M*. Lefevre. After she hung up, she looked perplexed and went to look for Ellen.

"Ellen, I just had the strangest phone call from *M*. Lefevre who said that Sebastian had not shown for his appointment. I, I have the feeling that Sebastian is in some kind of trouble. Oh god! Please don't let anything happen to him!"

"I'll call Peter and ask him what can be done to find him. Perhaps he had a flat tire or something. Did he take a cell phone with him?"

"Yes, but wouldn't he use it to call me if something happened?"

"I suggest you try calling his cell phone. With shaking fingers, Jill went to the house phone and dialed his cell phone number. He did not answer and all she could do was leave a voice message. "I'm scared. He would have called. I know he is in trouble."

Ellen was on the phone with Peter and relayed what had transpired.

"Love, don't panic. I will call the authorities and see if there is a report of an accident or – well, you and Jill stay calm and I will be over as soon as I call."

Ellen had put the phone on speaker and she turned to Jill. "You heard. Right now, there is nothing we can do except pray that he is okay. Let's go into the solarium and have a quiet moment."

Jill could only nod. The two women closed their eyes and each in her own way began to focus on Sebastian. Before they could get deep into it, there was a light knock on the door. Ellen sighed and asked who was there.

"Mama, it me – Magda and I have something important to tell you."

"Come on in Magda."

"Mama, I know you do not want to be interrupted, but this is important. I, I had a vision of *Oncle* Sebastian."

Jill sat up and gasped, "What kind of vision?"

"I, I was watching the others play and I had a vision of *Oncle* Sebastian in trouble. Some, some bad men stopped his car and took him away."

Ellen asked her, "How did they take him away and do you have a mental picture of the vehicle?"

"Umm, I have an impression of a black van of some kind. I think there were two men who took him."

"Thank you my darling. If you get anymore impressions, please tell us."

Magda nodded her yes and put her arms around Jill. "*Tante* Jill, I know he will be all right and please do not cry."

Jill wiped the tears away and hugged Magda. "I, I am so blessed that you have your psychic abilities. Thank you for telling us."

When Magda left the room, Jill asked Ellen, "Why would anyone kidnap Sebastian? He hasn't been involved with anything special since the Sarah scrolls. Do you think it has anything to do with the dagger?"

"I don't see how it could be a connection; however there is always that possibility. If – if it is, how could anyone know that he was going to visit Andre Lefevre? We have only told you, Sebastian and my brother."

Jill nodded her agreement.

Sebastian woke up with a massive headache and realized he was manacled on both wrists and ankles. He realized he was a captive of someone or a group of people. He was lying on a hard cement floor and there was no light. At first, he had a sense of panic and fear. He began breathing in and out to subdue his fear. His thoughts turned to Jill and the children. *Mon dieu, keep them safe. They are my treasures.* He had no idea of how long he had been unconscious, where he was or what was wanted from him. He fell into a sleep, and was awakened when he heard the door open. He squinted his eyes as a light was shone on him.

There were two captors and they spoke to him in French with an accent. He knew they were not French. He was pulled up and dragged over to a chair where he was made to sit. His head throbbed. The light on his face came from a torch one of the captors held. The questioning began.

"Tell us about the dagger. We know it is in the possession of your friends. Tell us what the symbols say."

"I, I do not know."

The man with the interrogator began beating him, while the one who first spoke continued to question him as to the exact location of the dagger and what had been deciphered from the writings on it. Sebastian continued to say that he did not know the exact location as he had never seen the dagger – only a photo and that he could not know what the symbols were.

The beatings and interrogations continued until the one with the torch spoke to the other in a foreign language. The sound of it was vaguely familiar and Sebastian passed out. He knew he had wet his pants.

The two people left Sebastian in the oblivion of his pain.

ΩΩΩ

~ Hy Brasil ~
400 A.D.

A DREAM AND A BEGINNING

In dreams begins responsibility.
~ *William Butler Yeats*

Awakening, Magdalena felt the darkness without opening her eyes. She was dreaming and began searching her awareness to recall the dream. Fragments would come and finally she stopped trying. The dream would come at a later time and now she allowed her mind to drift back to when she began training by the Druidesses.

Dawn was yet to come and she was beginning a test. It happened to be the year of her fifteenth year. After five years of rigorous training, she was being put to a test. Years of observing and learning to read and interpret the tracks of animals and people as well as years of stalking without being seen. There were also years of mind expanding exercises and breathing exercises.

A feeling of excitement came over her and she recognized the rise of her adrenaline. She knew she had to be careful because this could be a give-away. She allowed her mind to expand to nothingness and yet awareness of all that was around her. The first rays of the sun began to lighten the world around her.

She lay under scrub plants growing in the crags of the high tor. She used ashes and clay to cover her skin with a blending effect with the landscape. Her red hair was thick with the ashes and clay.

She scanned her view of the commune and she never tired of looking at it from afar. The center was the configuration of a five-pointed star and from it the buildings were placed in a definite spiral. She had been well taught that the commune was built on the energy lines of the earth. It was all part of living with the energy of the earth.

Her awareness told her someone was near. She knew it to be one of the young Druidesses stalking her. If Magdalena failed this test, it would be another year before she could take it again. She resolved to pass it this year

Slowly she focused her mind to be one with the earth. It had taken her many hours of focusing on a tree, a plant or a rock to become attuned to their energies. The stalker moved away and she knew it to be Regan who was considered the best stalker in the commune. She also knew no young Druidess had dared to become invisible so close to the commune and the stream coming down from the high tor would be searched for signs of a hollow reed sticking out of the water. For this test, she chose to blend with the scrubby brush and rocks of the crags.

A ram's horn sounded and she knew the test to be over and she had passed. She waited another full hour before the horn sounded again. Slowly she began to move and to allow her blood to begin circulating. She was reluctant to reveal her hiding place and she began to use the stalker's training of being invisible while she made her way to the commune.

When she arrived back to her group, she was greeted with cheers and hugging. The Lady was there to greet her and told her 'well done'. She was now ready to go into villages and Holds to further her art of invisibility.

Stretching, Magdalena smiled as she recalled the test. She also understood why she recalled the memory. It was at this moment of this day that a group of twelve Druidesses left the commune to journey to the far reaches of the northern realm. Cyran told her it was as good as done with Regan being the lead.

She also knew some would be dressed as old peddler women, and others as bards and minstrels. These women would be her ears and she knew she could rely on their reports. She smiled realizing another group of twelve was also departing. This time to the east, the south and the west. *Ah Cyran*, she thought, *Yew be leaving nothing to chance*. Arising, she faced the east and began her greeting of the day chanting with joyous wonder.

While Magdalena was dressing and beginning her day of meetings, the first group of twelve fanned out to cover the northern realm. Each well trained, and the Lady personally gave them instructions. They were to observe only and report any activity relating to the Skagerrak in addition to any potential dis-loyalty to Magdalena, the new Magentheld and Queen. They were to note arms and troops buildup in addition to conspiracies. The two groups of twelve had been thoroughly trained in the techniques of mind expansion. It was as though this assignment would be what they were trained for from the beginning.

As the day wore on, Magdalena contemplated her earlier meeting with her advisory council. The energy field of Brannon had been dark with anger and deceit.

Although his outward appearance seemingly belied it, she also observed him to be a heavy drinker and in the beginnings of liver distress.

In Oris, she observed his energy field to be vibrant with a love for his god. Life was an adventure and he respected the people. *This is why his Right Flank Army is so successful,* she thought. *He knows people and their weaknesses and there be much depth to him.*

Her contemplation was interrupted by the Chief Steward. "M'Lady, most honored Magentheld, I hesitate to intrude, however I be in a quandary. The Lady of Brannon—Lady Bertran, be insisting she and her entourage be garrisoned in the main part of the castle."

Magdalena smiled and asked him where the Lady Bertran and her entourage were usually garrisoned.

Wetting his lips, the Chief Steward, whose name was Hyfrin spoke. "M'Lady, the usual procedure is they be quartered in the west part of the manse grounds in the smaller manse. It be already repaired and be naow occupied by the wife, the General and their entourage."

Without hesitation, she told him there would be no change and if Lady Bertran had a quarrel, to come to her, the Queen. Smilingly broadly, the Chief bowed and left her.

She again reflected on her meeting with the advisory council. There were thirteen places at the round table and yet, there were only five men who were the advisory council. As her thoughts coagulated, she knew there needed to be women capable of filling the other seven spaces and that left one for her. She stood up and decided to walk in the gardens.

She walked among the roses and the flowers inhaling their beautiful scents. The bees were busy collecting nectar for their hives. She stopped when she heard the word 'guilds' came into her mind along with its implications. It was as though a scroll had unrolled in her thoughts. She smiled and turned to return to her room where she conducted business. Aye, she wanted to discuss this with Callan. Excitement rippled through her, and she knew this was a grand idea to benefit the people of the realm.

A new thought came to her of changing quarters. This brought to her awareness a point she was uncomfortable with. Her mother's chambers did not suit her needs and the thought of moving to her father's quarters was distasteful. She remembered a suite of rooms during her tour of the castle the previous day and she knew them to be suited for her needs. She called for Mireen and again for the Chief Steward. She told them of her plans. She noted the surprise in each of their energy fields, but they were too discreet to voice it. Magdalena informed them this move was to be implemented at once.

She knew the new quarters were well suited for her with the large circular room—or half-circular having windows to the north, the east and the south. There was also a small balcony facing the east and from this vantage point she had a magnificent view of the gardens with the far woods and mountains beyond.

She felt more excited as she thought about it. She stood in small entry from the hallway. To the right would be the sitting room before entering her large bedroom, which led to a large dressing and bathing room and beyond it a small bedroom for Mireen. To the left, another chamber to be used by Callan when she arrived.

She continued to her bedroom and found the serving people already pulling dust covers from the furniture. The big four-poster bed had its head to the north. She felt the mattress and knew it to be too soft and she gave orders to Hyfrin to bring a much harder mattress. "Before he could carry out his orders, Mireen informed them she had already taken care of it and the mattress was now on its way.

Magdalena smiled and was pleased Mireen had taken the initiative. Magdalena knew there were secret passageways riddling the manse and she knew how to enter them. Her new suite had only one secret entrance and she would see that no one used it without her knowing or permission. She looked around and pondered the layout of her wing. She realized the entrance to her chamber from the main hallway resembled the ancient ankh. The synchronicity of it made her laugh aloud. She felt like a child with a new gift.

The energy of the large consciousness of the manse and the surrounding Hold were pulling on her. This, she must guard against at all times. Her training with the Druidesses sent her many times into villages and Holds to test her ability for not giving in to the low energy field of the masses. It could lull one back into the enchantment of the physical body and the senses.

The move was accomplished quickly because Magdalena had no large amount of possessions. Mireen had laid out another red gown for her to wear at the evening meal. Inwardly, Magdalena groaned. She knew her attendance at the evening meal to be expected and that she would comply until after the burial of her father Sarenfeld. Somehow, she must create space for her to have alone time. This would be vital.

When Magdalena walked into the eating hall, a hush fell. Walking slowly and regally, she nodded and smiled as she made her way to her seat at the head table. She purposely looked at Lady Bertran while giving her a loving smile, which was met with downcast eyes. She was able to know from the energy field that inwardly Bertran was seething with anger.

The meal proceeded and for her, it was excessively long. She made her departure gracefully with few words. Waiting for her was Mireen who helped her undress and put on her nightwear. After braiding Magdalena's hair, she made her departure.

She lay upon her bed after making her evening prayer with the god within. She relaxed and allowed the energy of her new quarters to be filled with her own. Using her mind, she searched through the suite of rooms for any energy that would not be compatible with hers. Once she was sure it was clean, she began sweeping and radiating her energy throughout the suite. This was followed by placing a band of energy completely around, over and under the chambers for protection. When this had been completed, she knew there would be no unwanted intruders either in the physical or the astral realms.

During the time Magdalena was accomplishing this, the Druidesses in groups of twelve were making their way to all far corners of the realm. She smiled as she allowed her knowingness to follow their journey.

Sleep eluded her and she lay there reviewing the the day's events. *Dear Peppo,* she thought. *He had been her father's most trusted servant.* This day after high noon, she had met with him. With tears in his eyes, he asked to remain in her service. "M 'Lady, I be olde and what would I do? I 'ave no family and I 'ave no place I care to return to. I beg of you to allow me to remain here and serve you."

While the old man was speaking, she had a flash of insight. She knew exactly where he could serve. "Dear Peppo, your wish be granted. I 'ave the Druidess Callan coming to work with me. She will need an assistant and she will need to know the background of the castle as well as the lords and ladies. Yew will be of great assistance to her with the two of yew screening all callers who want my attention. Yere knowledge and background be valuable and necessary to me. I had hoped yew would want to stay. By staying, yew do nae forfeit the stipend which my father granted to yew."

Tears of joy ran down Peppo's face. "M'Lady, I do indeed accept this most worthy position. I, I am most thankful.,"

Aye, she thought. *Peppo's knowledge is priceless. Together with the knowledge of Cyran, the Historian and Kanen, Keeper of the Books, my reign will be reinforced.* She recognized she would need all the allies she could muster. It had been Kanen who had come for her at Argania. He was a soft man and not given much to talking. Her memories of him before her tenth year were one of gentleness and a deep well of knowledge.

The two serving women for her father had taken their stipend gladly. They would be returning to their places of birth to purchase cottages and to live the remaining of their years in peace among relatives.

She lay there thinking of the morrow and the burial ceremonies for Sarenhild. *What is meant by Kingdom of the Mind?* She felt her inner body rise. She knew she would have a conscious journey into another realm.

A FUTURE TIME

The empires of the future are the empires of the mind.
~ Winston Churchill

She felt her awareness sharpen and allowed herself to drift into a blue haze. The haze became a mist and she saw a blue temple coming out of it. She knew she was in a blue realm; however, she was not familiar with these surroundings. It was a vastly different aspect from what she had previously experienced.

She knew she was not in her physical body even though she had a sensation of walking up steps and into the blue temple. Her inner ears heard the sound of a beautiful harmonic. Some would call it a heavenly choir of angels. The further she went into the temple, the louder the harmonics became. Magdalena stopped and felt awed by the huge blue disc suspended from nothing. In the center was a brilliant flashing blue star. She could see that on the outside of the blue star were markings that she could not decipher. Somehow, she knew it was the key to all time and she felt in awe.

The moment she had the thought, the star disappeared and pictures appeared on the surface of the disc. It was of a time that she was not familiar with. She inwardly drew back as she was shown giant birds of prey that were brown, green and black mottled; they fought against one another while spewing flashes of fire from sticks that appeared to jut out of their belly.

The picture faded into another with more monstrous warlike things. They had no feet. Instead, they rolled upon the earth. Something that could have been their head swiveled around and around with a ugly belching tongue of fire. The grinding noise was horrendous. As she looked further into the picture, she saw trees torn from the ground and bodies of beings blown apart. This was a war as such that she could have never imagined.

    The heavy consciousness of the pictures was almost overwhelming. Intuitively she knew she was being shown a future time and it all had to do with her mission. She realized that by reviewing the kingdom of the mind that the past could be changed affecting the future. The pictures shifted and she viewed starving beings and some children coming to the surface of the disc. These beings had become lost in the elixir of enchantment. They were deep into their sensual nature and had forgotten who they were.

    A great wrenching of sobs brought Magdalena back into her physical body. The feeling was not pleasant and as she lay upon her bed, she allowed herself to cry for the humanity of the future. Even though Doretha was not there to hold her, she had a remembrance of her first night in the house of the novice Druidesses. At last, she drifted into a deep sleep.

Magdalena woke with a sense of smelling roses. A memory came of her early childhood. There was laughter, joy and a feeling that she could so anything. She remembered her mother telling her to always keep the feeling of laughter, joy and peace. She allowed these feelings to flow through her and she thought, *I must do this often.* Feeling at peace, she slept again.

    When she awakened, her journey to the blue realm was not as direful to her. She moved out of her bed to the Eastern window and greeted the day while paying homage to her god.

Mireen knocked on the door as though she had been summoned. Magdalena bade her to enter and Mireen came in with a steaming tray of cooked grains, a pot of honey and a small loaf of fresh baked bread. "G'day M'Lady. Tis truly a grand day."

Magdalena smiled and acknowledged Mireen before sitting down to eat her breakfast. She thought of the coming ceremony – the laying to rest of the body of Sarenhild. She smiled to herself because she knew he would be lurking around to watch the ceremony. She had felt his presence more than once since his death.

With a sigh, she stood up and allowed Mireen to assist her in dressing for the occasion. There was another red gown adorned with seed pearls and gold trimming. There were red slippers to match the color of the gown. *Again, she smiled to herself. It seems as though the Lady of Argania, Cyran and Sarenhild had planned this very well*, she thought. Mireen brushed her long wavy hair to a high sheen before placing the Crown of the Magentheld on her head. As she walked out the door, Mireen handed her the staff of office – the upright black lion entwined with a gold serpent.

Magdalena walked past her honor guard and slowly made her way down the stairs. Cyran, the Holy One was waiting for her. He walked two steps behind her when they entered the Great Hall where the lords and ladies were waiting. Sarenhild's body lay on a bier at the foot of the steps to the throne.

While she walked down the long hall, she felt very aware of the energy of the collective gathering. Using her *soft eyes*, she was able to assess all that was happening without looking directly at the large audience.

When she arrived at the bier, she knelt and paid homage to her father. She looked up for a moment and saw the astral or invisible body of him. Slowly he winked at her and it was all Magdalena could do to stifle a giggle. Those nearest her took it to mean that she was holding back a sob.

She stood up and walked around the bier and mounted the steps to the throne. In a clear voice that carried to the end of the hall, she welcomed them all and then turned to Cyran to commence the ceremony.

Intoning the sound of the *Ohm*, Cyran followed with a lengthy speech on the numerous virtues of Sarenhild followed by the invoking the netherworld to accept this spirit. Upon completion, the ram's horn began blowing. Slowly drums began to beat softly moving louder to a crescendo. Dancers representing the various regions of the realm emerged from behind the throne and began an intense dance telling the story of the human evolution depicting the various stages representing ignorance into awareness.

After the dancers had completed their part, one bard after another began singing of the feats and deeds of Sarenhild. During all of this, Magdalena sat quietly with an intense look of concentration on her face. Little did the collective audience know that within, she was carrying on a dialogue with Sarenhild and with Cyran. One could say it was a three-way communication.

Magdalena communicated her journey to the blue realm and the vision she was given. Cyran and Sarenhild reinforced that it was indeed possible to change the future by going into the past and changing it. What she had been given was a potential that could be changed.

She realized there was so much more to know about changing the past in order to change the future and this was neither the time nor the place to pursue it. She turned her attention back to the pageantry at hand.

Each member of Sarenhild's Council was taking turns extolling his greatness. As each one spoke, it was obvious to her which ones were sincere and those who were merely windbags such as Brannon.

It was long past high noon before the ceremonies were over. Cyran stood and bowed before Queen Magdalena, the new Magentheld, and requested that she accompany him to the burial grounds. With a fanfare of horns and drums, Magdalena and Cyran followed by the Council and then by the lesser Lords and Ladies left the Great Hall and began walking outside the castle to the burial grounds of former rulers and their lineage. The villagers had come to the burial en masse and many were sobbing.

Magdalena's thoughts after his body was lowered was that it had been interesting to see Sarenhild in his astral body stand at the head of his grave while his body had been lowered. He looked deeply at her and gave her a salute with his palms together and brought to his forehead. She returned his salute and the rest of the entourage assumed she was paying homage to her deceased father. When she lowered her arms and hands, she knew that Sarenhild had gone to the realm of another place. It had been ordained.

She then turned to the grave of her mother and the two deceased brothers' graves. She noted that there was no hovering there as they had gone on to another place. For just a moment, she felt weighted down with the heavy burden of responsibility. She knew there would be no feasting this night in the Great Hall. Custom dictated it was to be a night for quietness in order to allow the soul to move on.

Feeling drained, Magdalena was grateful for the remainder of the day and evening to contemplate what lay before her and to dream. After changing into her night robe, she sent Mireen away telling her to spend the evening in quietness because Magdalena would be fasting and wanted to be alone.

   Mireen had already lit the logs in the great fireplace and Magdalena sat before it and stared into the fire. With the flames leaping and dancing, she was transported into another realm of thought. And so, began a new era for Magdalena and the realm of Hy Brasil.

Magdalena of Hy Brasil

~ France ~
2013

Sebastian's Escape

Freedom is never voluntarily given by the oppressor; it must be demanded by the oppressed.
~ Martin Luther King, Jr.

Sebastian had been kept in the chair by his captors and as he slowly regained his awareness, he knew they would come again. He began praying for the courage to withstand their torture and that his family and friends would be safe. In his mind, he began giving gratitude for everything in his life and his love for his family and his friends. By holding an image of Jill in his mind, he began to feel a sense of courage. *Non,* he thought. *I will not die. I have too much to live for.* He passed out and knew no more until he awakened to a key turning the lock in the door.

The interrogator began his questioning and Sebastian held to his truth as he had told it already. There seemed to be a different person holding the torch on him. Finally, the interrogator turned to the torch person and speaking in another language that Sebastian now recognized as Arabic. Before he had a chance to think about it, the rope binding him to the chair was cut and his feet were unshackled. Then he was pulled up to a standing position. His hands were handcuffed in front of him. He almost collapsed from lack of blood circulation and was practically dragged out. The two people did not attempt to cover his eyes and he was placed in a van with lettering that was something about plumbing.

Another person was there wearing a ski mask over his head the same as the other two people. He forced Sebastian to sit on the floor and there were no tools or other items that could identify it. His guard held an assault rifle on him and he could feel the van turning corners until it came to a stop. A scarf was tied over his eyes and his guard left the van. He could vaguely hear their voices and all three sounded like males. Finally, the van began moving and he was alone. With his shoulder he pushed the scarf up and away from his eyes. There were no windows and he assumed it must be night. The van came to a stop and he heard someone opening the door.

There was only one man and he had no mask on. He also held an assault rifle on Sebastian and in French told him to get out as he was going for a nice long swim. Somehow, Sebastian managed to get out and saw he was on a bridge and he knew that he was going to be knocked out and pushed over into the river. He could hear the Metro running overhead and he knew this bridge was the *Le Pont de Bir-Hakeim*. Anger welled up in him.

The captor put the rifle under his arm and with a key unlocked the manacles that had held Sebastian's wrists. With great alacrity, he pulled the rifle away from the captor and with strength he didn't know he had, Sebastian hit the man in the head and the two grappled. A shot went out and the captor fell to the ground. Sebastian noted that there was a silencer on it.

Sebastian leaned against the van and began crying. The shot had not killed the captor and he stood up. Sebastian threw the rifle over the balustrade and lunged at the hurt captor. Sebastian knew he wanted to live and with a surge of strength, he managed to pin the man to the balustrade and with all his strength, he pushed him up and over into the river below.

    Panting and crying at the same time, Sebastian slid down onto the sidewalk. He knew not how long he sat there. Once, he managed to open his eyes and noted an automobile crossing the bridge and he did not have the strength to call out for help. He cried again, when a police vehicle screeched to a stop. Apparently, someone had observed him and the van, and notified the police. The first one to reach him shined a light into his face and somehow he managed to say "*Mon nom est Sebastian Gontard.*"

    How sweet freedom is whether one is conscious or unconscious.

ΩΩΩ

Recovery

Healing is a matter of time, but it is sometimes also a matter of opportunity.
~ Hippocrates

Peter was in a sound sleep and barely heard the phone ring until Ellen nudged him. He switched on the light while groping for the phone. *"La personne qui appelle?"* He listened as the officer from the *préfecture de police*, the 15th *Paris arrondissement* asked him if he was *M.* Peter Douglass. Peter replied, *"Oui."*

Ellen by now was wide-awake and she sat up, and saw a big grin come on Peter's face and knew it was good news. A shiver ran through her. She watched as Peter wrote down an address and then he said he would bring *Mdme.* Gontard immediately.

Peter turned to Ellen with tears in his eyes. "He is injured and the police have taken him to the American Hospital on *Avenue Victor Hugo*."

Ellen began crying for joy and the relief of knowing Sebastian was alive. "I will get Yvonne and Cerise to care for the children. And yes, I will notify Jacques and Marie."

"Okay and I will get Jill." Peter quickly dressed and went to the bedroom where Jill was. He gently knocked on the door. Groggily, Jill asked who was there.

"Jill, Sebastian has been found. Please get dressed as soon as possible and I will meet you downstairs. He is in a hospital in Paris."

With a shriek, Jill began laughing and crying at the same time. Before Peter could get to the top of the the steps, she was out and hugging him. "Oh Peter! Thank god! The children?"

"Ellen is seeing that they are taken care of. I am having a car ready and the three of us will go to the hospital. In the meantime, you dress and I will meet you in the breakfast room."

By the time Peter reached the breakfast room, Marie was already there with hot coffee in a large thermos and croissants. "Ah *M.* Peter, I am relieved." She began crying.

At that moment, Jacques came in and said that the automobile was ready. Tears were welling up in his eyes. Peter told them that *M.* Sebastian would recover and to pray for him.

Once Peter, Ellen and Jill were on the road to Paris, Jill asked what hospital they were going to, and Peter replied the American Hospital. "The police wouldn't give any details other than he was taken to the emergency room and we were to meet them there. I also called Alain and he said he would meet us there."

Jill was sitting beside him in the front and said. "Thank you."

Ellen was sitting in the back and knew there was really nothing else to say. She looked out the window and felt numbness in her brain. *Was this in connection with the dagger?* She asked herself. *What in god's name was its importance?* She sighed as she continued to look out the window. She noticed the clouds were scudding over the bright full moon. *Could the clouds* and the moon be a sign that there would be a breakthrough?

Peter was concentrating on his driving. He knew this was not the time for idle chatter. He also wondered what the connection was to the dagger. It was now close to 4 a.m. when Peter pulled into the parking lot of the Emergency Room and the threesome entered. Peter went to the desk and gave his name, and then asked if the wife of Sebastian Gontard could see him. Told that a doctor could be with them soon, Peter relayed the information and the threesome entered the crowded waiting room.

Jill held Ellen's hand while managing to hold back her tears. "My emotions are going wild and my thoughts are churning."

Ellen gently squeezed her hand. "I know he is going to recover and all we can do is just love him"

"You're right. In one way I am angry because someone or some people harmed him and in another way, I am relieved that he is alive."

At that moment, Alain arrived followed by an inspector detective from the judicial police who came to them and introduced himself as *M'sieur l'inspecteur* Jules Fortier. Peter introduced himself, and then Jill followed by Ellen. The *l'inspecteur* acknowledged them and speaking to Jill, told her that when the doctors had completed their examinations, *M.* Gontard would have to be questioned before she could see him. He regretted the delay and went on to say that it was imperative that the questioning take precedence so that whoever had kidnapped *M.* Gontard could be apprehended.

Alain stepped forward and told Fortier that he was the *advocate* for *M.* Gontard and family. Fortier asked for his credentials and Alain handed it to him.

The *l'inspecteur* asked them to follow him and they went with him into a small room where they were to wait. He asked *M.* Delacroix to come with him and they left the room.

The threesome sat with each going into their own meditative mode.. Jill was the first to move into a state of awareness of where they were, followed by Peter and then Ellen. An hour had passed with no information forthcoming. Jill was the first to speak, "I, I know he is going to be healed. I sense that it will be a long process."

Ellen shared what she had sensed and agreed. "Yes, he is going to recover from this ordeal. I had a vision of this being connected to that damn dagger."

Peter reached over and took one of her hands. "My love, it probably is and right now my only concern is Sebastian's recovery. I am sure it has made the news and we must be aware of this. Hopefully, the dagger will not be mentioned."

Jill nodded in agreement. "We all have been through trying times and I know that we will live through this. I wonder, do you think that the dagger could be connected to the Magdalene?"

"Possibly," replied Peter. "Let's not dwell on this now. I am going to the car and get the coffee and croissants Marie prepared for us." He stood up, bent down to kiss the top of Ellen's head, and left the room.

Jill was the first to speak. "Well, my friend. Who would have ever thought that we would still be friends when we first met at the University?"

Ellen smiled. "You are correct. Never in my greatest imagination did I think we would have the mishaps and adventures we have had and are now having."

Nodding her head in agreement, Jill said, "I can't say that I have enjoyed many of the events that have occurred, but I think they have strengthened me."

"Umm. I agree. Life certainly has not been boring for the most part. I have thought about these events and if they hadn't happened, we wouldn't be married to the beautiful men that we have nor have the children we have."

"Yes. After this is cleared up, I think Canada will be a great change for Sebastian, the children and me."

Before Ellen could answer, Peter opened the door and brought the thermos and basket in. "I spoke to a nurse at the Emergency Desk and asked if the doctor or doctors could give us an update on Sebastian even though not allowed to see him until have he has been interviewed, and she said she would."

Ellen smiled as Peter began pouring the coffee from the thermos. "Ah, just what I need." she said.

Jill took the cup of coffee from him. "Thank god for you! I sense that we are in for a long wait."

"Well Jill, I agree and I recall other long waits in a hospital. I'm just happy Sebastian has been found and is alive."

The threesome lapsed into a silence – each within their own thoughts. After what seemed like a forever moment, the door opened and a doctor came in with his surgical mask around his neck. Speaking in French, he asked which one was *Mme.* Gontard. Jill stood up. "*Je suis.*"

The doctor informed them that he was *le médecin chirurgical,* Marcel Allemande, and shook each of their hands. Speaking in French, he told them that *M.* Gontard was being moved to a recovery room after surgery for a broken nose and jaw. Sebastian also had a mild concussion, and he went on to say that other than some severe bruising, Sebastian would recover. "*M.* Gontard will be under sedation for possibly several hours.

Tears began rolling down Jill's face. She asked when she would be able to see Sebastian and he told her that it could be several hours after the sedation wore off. He went on to say that they could now move to the waiting room outside the recovery section.

Again, shaking hands with each of them, he left. Peter was the first to speak. "Okay, we move now to the waiting room."

Once they were in the waiting room, Peter said he was going to call Nance and let her know what has happened. He soon returned with Alain who told them, "Be prepared for reporters who could come in wanting an exclusive with you." At that moment, *l'inspecteur* Fortier entered the waiting room. He came over and spoke to them.

"Since *M.* Gontard cannot speak with a broken jaw and he is under heavy sedation, I am placing a guard here to keep out unwanted persons. According to *M.* Delacroix, *M.* Gontard had an appointment with a professor. Can you tell me what it was about, and the professor's name?

Jill swallowed hard and daubed her eyes using a tissue. "Yes. Sebastian was on his way to speak with a colleague regarding a translation of a language that Sebastian was not familiar with and wanted advice."

"And what is his name *Mme.* Gontard?"

"I believe it was *M.* Andre Lefevre."

"Can you give me the name of the language to be translated?"

"I, I have no knowledge of what language it was. Sebastian keeps his newest translations to himself."

"*Merci*." He was about to enter the Recovery Section when Peter asked him if he could keep the reporters from coming into the waiting room. Fortier replied that he had an officer standing outside and would do that.

Alain did not follow and told them that he already knew Sebastian was heavily sedated and that Fortier had gone in to check with the officer who was already at Sebastian's bedside. Fortier promised him that he would not attempt to interview Sebastian unless he, Alain was there also. "I am not going to say much more and I think it is best that we go and have something to eat. I need to talk to all of you."

Jill had been reluctant to leave, however she consented to go with them. The foursome knew it was early and that there would be few in the cafeteria. Once they secured what each wanted along with a *café au lait*, a table was found that was in a rather isolated corner.

Alain spoke first. "I am relieved that Sebastian is going to recover. What I am concerned about is the possible connection with the murder of *Mme*. Gillet. I do not know how lucid Sebastian will be for the interrogation. However, when the authorities found his automobile, there was nothing to indicate a connection with the photo *Mme*. Gillet had in her shop. He turned to Jill. "Can you recall anything Sebastian said to *M*. Lefevre?"

"I, I remember hearing him making the appointment and as I recall he said that he had been sent a document with interesting markings and would like to consult with *M*. Lefevre as he, Sebastian was unable to interpret or decipher them. He did not mention a dagger."

"This is good. Let us only hope that Sebastian is too groggy to mention it was about the dagger you received."

Peter said he agreed with Alain. "Well, we can only hope that Sebastian will not be too intimidated by the interrogation. The primary goal is to assist him in his healing."

Ellen asked the question directed to Alain, "Will you have someone there with you to record the interview?"

"But of course. I have already asked my secretary to be prepared to come with a recorder and I am sensing that Sebastian is – or will be unable to answer all of their questions now. It might be a few days because I am sure the interview will happen when he gets all of his faculties together. Now, I have other phone calls to make so I will leave you now."

Peter looked at Jill and Ellen. "I have a suggestion. Let us go outside and take a walk. It will be another hour or so and I think the fresh air and being away from the hospital atmosphere will help each of us immensely."

Ellen and Jill agreed. Once they were outside the hospital, Jill exploded. "A damn dagger comes into our lives and Sebastian is the one who is kidnapped and hurt! Yes, I am pissed off!"

Peter suggested they start walking and with Jill between them, they walked through the parking lot on to the Victor Hugo Blvd. He steered them towards the Marriot Courtyard Hotel not too far away. "I have my cell phone and I left word with the hospital to call if there is a change. I understand your anger and frustration."

Jill stopped with tears flowing down her face. "Isn't there something Alain can do to stop the police from interrogating him?"

Peter took out his cell phone, and called Alain's office and was through to Alain immediately. He asked Alain about the possibility of delaying the interviewing of Sebastian.

Alain replied, "I am already on this and have assurances that there will be no interviewing until the doctors give permission. In the meantime, I suggest that all of you relax because Sebastian will recover and I am following up some leads regarding *Mme. Gillet.*"

Peter had put the volume up so that Jill and Ellen could hear. "*Merci* Alain. We will do that." He looked at Jill. "I suggest we relax and allow the healing to happen. And, for the moment I suggest we go to the Marriot and have something to drink. Even though the hospital has great amenities, I think a change of atmosphere will do us good."

Ellen smiled. "I second your idea. Let's go."

Jill nodded her agreement and the three began walking to the Marriott. Once they were there, they decided to have something on the terrace, as the weather was clear and nice. Once they had ordered light luncheons, Ellen was the first to speak. "I know I have shared with both of you my contemplation of why I seem to appear to be the 'chosen' one to find scrolls or have them brought to me along with the dagger." She sighed. "Do you have any ideas?"

Jill smiled. "I have thought of this also and what if – and I am saying again what if you were of the lineage of Mary Magdalene and Jesus? However, I don't know how the dagger fits it, but there must be a connection."

Peter said that he agreed and that he and Ellen had discussed this a number of times. "I feel that the *'what if'* is a potential, however I also know that attempting to discover one's lineage going back two thousand years is a challenge, however we found something interesting in a book by Michael Bradley. Ellen can tell you."

Ellen smiled and went on to say, "Yes. We read his book *Grail Knights of North America,* and learned something interesting. Apparently, the Knights Templar had brought the bloodline to Nova Scotia. It is a possibility. Bradley's research leads him to Montreal where he learns that Edward, the Duke of Kent called the "de facto King of England," was assigned to Quebec City in 1790 as the governor of New France – now Canada. It is a long story, however he had met a woman when he was assigned to Gibraltar and she became his mistress, and later his wife by way of a Catholic ceremony, which was kept quiet. Her name was Thérèse de Mongenet and while in Gibraltar was known as Julia. Peter you tell her what happened in Canada."

Picking up the thread, Peter continued with "It seems that while in Canada a second marriage was performed at the Quebec cathedral in a Church of England ceremony. Bradley goes on to say that the couple had 5 children and this was okay because he was not the King. This was still not okay with the Crown. The couple were married for about 26 years when the King died and Edward became King of England where he married a German princess. Their offspring grew up to be Queen Victoria.

"A long story short, there are or were records in the Quebec Cathedral that Bradley had access to and since Edward was now King, he had to hide his children. They were given the last name of 'Wood and Green. This is another story that has some merit. Where the children were taken, it an unknown. What we did learn is that in Ellen's lineage, there is a family name of Wood.

"Ellen and I have tracked this and we learned that many bloodline family trees only go back as far as perhaps a thousand years or more and many of those are dubious."

Jill nodded in agreement. "I have often wondered how many of these family trees are actually realistic. Since the time of Mary Magdalene and Jesus there have been too many wars and the destruction of libraries for lineages to be kept."

Ellen added to this, "I think the best kept records were from the Egyptians and we only know from a few records the dynasties along with the pharaohs' names. There is a possibility that the *Priory of Sion* originated in Egypt and has kept a record of the bloodline since Mary Magdalene's origins are in Ethiopia and Egypt. It seems so long ago and I also am wondering how these records can be kept and handed down through wars, changes of rulers and god knows what else.

Peter smiled and reached for Ellen's hand. "You are right in this. I think it is time for us to return to the hospital."

ΩΩΩ

~ HY BRASIL ~
400 A.D.

REVELATIONS

Three things cannot be long hidden: the sun, the moon, and the truth.
~ Buddha

Two days after the burial of Sarenhild, Magdalena sent a message to Cyran asking him to meet her in the rose garden at the hour called 10 in the morning. Her thoughts were in turmoil with unanswered questions. She knew this to be the time for her to have some answers from Cyran. She already knew he would be there waiting for her by the rose bush that had been her mother's favorite. Cyran was bending over smelling the fragrance of a blue rose.

"Greetings Holy One. I knew yew could nae resist the blue rose as it be my mother's favorite."

He bowed. "Greetings "M'Lady Magentheld. Tis a grand day to be smellin' the roses," he said with a twinkle in his eyes. "Shall we move to the garden pavilion?"

She smiled and led him to it and asked him to sit across from her on the bench circling the round pavilion. "I know no thing of my heritage or my ancestors and I find this a breach of faith if I be the Queen – the Magentheld of Hy Brasil. I be asking yew to tell me all yew know about the history from whence I come."

He nodded. "Aye, tis tyme yew know and aye, I be trained in Druid oral history." Thus, Cyran began reciting the ancient history as if in a trance. "Long, long ago in a land named Aigyptos[2] across the waters beyond the mists, there be great and noble people. There be a king with a title of Pharaoh named Amenophis[3]. He later took the name of Akhenaton whose ancestry be far back into the beginnings of tyme. Six daughters he sired. The story handed down be a pestilence came into the land. There be a history this Pharaoh left Aigyptos and took with him his people. Nae to the West, but to the East where the great purple dye came from.

"There be one daughter said to be married to a prince of Hellas.[4] "The daughter's name be Meritaten who survived the pestilence. The annals of history as handed down say she married a Greek prince whose name be Gaythelos. The two set sail with many ships and what be left of her people seeking a new land fer them. They sailed west. Leaving her country, Meritaten be named Scota. The first landing be in ancient Iberia. A tyme 'erefore the Romans. Iberia be of two Iberians' with one nearest Hy Brasilia. The tyme in this place sought by Scota and Gaythelos nae be long. It be nae their final home.

Cyran be speaking as if in a trance, reciting the ancient history, and he continued on "Scota and her peoples set sail fer another land. The annals of history say they found a large island peopled by tribes. It be named Erin. It be nae the final place fer Scota's people. There be war with Tuatha tribe. Tis said Scota's body be buried in Erin. After long ans, some traveled to other

---

[2] Egypt
[3] Greek name for Akhenaton.
[4] Name for Greece

island to north and others came here. Yew be of the ones who arrived here.

"After many ans, there came to this place a great woman but tarry she nae fer long. Her name be Magdalene. She taught much to people of Scota. Scota be passed into another plane long 'erefore. The Magdalene descended from great peoples of Aigyptos. She be great teacher. Her husbandment be Yeshua ben Joseph, another great teacher. He be nae with her. Later, her daughter's daughter came to be a Druidess. Her name be Morgance. Morgance came here to escape the Romans. As yew know, during the spring rites it be the will of the Druidess to mate with the Horned One and bear a child. The Horned One be of the heritage of Scota and Gaythelos. Morgance be of the heritage of the Magdalene and Yeshua ben Joseph. Yew be of the heritage of Morgance, the Magdalene, Yeshua ben Joseph, Scota and Gaythelos."

Cyran became silent as well as Magdalena. She was assessing what she heard him say. "Yew tell me a portion of this heritage. I know there be more to know, such as how this kingdom came into being and titles of King, Queen and Magentheld. I ask yew speak more of this."

He smiled, nodding his head and began. "Many eons in the past 'erefore the Druids and the Celts, this world as yew call it be beautiful – even more so than 'tis this day. Beings from the stars came in sky boats bringing with them new great knowledge. Leaders of these beings be twelve in numbers and began to create other beings by mating with the inhabitants naow here. More eons passed and these star people became known as gods. Each of the twelve be given a part of this Gaia – meaning ruling twelve portions.

"The star beings chose to return to their place among the stars. 'Erefore they departed, a leader be chosen to oversee each of 12 parts. Within each portion, Twelve clans be created with each clan having a chieftain." Cyran paused and Magdalena sensed he was scanning his memory for more information.

"This be a tyme of the learning and this be a blessing from star people. After many, many changing of winters a seed of change brought forth something new. This be named power. The rulers and chieftains began warring fer power and from this came greed." He stopped and looked at her. "Methinks yew 'ave be chosen well."

"Why?"

"There be a small cove on the setting sun side and yew already know star ones come from tyme to tyme and seek the Magentheld ear. There be much more fer yew to know. Fer naow, tis a tyme to contemplate what I 'ave spoken."

She nodded and stood up. "I thank yew Lord Cyran and naow I must attend to other matters. I be sensing there be treachery abroad."

"Yew be correct. Go in peace and knowing."

Magdalena continued walking and pondered all Cyran told her. Aye, she had been aware of the star boat people and had placed it in the back of her mind. She remembered hearing about them soon after she was sent to the Druidesses. What was it she heard? *Aye, they be beings from beyond the northern star and had drawn descendents of Scota to settle here. It be they who be the overseers and brought new ideas. Aye, t'was said this be why there be always a mist around this land in the midst of the great water. Hmmm, I want to meet with them and since I be the Magentheld it will happen.*

PLOTS AND SCHEMES

Society bristles with enigmas which look hard to solve.
It is a perfect maze of intrigue.
~ Honore de Balzac

While standing at the great window of her bedroom, Magdalena stared out at the gardens and beyond the lake. It was the time of the planting season. She sighed, thinking she would not be part of the planting at the Druidess Commune. Instead, as she looked out the window, she knew others were doing the planting here. This was the Mother's time to awaken from her long dream and to bring forth new life in gardens, the fields, meadows, forests and mountains. The knock on her door moved her out of her reverie. Turning, she bade "Come."

The door opened and Callan thrust her head in. "M 'Lady, if I be intruding…" Before she completed her sentence, Magdalena held out her arms to embrace her. Laughing, Callan closed the door and met Magdalena halfway in the room and the two embraced.

""Ah Callan, dear Callan. What be I without yew? It be blessed I be to 'ave yew be my ears and eyes. And methinks there be mischief abroad from yere countenance."

"Aye. Yew read me rightly. The reports from our travelling Druidesses indicate that Brannon be plotting to overthrow yew. I know this be no surprise to yew. What be reported be during this season of planting, he be sending his trusted ones to the Holds fer stir them up and to throw in with him. His reasoning be the Magentheld should be a strong man and a female only weakens the realm."

"Yere right Callan. Tis nae surprise. I question his doin' so at the beginning of the planting season. We 'ave a weakness in Rath. Naow, he be loyal, but his willingness to try new ideas be slow in coming. Methinks it best to replace him. I 'ave been contemplating how to do this diplomatically. He has some loyal followers."

"M 'Lady, yew be correct. I too 'ave contemplated this. It be perhaps he travel abroad to other lands and study their methods of training and armaments?"

"Callan! This be a brilliant idea! He does need to feel important. I will tell him this be an important secret mission and he be travelling under the guise of opening up possible trade exchange with them"

Clapping her hands, Callan laughed. "Brilliant! We could send Matran, Master of Potters and Frint, Master of Gardens to assist him. They can teach him the correct information to make him sound plausible."

"Good choice. Perhaps it be wise to send one of the Druids to assist them in their arrangements fer travel and accommodation. Perhaps something such as a personal scribe."

"I agree M 'Lady. I also know the perfect one. His name be Hopenth and he be quite adept in the things yew want him to do. He be also a great tyme traveler."

"I applaud yew fer yere ability to know what be needed. I 'ave also heard great things about Rath's assistant Joffen. He appears to 'ave a willingness to try new things. Do yew 'ave any reason to doubt his ability?"

Callan looked as though she was assessing the one to replace Rath and then replied, I deem he being very loyal. From the information I 'ave received from my assistant, yere father chose him with care, as he knew Rath 'ave to be replaced. Joffen comes from the lineage of yere uncle, Jaxon twice removed."

"Aye, I know. I deem it advisable to 'ave him teach me the fine arts of guardmanship. I want this be done quietly."

"Yew, Magdalena?" blurted out Callan. She realized what she had done and apologized for her outburst.

Magdalena laughed. "Why nae me? I be the Magentheld and to know how the army and the Garenfeld guard be trained, will be to my advantage."

"Well aye, I can see the value of it. Together with yere training as a Druidess, yew will be a formidable Magentheld. I will arrange fer yew to meet quietly with Joffen, and iffen yew want I make an appointment for yew to meet with Rath?"

"Yes, and schedule Rath fer this afternoon. I prefer to meet with him 'erefore the morrow. I find it telling Brannon did nae retire to his Hold for the planting. He be a sly and astute one."

"Aye, he be that. It be also known his lady be stirring up her own jealous faction. If I may suggest, and it feels right with yew, why nae create a position of importance fer her. It be taking the sting out of the nettle."

"Brilliant! If it be me to bring forth a kingdom

of mind, then we create a unique position to expand the mind of Bertran."

Moving to the great window, Callan stared at the garden fer a moment erefore turning to Magdalena. "M 'Lady, it be most fitting iffen she be sent about the realm to study the plight of the women. There be much lacking in the attitudes of the masses toward women and their capabilities."

"Aye, Callan. I be thinking much along those lines and methinks it be the position fer Bertran and do make a list of the aspects fer she to study. I want to know how many be abused and the number who be nothing more than chattels to their husbands."

"Aye. I be getting thoughts swirling in me head. We can ask what their skills be and emphasize we want an unbiased picture of the roles of women. I be 'aving her meet with yew two days hence to present this to her. By the tyme, I be 'aving a clear and concise outline of what her duties be. It be most interesting to observe the expansion of Bertran's mind."

Callan turned to leave and Magdalena stopped her. "I understand Peppo tis being of great assistance to yew. Yew do 'ave a way with people."

Smiling, Callan curtsied. "I 'ave excellent training."

After Callan left the room, Magdalena turned back to the window and thought, *Aye, there be much mischief afoot. Getting Rath away within a fortnight would remove a weak point. The sooner I send Bertran on her journey will do much to relieve the jealous faction of the women. Perhaps it would be well to meet with the ladies of the realm.*

⛫⛫⛫

THE PLOT THICKENS

Opposing a queen is as dangerous as keeping company with a tiger. ~ Anonymous

The meeting with Rath took place after mid-noon. Magdalena began by asking for advice regarding the Skagerrak and the status of their rebellion. She observed him as he puffed himself up with importance. Rath gave a rather lukewarm dissertation, which indicated his ignorance. "*Aye*," she thought, "*It needs to expand his limited mind to travel abroad.*"

With skilled diplomacy, she broached the subject of sending someone abroad to observe the arms types and buildup in other realms. Using her insight, she brought Rath around to agreeing it be a splendid idea. She accomplished this so adroitly that he actually believed it be his idea. This was as Magdalena intended it to be.

"Rath, you be brilliant!" she said with a lilt of surprise. After much discussion, she asked him whom he thought would best go with him, and of course, the real motive would have to be a secret in disguise.

"Ummm, M'Lady, there be so few who 'ave the talent fer such an undertaking. I be 'aving to think upon this point."

"Rath, why nae yew go? It be your idea and I can think of no one better qualified to observe and report."

Sitting up straight in his chair, Rath preened himself like a peacock. She could feel the thrill ripple through his being. "Ah, um, M'Lady, I, I had nae really thought of me self. Ah, um, aye. I gladly undertake this journey."

With relief at the simplicity of persuasion, she thanked him and suggested he leave at the first harvest. "Perhaps to make your real intent concealed, yew will include Matran, the Master of Potters. It be of benefit to our trade to 'ave our potters' wares traded abroad."

"Ah, um, , this be a splendid idea. With my undertaking this be a very private expedition, I deem it wise to place Joffen as the temporary head of the Guardsmen. That be, unless yew 'ave another in mind."

"Yew 'ave chosen well and I accept Joffen because yew know he could temporarily take over yere duties. Until such a tyme all arrangements be made, I insist our agreement be kept quiet. I know I can count on your silence."

"Of course, M'Lady. I give thee my oath."

"Thank yew. Naow there be arrangements to be made and I will see to the arrangements."

After Rath left, she sat and contemplated deeply this coming venture. *Could Rath be trusted to keep his mission secret? It would be normal fer a man to share something of this importance with his wife, or a trusted friend. Of course, Joffen 'ad to be apprised of this mission as well and Matran and Frint.* This was having a ripple effect with Callan knowing along with Cyran. "*Aye, I will send Hopenth with him as his scribe.*" She knew Hopenth to be a Druid, a scribe and a time traveler. There could be more benefits to this with Matran the Master of Potters and Frint the Master of Garden.

As she thought more about this venture, the thought came to her, "*What if a rumor be initiated that *held within it a bit of truth. This might satisfy the wolves. Aye, a nice rumor can do."* She smiled as she thought about it.

Ah a rumor. Magdalena continued her contemplation and she knew it was wise to spread it abroad of Rath and his party going to Hibernia requesting the aid of the ruler to assist the new Magentheld in her fight with the Skagerrak. *Aye, Brannon be indeed loving this. This provides the false scent while I set about strengthening the forces.* What is not to be shared is the real reason for this trip and its extension to other realms.

Now to seek out Callan. Before she could move to leave the chamber; there was a rap on the door. "Come." Callan entered and curtsied. Magdalena smiled. "I can see yew be pleased about something. I deem it might 'ave something to do with Lady Bertran."

"Aye, M'Lady. Peppo be a wealth of information. He gave me an excellent background fer Lady Bertran and others. It appears as though the marriage of Brannon and Bertran be not one of love and respect." Callan paused and then continued. "There be few marriages be loving or respectful, and fewer contain both. Nonetheless, Bertran's treatment by Brannon be named bordering on the cruel side. I 'ave arranged fer yew to meet with her the day following the 'morrow. That be, if it meets with your approval."

"Ah Callan, it be desirable if mutual respect could be 'ad by all. Perhaps one day it be coming about." Magdalena proceeded to relate visions she had of the future and horrendous scenes. She finished by saying, "At tymes I feel so inadequate. How be I to lead this realm into the expansion of the mind in order to correct the future?"

"M'Lady, these words I speak be only trite words, but I do believe – nae, I know it all unfolds and I be happy I be here to be part of this with yew. I suggest yew meet with some of the women in addition to creating an avenue of altering the beliefs of the women.

"Yere suggestion be well taken and I be contemplating this." She went on to relate to Callan her vision of the future and the horrendous scenes. Magdalena finished saying, "At tymes I feel inadequate. How be I to lead this realm into the expansion of mind in order to correct the future and I be not understanding why I be called to do this."

"M'Lady, these are only trite words, but I do believe – nae, I know it will all unfold and I be most happy I be here to be part of this with yew."

Magdalena embraced Callan and told her she felt lighter in countenance. "Naow, to other things. Rath, as yew know, agreed to our plan. I want to meet personally with Matran and Frint, and each separately. When Hopenth arrives, send him to me straightaway. The details I leave to yew. It has come to me a nice rumor needs to be spread about." She related to Callan her idea and the reasoning.

"Oh M' Lady! Tis a grand idea and I know just the person to begin the rumor. Peppo told me of a personage named Kitrak. I be told his tongue be loose. My knowingness tells me Peppo be trusted. I be asking him to plant the rumor with Kitrak. Tis grand to stir the pot so nae one knows what be cookin'. I also 'ave taken the liberty of quietly arranging a meeting with yew and Joffen fer this night after the dining hour."

"Thank yew, my dear Callan. Little did we realize what our work be entailing when we be young novices."

"True M'Lady. True. Naow I be off to confer with Peppo. Would I 'ave more like him. He 'be a wealth of knowledge."

As the days passed, Magdalena later wondered how she had the stamina and patience. Bertran had snapped at the opportunity to travel around the realm and to insure her importance. True to character, Brannon had come to her in a rage. How dare her to interfere with his marriage! *Indeed*, she mused. It had been a tense exchange and for a moment, she felt his spleen about to explode. It was after she pointed out how it enhanced his own position that Brannon left with a happier countenance. She could see ideas spinning in his head. Aye, he was already plotting to have this work to his advantage.

She and Callan agreed there could be obstacles in sending Bertran; however, they were sure she would never divulge the true state or plight of women to her husband. This was her secret and ultimately her freedom. With the Druidesses travelling around the realm, it was assured they would be watching and reporting Brannon's moves.

Joffen proved to be an excellent teacher. In the beginning, he was taken aback at the prospect of teaching a woman and especially the Magentheld. Warring and fighting had always been a man's job. However, with the gentle persuasion of Magdalena he agreed. She made it a policy of not always attending the evening meal with others, as Sarenhild chose. She knew she had the eyes and ears to keep her informed of the goings, comings and plotting within the Garenfeld. Most of her evenings were spent in learning how to fight with the sword, the lance and other weapons. Joffen was astounded at her prowess and swiftly moved her into strategies and mapping. Again, she proved to be an apt student.

It was not until the moon before the Beltane that she approached Joffen regarding him becoming the replacement for Rath. Shocked, Joffen could only look at her while a flush came over his face. "M'Lady," he stammered. "It tis a great honor, but I be nae intruding upon Rath's domain."

"Well put. However, Rath has agreed to undertake an important mission. I be sure you 'ave heard the rumors."

Joffen replied that he had. She noted that strong as he was in the ways of guardmanship and fighting, was backward in his attitude with women and especially her. She knew she had assessed his capabilities and all it needed was a fine-tuning. She was delighted with the progress and thought, *Working with me be certainly expanding his mind.*

It was agreed Joffen would assume his new duties ten days before Rath's departure. Her lessons in horsemanship were to wait until the group departed. What Joffen did not realize was she was already skilled in the ways of riding a horse until her mother died. She often rode with Sarenhild and he trained her very well.

Quietly, her plans fell into place, as she knew they would. Much would be accomplished and now the play would unfold.

Magdalena of Hy Brasil

~ France ~
2013

Interrogation Postponed

Remember when life's path is steep to keep your mind even. ~ Horace

When Jill, Ellen and Peter returned to the hospital, they were told Sebastian would be moved to a private room within the hour. They all breathed a sigh of relief when the doctor said that Jill would be able to see him as soon as he is settled in the room. She asked if Ellen and Peter could also visit. The doctor paused a moment and replied that it would be possible as long as their visits were short. At this moment Alain returned and given the latest information.

"This is good news and I have been in touch with the *l'inspecteur* Fortier. It is uncertain when he will be able to interview Sebastian as *le docteur* has said no due to Sebastian's concussion," he told them.

Jill came over to him and hugged him. "I am so relieved and thank you for all you are doing for us."

He took her hand and kissed it. "I am most happy to do this for all of you. After all, if the four of you had not been involved with the scrolls of Sarah, then I would not have met Louise Bianchi and after the death of her husband become the a*vocat* for all of her holdings. And now I must leave as I have another appointment." With embraces to the three, Alain left for his appointment.

Jill was the first to break the silence. "I, I am wondering how bad Sebastian looks. I only hope I don't breakdown and cry when I see him."

Ellen reached over and touched her hand saying, "You have the courage to ignore the way he looks and just love him."

"I, I know, but lately we have been quarreling, and I feel so horrible about that." She began crying.

Ellen and Peter allowed her to have this moment of release. Peter broke the moment by suggesting they leave and find some water or something else to drink. "It will take some time to get Sebastian moved and settled.'

He and Ellen walked with Jill between them to the elevators and went down to the cafétéria, where they each ordered a mineral water, and found a table. Ellen broke the silence. "Would you like to talk about your feelings?"

Jill nodded a yes. "I am the one who has pushed him to take the teaching position in Canada. He, he really did not want to do it. I, I just felt stifled in *Toulouse* and wanted a change. Even though he accepted the position, he wanted to cancel it. Oh gawd! I love him so much and I have been a bitch about this."

Ellen found some issues in her handbag and gave them to Jill. "My dear friend, beating yourself up isn't going to help him recover. Now put a smile on your face and practice smiling in a loving way when you finally are allowed to see him."

For a moment, there was silence and then Peter started laughing and in a moment both Jill and Ellen were laughing with him.

The ever aware Peter seemed to have an inside time ticker and when they had finished laughing, suggested they go and see if Sebastian was ready for Jill's entrance. More laughter followed this.

Only Jill was given permission to go in and see Sebastian. She was told that she could not remain in there more than 10 minutes.

While she was in the room with Sebastian, Peter stood up. "Ten minutes isn't long enough. God I want the bastards captured who did this!"

Ellen had tears in her eyes. "I agree. I still cannot imagine how or why this dagger was sent to me. I pray that Sebastian will recover quickly."

Peter, "Amen."

ΩΩΩ

Memories

A whole stack of memories never equal one little hope.
~ **Charles M. Schultz**

With trepidation and her heart beating rapidly, Jill entered the hospital room, and walked to Sebastian's bed. She almost gasped when she saw his face. She hardly recognized him with his blackened and bruised face and his jaw wired shut. The nurse had told her he was heavily sedated, and therefore might not awaken to her presence. Jill stood there with tears rolling down her face. Her silent thought was *Thank God he is alive. What insane demon person could have done this to him?* Anger welled up in her. She turned and left the room walking past the guard posted outside his door. She walked to the small waiting room where she had left Ellen and Peter. When she saw them, she threw herself into Ellen's arms.

"I didn't recognize him. His face is bruised and puffed up. I, I am so goddamn mad! He, he is under sedation so I didn't try to talk to him. One of his fingers is in a caste and god knows what else his body looks like." She began sobbing against Ellen's shoulder.

Ellen looked at Peter and even she had tears in her eyes. "It's good to cry. Don't stifle your tears or your anger. Let us be thankful that he is alive and will recover." She led Jill to a chair and had her sit down. She and Peter pulled up chairs to be close to her.

When Jill's crying had subsided, she looked at both of them. "I don't know what I would do without you being here for us. I want to go back to him and stay there until he wakes up and if necessary through the night. Do you think they will allow me to do this?"

Peter stood up saying, "I will go and get the permission. You and Ellen stay here."

Ellen took Jill's hand and said, "When Peter comes back, we will leave you here. We will go home and check on the children. Then we will come back with a change of clothes for you and some toiletries. Is this okay with you?"

"Yes. I appreciate this and, and I will work through my anger because I know he needs my love more than ever. I find it despicable that, that there are people who will torture others. Don't say anything to alleviate my feelings. I have to vent this now before I go back into the room."

Peter returned at this moment with a smile on his face. "You have permission to stay. I have talked with Alain and he is doing his own search for whoever did this. Ellen and I will be back before evening. In the meantime, do you have your cell phone?"

She nodded yes and stood up to go back into the room. "I can't begin to tell you both how much I love you and my appreciation for all you are doing." Giving each of them an embrace, she left to return to Sebastian's room.

"Okay sweetheart, let's be on our way home."

Jill nodded to the guard sitting outside Sebastian's room. She pulled up a chair next to his bed and sat there holding the uninjured hand. She began speaking to him softly. "My beloved husband and lover, I love you. I know there have been times when I have been a bitch and wanted everything my way. I apologize and when you get better, I will be with you and we will see better days."

Memories of the first time she met Sebastian began flooding her mind. She smiled when she remembered how with Ellen and Peter she had met Sebastian at *Lourdes* when he was a priest and on the brink of suicide. Peter had already told him about the scrolls found in the cave that appeared to be in Greek and asked him if he would translate them. Sebastian said yes and the foursome were off to Toulouse where he had a small house. From there the foursome moved to a house outside of Toulouse belonging to his friend Paul, who was away working in South Africa.

Sebastian was excited and thrilled over the potentials of these scrolls. She closed her eyes as she began the remembering of their courtship. Ellen and Peter had already fallen in love and left to be the potential bait if others were seeking to find the scrolls. They already knew that the news was out as a shepherd boy had seen them coming out of the unknown cave.

She sighed as the memories continued and she even emitted a chuckle when she thought of how she had seduced Sebastian and from there love blossomed.

She did not know how long she sat there and she might have dozed off. It had been a long day since she, Peter and Ellen had driven to the hospital after hearing that he had been found. She wondered about the circumstances of why he had been found on the bridge. *Oh well, I will learn soon enough. I am just thankful he is alive.*

ΩΩΩ

Sebastian's Interrogation
An interview is like a minefield.
~ Michelle Williams

Three days after Sebastian entered the hospital, the doctor gave *l'inspecteur* Fortier permission to interview Sebastian with the stipulation that if Sebastian indicated he was unable to respond, then there would be no interview.

Fortier had met with Alain and the two came up with the idea that since Sebastian was unable to speak that they ask him to blink his eyes with one blink meaning 'no' and two blinks meaning 'yes.' Alain also stipulated that *Mdme.* Gontard be allowed to witness the interview. At first Fortier was against it until Alain said that Sebastian would be more amiable if she were present. Fortier acquiesced.

Jill had been given advance notice that she was to observe only. At no time was she to make a sound. She agreed and the interview began.

Fortier entered with his stenographer and Alain entered with his own stenographer with Jill sitting in a corner as the observer.

Fortier, speaking in French asked Sebastian if he had any memory of being stopped on his way to see *M.* Lefevre and he blinked twice for yes.

"Did you recognize who stopped you?" Sebastian blinked once for no.

"Were there more than one person?" Sebastian blinked twice for yes.

"Were there only two?" Sebastian blinked twice for yes.

"Were they men?" Again Sebastian blinked twice for yes.

"Were you given something to sedate you?" Again, Sebastian blinked twice for yes.

"Were they another nationality and not French?" Sebastian blinked twice for yes.

"Were they Algerian?" The blink was once for no.

"Were they Egyptian?" The blink was twice for yes.

"Ah, M. Sebastian you are to be commended for your bravery. Were these two men masked? Sebastian blinked once for no.

"Would you recognize either of them if you were given a photo?" For a moment, Sebastian just looked at Fortier and then blinked yes.

Fortier looked at Alain and said, "I think this enough for now. Once we have photographs, we will return. *Merci M.* Gontard. *Adieu.*"

Sebastian blinked twice and then closed his eyes as the group left the room. Once they were gone, he opened his eyes and saw Jill standing by the bed. Tears began flowing out of his eyes. She reached over and kissed his forehead.

"My darling, I am so proud of you. We will take you home in a few days. I won't leave you."

He blinked twice and closed his eyes. A nurse had entered and checked the medication in the tube that held a liquid sedative. He drifted off to sleep and Jill left the room to seek Ellen and Peter who were in the waiting room with Alain.

Alain suggested they have lunch at the hospital's restaurant, *The Garden*. Once they were seated and had ordered, he spoke. "Sebastian gave us some leads, which I will pursue. The man who Sebastian fought with has been recovered from the *Seine* and I will get the autopsy results perhaps this afternoon. In addition, Sebastian indicated there were two men and they are Egyptian. These are strong leads."

Peter nodded. "Yes, I have to agree with you. We now know the dagger is of Egyptian origin and now we have two Egyptian men apparently wanting the dagger."

Ellen let out a big sigh. "I am growing weary of this new so-called gift sent to me. I have wracked my brain attempting to figure out why and I keep coming up with a blank."

"Why?" Jill asked, and then went on to ask, "Haven't you thought that you were of the lineage of Mary Magdalene?"

"Umm, yes I have. We have already shared with you that Peter and I have been working on my genealogy and have not come up with anything concrete that would indicate that I am. When I think of it, I cannot see how a lineage could truly go back that far unless the Priory of Sion goes that far back. Think of Europe at the time the Magdalene brought her children from Egypt. The Romans were expanding all over France, Spain and Germany. I do not see how records could have been kept.

Alain interrupted, "I ask that you forgive me for leaving now, however I do have an appointment I must keep." He stood up and said that he would take care of the lunch bill and kissed Ellen and Jill on their cheek before leaving.

Peter watched him leave. "He does appear to be happier now that he is working for Louise."

Ellen and Jill both agreed with him. Jill said that she wanted to get back to Sebastian and left them.

Peter and Ellen looked at each other. "My love, it is just the two of us. Do you have any plans while we are in Paris?"

She laughed. "Not at this moment. What I would really love to do is go home and relax in the sauna. Will you join me?"

"Ah, I never thought you would ask."

ΩΩΩ

~ HY BRASIL ~
400 A.D.

A HISTORY

Surprise is the greatest gift which life can grant us.
~ Boris Pasternak

Magdalena stood looking out the window from her bedroom. She felt a nagging within her brain and it had to do with sending Rath out into the other world. *Something be missing.* The idea came to her that perhaps Cyran did not tell her all the history. *Aye, that be it. There must be more fer me to know.* At that minute, Mireen knocked on the door and brought her the usual breakfast.

"Thank yew Mireen. I 'ave an errand fer yew. Send a runner to find Lord Cyran and ask him to meet me in the library within the hour."

"Aye, M Lady."

Magdalena sat down to eat her breakfast and continued to think about the missing information that Cyran had not given her. She knew it had something to do with Rath's trip. She could not allow him to leave until she had more information.

Magdalena was already in the library when Cyran opened the door. He bowed to her and she returned the bow. "Welcome Lord Cyran. Please sit as I 'ave questions fer yew."

"I 'ave been waiting for yew to ask and I be here to perhaps give you the answers yew seek regarding the trip Rath is to take."

She chuckled. "Yew be astute. When yew told me the history of Hy Brasil, yew did nae tell all of it. I remember yew told me there be more. "

"Aye, I did and 'ave held back until yew realized there be more. This I can tell yew. The star boat beings come from tyme to tyme. The truth be they seeded our people here as an experiment. This experiment be that the evolution of our peoples will be beyond what the other peoples elsewhere be. They brought us many inventions as they named them and 'ave yet to be introduced in places beyond here. They do nae intrude into the affairs of Hy Brasil.

"It be nae Scota or Gaythelos who came here. The Tuatha de Danaan who be of the island of Erin bringing with them women and men of Scota when Gaythelos and sons fought the Tuatha and won. Peoples of their lineage came to establish a new country and be called Hy Brasil many ans ago. Thus after more ans, there be a mating with Morgance, daughter of Sarah, who be daughter of Mary Magdalene and Yeshua ben Joseph, and thus began the lineage of the Magentheld when a group of Scota's peoples arrived here in Hy Brasil with the Tuatha de Danaan..

"What the star boat beings 'ave done is bring forward knowledge from the future and it be many ans ahead. We naow 'ave water running through pipes here and in many hovels. We 'ave a source to dispose of our waste. New grains and seeds be introduced. They allow us to advance while other worlds such as the one yew be sending Rath to be nae privy to our knowledge. Rath and his group will consider them backward, and they be that. Tis not our place to teach them.

"Aye, we be 'aving wars. Nae many as our mists keep many away. The Star Peoples allow these wars fer a tyme. We 'ave always won these wars."

She was quiet and contemplating what he told her. "When will I meet the star boat people?"

"Tis nae fer me to say. They come in the night when least expected."

Magdalena drew in a deep breath. "I be apprising Rath and his group of the backwardness of those he be meeting. Be there more I be to know?"

"Aye M' Lady. There be an outlaw Druid who left the teachings. He thinks he knows more than the others. He uses a wicked mind and yew best be aware of him. His name be Wexon and he claims he be part of yere lineage."

"Yew mean he could be part of my kin?"

"Perhaps, but do nae take him lightly."

"What part of my kin?"

"Tis spoken he be a son of yere father's brother, Jaxon."

"I 'ave heard naught of Jaxon."

"Aye. Jaxon perished in a battle with the Skagerrak. He be unable to breed children due to injury. Wexon's father nae be known. The mother of Wexon passed this plane soon after his birth. He be taken in by Druids to care for and teach. Beware of him."

"Thank yew Lord Cyran. Tis always wise to be aware. Naow, I go to Callan and seek to give Rath a history lesson."

Before she left him, Cyran told her the beings from the star boat ships had also brought the people a game be called Chess – a game of life.

PLAYING THE GAME

Chess is an infinitely complex game, which one can play in infinitely numerous and varied ways
~ Vladimir Kramnik

Drip, drip, drip. Slowing the sound awakened Magdalena. The darkness was deep and she knew it was not the time of the rising sun. Awareness grew as the dripping sound continued. *Ah*, she thought. *Tis raining and the beginning of Beltane.* Settling back under her covers, her mind began to race with ideas and things to do until she recognized her mind was akin to a runaway horse.

She quieted her mind by focusing and blessing the Great Mother Earth and to give thanks for all she was. She knew impatience could undo all the most careful laid plans.

She drifted back into sleep and the dream began. Magdalena foresaw Oris being wounded and taken prisoner by Brannon. She watched him deep in a dungeon chained to a wall with his wound unattended. Before she could determine if he was to live or die, she awoke with a deep sense of grief. Calling forth her training, she went back into the dream. She knew she could change it.

She saw Oris in the dungeon chained to a wall and she began to imagine a figure opening the strong door and silently moving to Oris with a key in the hand. Silently the chains fell away from the lock and the figure picked up Oris and swiftly left the cell. Quickly the figure with Oris on its back moved past a sleeping guard and up the stairs moving through passages out of the Hold to waiting horses. The horse's hooves were wrapped in skins to muffle the sounds. Oris was freed at last.

Magdalena continued to imagine in her dream his arrival at the safety of her camp and his complete healing. When she felt complete with the dream, she woke up to a sense of well being. She continued to lay in her bed contemplating the dream of a possible future event. Becoming aware of another presence in her chamber, she opened her eyes and focused in the darkness. She recognized the Druidess Regan. "Regan! How did yew get in?"

Smiling, Regan gave her the greeting of the Druids. "Me sister, 'ave you forgotten we be trained to walk through walls?"

"Aye, and also that we transport ourselves in order to be in two places at once," Magdalena replied. "I placed a spell around my quarters to keep intruders out. How did yew manage to come through?"

"I became yew and yere frequency."

Magdalena even though perplexed, smiled. "Naow, my dear Regan, what brings yew to my bedchamber at this hour?"

"M'Lady, tis indeed no social visit. Brannon enlisted the assistance of a renegade Druid. Aye, occasionally there be some who reach a point where they deem they can be taught nothing more and become intoxicated with the power they 'ave gained. It be unfortunate fer humankind and even more tragic fer the soul."

"I 'ave heard tales of a Druid named Wexon, if he be who yew be referring to."

"Aye M'Lady. His black magic be nothing to blink one's eye at. He has a burr under his skin as Sarenhild refused to dally with him. Wexon be sore to the bone about his banishment to the hinterlands and my feeling and knowingness be he has subtly created this move."

"'ave yew alerted the Druidesses and Lady Alinor?"

"Aye, that I 'ave. Lord Cyran also knows. I deemed it best to alert them first so necessary fields of spells can be placed."

"Thank yew Regan. Yew be most wise and yew 'ave trained well. Wexon also be trained well it seems. Power be a heady thing and may I never abuse mine. This be indeed a most interesting turn of events. I must contemplate naow and I honor yew fer bringing me this bit of news. May our next meeting be one of mutual light heart."

Each saluted the other and in a twinkling of an eye, Regan was gone. Magdalena stoked the fire and sat near the hearth. A cold chill had gripped her for a moment. She stared into the fire and began to have a vision of Wexon – a man of great stature with light colored hair. The color of corn silk. Some could call him handsome. His beard and mustache were well trimmed. Now he was in deep discussion with Brannon.

For a moment, he looked up, and his deep grey eyes searched the room and then he looked down at the map on the table. Brannon asked him what he was looking at and shaking his head, Wexon replied that he was searching to see if there were spies about. Brannon laughed and said there were no spies today or this night.

Bringing her attention back to the fire, Magdalena sighed. *So, Wexon is in the Garenfeld. With the great heavy rains it be doubtful fer him to travel, so it must be either he be in two places at once, or Brannon smuggled him in.* Mentally, she checked the frequency spell placed around her chambers and the wing she used in the Garenfeld. They be still intact. She used her mind power to summon Cyran to meet with her in her chamber.

She stood up and went to the window where she began her morning salutation for the day. When she finished, she completed her toilet and dressed for the day. A knock sounded on her door. "Come."

Mireen entered and before she could announce his arrival, Cyran entered upon her heels. Magdalena smiled. "Thank yew Mireen. Please bring a meal fer two."

"Aye, M'Lady. It be good as done."

After Mireen left the room, Magdalena and Cyran greeted each other. "M'Lady, I can see that yew 'ave received the message from Regan."

"Aye, I received her message and after she departed, I began using my second vision. Wexon is meeting with Brannon in the Garenfeld. I observed them reading a map."

"Hmm, it means he could be in two places at once, or Brannon smuggled him in. I 'ad nae expected him to show his hand so soon. There be no accidents, so tis well we be aware."

"Yew knew he be already involved? Why be I nae kept abreast of this potential development? Moreover, what else be it I 'ave nae been told? Or would it spoil the game?"

While tugging at his beard, Cyran looked at her with a twinkle in his eye. "Naow, M'Lady, yew very well know yew agreed to play this role 'erefore yew be born to Sarenhild and Golornia. Tis all unfolding according to plan."

By now, Magdalena was seething with indignation. "How dare yew tell me it be unfolding according to a plan! Whose plan? If I agreed to this *game*, why do I nae remember?"

"M'Lady, forgive me. I can see yew do need a few more explanations. How much do yew know about tyme and dimensions?"

Magdalena's countenance changed and she thought a moment before replying. "I 'ave been taught tyme be nae a straight line, and it be of many dimensions according to its frequency." She stopped as though searching for a further explanation.

""Aye," replied Cyran."It be very much akin to a chess game in three dimensions. There be events happening at the same tyme – only on different levels. Be yew understanding this?"

Magdalena nodded her head in agreement and Cyran continued. "An event in the past can be affected by a future action since it be all happening at the same tyme. Therefore, one in the present can affect the streams of both tymes."

With understanding brightening her countenance, Magdalena nodded again in agreement. "Then life be a large game of chess and the major decisions we make or by our thoughts and actions, we create a ripple effect into other dimensions."

Cyran smiled, as he was happy to note the grasp she had in the understanding. "Once one fully understands this, one be empowered to choose one's destiny. The past can always be undone and there emerges a change in any future event. It takes consistent action in the present."

"And, what be it I am to change in this past I be living in? Or, what event or events be I to affect?"

"Very astute questions M'Lady. Our renegade Druid Wexon has tasted the elixir of power. He wants to establish the old religion of *Aowe*. He wants to place himself as the spokesman fer *Aowe* and he becomes the supreme tyrant."

She shuddered, arose from her chair and stood by the fire. "This could mean the total control of the people and with results in a future of jealousy, hate and great wars. Cyran, I be nae sure I be capable fer this responsibility. Be there some other way?"

Cyran smiled and came to stand by her. "M' Lady, yew be well prepared. Yew cannae change the course of events naow. Yere god has committed yew and it must unfold. Tis why it be important for yew to initiate an era of the expansion of mind. People who be aware of their inner potentials and possibilities cannae be ruled by tyranny."

She was about to reply when Mireen knocked and reentered the chamber with their morning meal. While she prepared the table, Magdalena stared into the fire. The flames leaped and danced. Turning back to Cyran, she invited him to sit at the small table. Mireen had discreetly left the chamber.

"Ah Cyran, yew be as usual correct. Tis only a coward who runs from the challenge. I can nae do this to my god. Be there some person who could scan. "Wexon without his knowledge? There must be a weak point in his countenance and I intend to ferret it out."

"Aye M'Lady he could be scanned. It will nae be easy. Tis rumored he has a weakness fer young lads. Perhaps this weakness be his downfall." Cyran frowned with distaste as he spoke.

"She sighed and arose from her chair. She walked to the window. The early morning sun was radiating golden brilliance as it made its way up past the far off mountains. The beauty of the scene gripped her being and for a moment, she forgot where she was. "It be indeed a distasteful weakness, but use it we must. Do yew 'ave anyone in mind?"

"Methinks there may be a young Druid lad who be an excellent scanner. This be a wonderful test fer him"

"Naturally you would already 'ave someone in mind. Yew perhaps 'ave all of this plotted out to the last character."

"Naow M'Lady! I do keep tabs on the Druids and Druidesses. I also study my so-named adversaries in depth. Tis all part of life if one wants to remain free."

"Thank yew Wise One. Yew 'ave made a very valid point. In my vision this early morn, I noticed a large map, which Wexon and Brannon be poring over. I deem it advisable to 'ave a copy of it. I be asking Callan to initiate this."

"Tis indeed a good ploy. And naow, another matter. I ask yew to consider adding the Master of Science to a Council position along with the Master of Music. The present Council be heavily laden with men whose only consideration be arms and war."

"Cyran, honored Wise One, yew be reading my mind again." They both laughed. "Callan be already screening the realms fer committed and knowledgeable peoples. I also know it be my choice to enlarge the Council membership. With Brannon and Wexon plotting my overthrow, this perhaps be a good tyme to initiate this action. It could be another diversion in conjunction with my 'rumor."

"Aye. Spread their attention to many areas and it weakens their center as well. I be sensing yew have other actions as well.

Magdalena's countenance brightened. "Aye. When I 'ave selected the most able of science and music, I be 'aving a search made of the realm fer students with potentials. It be my intention to establish an academy where young minds expand and learn. Perhaps they be surpassing their teachers and this will truly expand the mind of the populace. I 'ave also contemplated guilds of music, law, artisans, weavers, and scribes. However, first things first. The matter of Brannon and Wexon must be settled. I also understand Wexon has a small cadre of seers who be powerful. The coming battle will be of the mind."

"M'Lady yew be indeed a most worthy Magentheld. Yere selection of guilds be worthy causes. If I 'ave yere permission, I naow take yere leave and be about my business."

"Granted. Thank yew for coming."

After Cyran departed, Magdalena sat down before the fire. There was much to think about such as Wexon and the misuse of power. Smiling ruefully, she recognized the ageless battle of good and evil. *Ah well,* she thought, *of opposites. And nae until the planet evolved to another frequency this be resolved.* In the meantime, she knew she had to plan her next step carefully. *I need to know all I can about my adversary.* Mentally she sent out a call to Callan and returned to the flames of the fire.

It was not too long before there was a gentle tapping on the door. "Come."

Callan entered with a smile on her face and saluted Magdalena. "I be here as yew called me."

"Callan, what do yew know about the Druid Wexon? I also want Peppo's knowledge of him. He has proven to be a well of knowledge and perhaps he can enlarge on what we already know about Wexon."

Callan looked into the fire and then at Magdalena. "So, Wexon be at last showing his hand. I 'ave wondered if he be involved."

Magdalena began giving Callan the details of Regan's visit during the early morning hours, and of her conversation with Cyran. "I 'ave to know my adversary in depth if I complete me mission."

"Aye, M'Lady. What I do know is he left the Druids some seven ans ago. It be said he had a great disagreement with the Arch Druid. He disappeared fer three ans when he resurfaced. Tis said he applied to Sarenhild fer a position as court seer and he be refused. He again disappeared and tis rumored he be trained a small group of seers fer what purpose I know nae of; however I can perhaps guess."

"Perhaps we need to speak with the Arch Druid. I know Cyran knows more than he 'as told me, but it be his way of allowing me to ferret these things out fer meself. It be why he be the Wise One. I deem it necessary to ask the Arch Druid to transport himself immediately."

Magdalena and Callan sat before the fire and mentally sent a message to the Arch Druid to come to the Garenfeld. Once satisfied the message be received by him Callan departed to find Peppo and bring him to Magdalena.

Magdalena walked to the great window and watched the sun dance upon the great trees and gardens blanketed with raindrops. She mused, "Soon Beltane. I must meet with Druidess Jurist soon."

At this moment, Mireen knocked and entered to take away the dishes and also to tidy the table. Magdalena asked her to prepare tea for three. Mireen curtsied and replied, "Aye, M'Lady."

Mireen soon returned with the tea and cakes and as she left, Callan arrived with an apprehensive Peppo in tow.

"Ah dear Peppo, I be hearing great things of yere knowledge and accomplishments. Callan speaks most highly of yew."

His look of apprehension faded and a large smile graced his face. "M'Lady, tis most kind of our Lady Callan and yew to call me here. I be honored to remain in the service of the Magentheld."

Magdalena smiled. "It be known that yew hold a wealth of knowledge about people. What can yew tell me about the seer Wexon."

Peppo frowned as if he be thinking. "He be a most distasteful person. He 'ad the audacity to approach the then Magentheld Sarenhild and ask him to give him the position of court seer. Nay, he did nae ask. He demanded. Our Lord Sarenhild told him he would nae be blackmailed, and banished him from the realm. Be he back?"

Magdalena nodded yes, and asked Peppo to tell her all he knew of the man's background. Peppo laced his fingers together and looked at the ceiling before he began speaking. "M'Lady, it be said he be born of a maid in the Hold of the deceased Lord Fallon. Some say he be a bastard born of Fallon."

Magdalena held her hand up to hold him from saying more. "I be told he be a son of Jaxon, my father's brother."

"Nay! M'Lady. Lord Jaxon could 'ave never bred him or any other child."

"Why be this?"

"M'Lady, Lord Jaxon had an accident as a child and he, he lost his member and he never married due to his shame."

"Thank yew Peppo. What else can yew tell me of Wexon?"

"As I recall, he be known as a bright child and when he be ten ans he be sent to the Druids fer training.

Tis said he favors lads. It be after this episode he disappeared and resurfaced to approach Lord Sarenhild with promises of power and wealth if he be appointed court seer. Moreover, M' Lady this be all I know at this moment. At your bidding, I will make discreet inquiries."

"Thank yew Peppo. I think inquiries at this tyme be inappropriate. However, if yew hear of something, please inform Lady Callan. Yere service be truly appreciated."

When Peppo left, Magdalena asked Callan to remain. With the door closed, she asked Callan to ferret out where Wexon had gone when Sarenhild banished him. If he had left the realm, then another country had to house him. She also wanted to know everything about the Hold of Fallon.

Callan consented to do as she requested and in the meantime, she reminded Magdalena of meetings in the afternoon with Matran and Frint with each meeting being separate. There was also a scheduled meeting with Bertran.

The remainder of the day passed with meetings and appointments which were productive and harmonious. It was agreed Matran, Frint and Rath would depart with Hopenth as their valet and secretary one moon from Beltane. Matran and Frint were enthusiastic over the prospect of opening up new markets in other realms for trade, and to observe the ways of others. Magdalena was impressed with their knowledge and their dedication.

The meeting with Bertran was different from their first meeting. Now that Bertran realized the import of the mission given, her manner markedly improved. Gone was the jealous woman. The value of her worth grew within her. She too, would depart a moon from

Beltane. Magdalena had managed to place a young Druidess as Bertran's secretary. Bertran was only too happy to have the young maiden as it increased the importance of her mission. Magdalena knew she would be receiving an accurate report.

After Bertran left, Magdalena decided to walk to the village and have a chat with the Druidess Muirno. The village had been built outside the walls of the Magentheld abode, which housed its stables, kitchens, the hospital and housing for visitors. She requested Callan to accompany her. The village had grown since she was a child. She felt a deep stirring of emotions in remembering her mother who loved to come and talk with the villagers.

The road still had mud from the rain and it was now beginning to dry. She took note of the smoke coming out of the homes and the thatched roofs appeared to be well kept. She and Callan nodded to the Villagers they met while they were walking. They noted there was a new inn for visitors and travelers along with the open stalls containing meats, foodstuffs, implements and various other items. When they reached the house of Muirno, she was there waiting.

"Greetings M'Lady Magentheld, welcome to our village. I invite yew to enter my abode and 'ave a cup of tay." Her eyes twinkled as she spoke.

Magdalena was taken with her lightheartedness and took her hands while looking deep into her eyes. "Thank yew. This be Callan and we be honored to sit with yew."

The house was small and kept neat and clean. Magdalena felt a sense of peace and calm. Once they were seated and the tea poured, Magdalena spoke first. "Lord Cyran told me yew be the Jurist of this village."

"Aye, tis right. I be that." She went on to tell of her duties, to settle disputes, arrest wayward people who be robbers or murderers and delivering her edicts to the Magentheld.

Magdalena thanked her for the information and asked if there be any Druids who were not local within the village or the nearby countryside. Callan was mentally taking note of all that be said.

"Aye, M'Lady. Tis well yew came to me as I 'ave seen some who be nae of the kind I know. I 'ave seen them entering the inn and within me it bode nae goodwill. Methinks one be named Wexon."

Magdalena thought this to be true. "I 'ave heard Wexon be a renegade Druid and I be askin' yew keep me apprised of who comes with him and what news there be."

"This I do. Me senses tell me they intend harm to yew and this realm. Tis nae good fer yew. What I know be Wexon meets with General Brannon from tyme to tyme."

"Aye, I 'ave learned he does. I ask if Wexon or any of his Druids come to the village yew alert me. He be a troublemaker."

"I 'ave heard he wants to change the villagers worship to a being called Aowe. Tis well yew came to visit me as I be going to come to yew with the whispers."

Magdalena stood up. "I thank yew for yere tay and yere news. Yew may always come to me with news."

Magdalena and Callan did not speak until they were out of the village. Callan spoke first. "Tis well yew came. I find Druidess Muirno most observant and trustworthy."

"Callan, since yew be my eyes and ears, I charge yew to keep abreast of what be happening in the village."

Later in the early evening she had training with Joffen before retiring to her chamber for the evening. She asked Mireen not to disturb her until she called for her. The fire was dancing merrily in the large fireplace and she sat down on the great hearth to contemplate how she could meet the challenge of Wexon and his band of seers. She knew the challenge to be great as it involved the power of the mind. As she continued to stare into the fire, she began to dream the dream of her mastery over Wexon's involvement. She imagined the outcome repeatedly until she knew her god had received it. With a knowingness that it is done, she fell into a deep sleep. It was a dreamless sleep.

Magdalena of Hy Brasil

~ France ~
2013

Sebastian's Homecoming

Healing is a matter of time, but it is sometimes also a matter of opportunity ~ Hippocrates

Ten days after his abduction and his escape, Sebastian was allowed to return to the chateau. The children had decorated the gates entering into the chateau with colored balloons and were eagerly awaiting with anticipation his arrival. They had been forewarned not to overwhelm Sebastian as he was still recovering from his injuries. When the word came from the gatekeeper that the limousine had just passed through, the children began jumping up and down and waving their own balloons. Aimee and Eleanor were the youngest and the smallest, so they were told to stand in front. When the limousine stopped, the cheering began.

The chauffeur was the first to get out and he opened the door for Sebastian and Jill. As he stepped down, there were tears streaming down his face. Due to his jaw being wired, he could not speak. Instead, he bowed with his hands clasped under his chin.

Jill stood beside him with her eyes teary also. Aimee and Arthur were hugging Sebastian's waist until Jill asked them to step back. Magda stepped up and began reading a welcome home poem.

Beloved Oncle, Father Sebastian
Over adversity you did win
A mighty warrior you be.
For all the world to see.

Magdalena of Hy Brasil

*You dealt a major blow
And brave you are we. know
Accept our love and never fear
Because we all hold you dear.*

    The children stepped back to allow Marie and Jacques to welcome him. The couple stepped forward and told him how happy they were to have him back and that as soon as he was able to eat and speak that Marie would prepare a feast for him.

    Again, Sebastian's eyes teared up. Jill told them how grateful she and Sebastian were for their love and honor.

    Peter now took charge and asked the children to go and play and if they wished, they could draw pictures for Sebastian. Ellen was beaming and hugged Jill and told Sebastian that she was delighted to see him back where he belonged..

The healing period for Sebastian had been forecast to be for approximately six weeks. He was able to walk around and with Jill they took long walks in the woods. The office near the lake that he and Jill had used when they were translating the Sarah scrolls was now his to use for his research. He also had a laptop that he used when he chose to remain in the chateau. He always carried a tablet and pen with him so that he could write a reply or request something and appeared to be patient with his long recovery. As he wrote to Jill, he was using his quiet time for inner guidance and reflections.

    At one point, Jill asked him if he still planned to take the position in Canada. He paused for a moment and then wrote, "*Non.* I cannot leave until I have deciphered the information on the dagger."

"But, but!" She sputtered. "You almost lost your life! What good is deciphering some symbols on a dagger going to do for you?"

There was a twinkle in his eyes and he wrote, "Ah, I will not run away from this. It is not over and I sense that there will be another attack to steal the dagger. I do not think it will be me. However, this is not over. I am on sabbatical from the *Université* and we are here."

She sighed. "Yes, I know we are here and the children are attending school, but I thought you were bored with the *Université* and wanted a change."

He responded by writing, "*Oui*. Until I met you, my life was boring and I wanted to die. You changed all of that and you are my love. *Oui*. The *Université* has become boring and I wanted change. I received it, but not in the manner it happened."

"All right my beloved husband. I will stop badgering you regarding Canada. You are the love and light of my life and I will work with you." She reached over and kissed him on the forehead. "In the meantime, I will leave you alone.

Inwardly, she smiled as she no longer wanted to move to Canada. She began thinking, *What if we find a place nearby to Ellen and Peter to rent.*

That evening after the children had been put to bed, Ellen and Peter decided to go to bed early. Once they were in bed, Peter approached Ellen with an idea. "I learned today that the property next to the chateau has been placed up for sale. Nance learned of it through her own sources."

"And, what is it you have in mind?"

"With the death of Agnes Pettigrew, the estate is up for sale. Apparently, none of her children want it. From the photos Nance secured for me, it isn't all that large. There are about five bedrooms, three baths and is on about 2 and one-half hectares."

"Yes, I remember meeting her. As I understand, it was once a guest house and the Pettigrew family added to it for Agnes."

"Since, Sebastian is not going to Canada and does not want to return to the *Université*, I thought perhaps we could purchase the property and give it to them to live there. They need to own their own home."

"My beloved, I think you have been reading my mind because I want them near us. They are our second family and I was dreading having them so far away."

"I'm glad to know that you agree with me. I had a talk with Sebastian the other day, and asked if he was accepting the position in Canada and he replied by writing his response. He has been offered a position as a translator of old documents at the Sorbonne and he is considering having his own private translation business. He has told Jill that he no longer wants to go to Canada."

"What? Jill hasn't told me this!"

"Whoa. Perhaps he told her about this and she is waiting for the right moment to tell you. However, with your permission I will purchase the property."

"Well, big guy! You are brilliant and yes! Please buy it now."

He looked at her sheepishly. "I thought you would say yes, so I made an offer."

Ellen began laughing. "You know me so well. You already knew I would say yes."

"And now my beautiful love, it is time to make love. Shall we?"

"I thought you would never ask."

Slowly and with an intense heat of love, their lovemaking exploded. When the two were finally satisfied, Ellen cuddled in his arms. "It's never the same is it?"

He kissed the top of her head. "Thank god it is never the same. Sweet dreams."

ΩΩΩ

The Move

Where we love is home - home that our feet may leave, but not our hearts. ~ Oliver Wendell Holmes

It was several weeks after Peter and Ellen had their conversation regarding the purchase of the house and property next to their chateau, when Jill had asked Ellen to take a walk in the woods with her. The two women were admiring the changing leaves, and stopped at one of the benches that had been along the path. Jill was the first to speak. "Well, my friend there is change in the lives of Sebastian and me."

"Do you want to talk about it?"

"Of course I do. This is why I asked you to walk with me. Sebastian turned down the position in Canada and has now accepted a position at the Sorbonne. I, I am relieved as I felt so far away from you, your family." Her voice trailed off and Ellen did not say anything. "I, I am actually excited because I felt so far away in Toulouse."

"When will he begin his position? And, what will he be doing at the Sorbonne?"

Jill laughed. "What he dearly loves doing, and that is translating old documents. I think he will be much happier there."

Ellen reached over and hugged her. "I am relieved that you aren't going to Canada, and in fact, I a delirious with joy!"

The two women giggled like young schoolgirls. Jill told her that Sebastian was progressing quite fast according to the doctor with his healing. "I will be so happy when he can speak. I miss hearing his voice. I also miss our lovemaking. But, this will change."

"Yes, it will change. I can hardly wait to tell Peter – if that is okay with you."

"Sebastian told me he had already mentioned it to Peter. I think he was afraid to tell me first and I felt a bit miffed, but actually I am happy and relieved."

Once the news had been shared regarding Sebastian's new position and his recovery was moving faster than what the doctor had predicted, Peter and Ellen decided to offer them the new property to have as a gift. The papers were ready to be turned over to them.

A few evenings after Jill shared the news with Ellen, the two couples were able to talk once the children were in bed. Peter had brought out one of their prized red wines, a *Petrus* from the winery located in *Pomeral* in the *Bordeaux* region. Sebastian was drinking his through a straw. He had written that he would not be without red wine.

Peter began by toasting to Sebastian's new position that would begin after the first of the year. "To our beloved Sebastian and Jill, here is to a wonderful new beginning. We are delighted that you will be near us. That is, if you will consider living on the property next door to the chateau."

Sebastian almost choked and Jill's jaw dropped. Somehow, Sebastian managed to keep the wine down and he quickly wrote on his tablet, "But that property is for your business."

Ellen smiled as Peter went on to say, "That is not the property I am speaking of. I am talking about the property on the other side of this one. It came up for sale, so Ellen and I purchased it and if you so desire, it is our gift to you."

Jill was speechless and Sebastian looked dumbfounded until he managed to write, "I don't see how we can accept a gift of this magnitude."

Ellen looked at her two friends. "If you recall, this chateau was a gift to the four of us by Alain, and he put it in the names of Peter and me with the stipulation that it was also your home. We have made changes and upgraded it. Therefore, it is only proper that the two of you have your very own home."

Jill began crying and Sebastian had tears flowing out of his eyes. Jill replied, "We are overwhelmed. I, I accept on behalf of my husband and our children." She looked at Sebastian, and he managed to nod that he agreed.

Peter had a folder with him and he brought out the papers for the new home and gave it to them. "Now, this has been recorded in both of your names and you must go to the *Notaries'* office to complete the details and get the official deed. Tomorrow, Ellen and I will drive you to the *Notarie.* "

Ellen nodded in agreement. "In the meantime, the two of you can look through this portfolio that Peter had Nance to put together. It is not as large as this home; however, it does have five bedrooms. At one time, it was a small carriage house. When Agnes Pettigrew came to live with her daughter and son-in-law the carriage house was renovated with additions." Ellen smiled after she handed the portfolio to Jill.

"I, I never thought that Sebastian and me would ever have our very own home such as the one shown here in this portfolio." She began crying.

Sebastian squeezed her hand while tears streamed down his face. The two looked through the portfolio and were amazed at the size of it.

Peter said, "It's been a long time coming and we did not want to dissuade you from going to Canada. Now, that there is a position for Sebastian in Paris, we knew it was time for you to have your own home. I promise you that I will have security placed around your home. Now, tomorrow Ellen and I will take you to your new home."

"Peter and I will now leave the two of you to go through this portfolio and we will see you in the morning. I love you both so much."

Jill's eyes glistened. "We love the two of you also and there are not enough words to express our love and joy."

The following day, the foursome drove to the *Notarie* in the nearby village where the documents were signed and the deed handed to Sebastian. It was a momentous occasion for both Jill and Sebastian. Peter handed them the keys to their new home and then drove them so they could walk through their first home.

Ellen was still daubing her eyes from being teary-eyes, when Peter drove to the gate and pressed in a code that he had already given to them. When they drove in, they could see a stone fence had been built between their new home and the original chateau. The gravel driveway came to a circle with a fountain in the center with fall flowers. When Peter stopped the car, Jill gasped. "Oh my god! It's lovelier than the photos!"

Sebastian could only nod his head with tears streaming down his face. The outside of the house was made of gray stone with the entry under a small peaked roof. The windows on each side of the entry were glazed glass of small panes. There was a garage that was attached to the house with its doors white. The second story had a peaked roof with two chimneys. Apparently one was for the kitchen and one for the family room.

Once they were inside, Jill and Sebastian were shocked as the previous owners had left all the furniture in it, even to the linens and towels. It all came with the house property. Jill turned to Peter, "How on earth did you manage this?"

"Actually, I did not. The children of Agnes Pettigrew have also sold the chateau and with this one, they did not want to bother with any of the furnishings once Agnes died. So, this is an added bonus."

Slowly the foursome walked through the house once again before seeing what the rest of the property held. To the left of the living room, there was a terrace and apparently, a pond had been created so Agnes could sit out and watch the wildfowl as they came and swam. Peter told them that Nance had learned that the old woman and her caregiver always took their meals here when the weather was warm and not raining.

Jill replied, "I know the children will love this, and I can see the children now exploring every inch of this property. Is there anything else you haven't told us?"

Peter cleared his throat. "Well yes. There is one other item the family decided to leave. Here, let's go to the garage."

When he opened the door, Jill almost choked. "Oh my god! A car!"

Peter smiled as he opened the door on the driver's side. "Apparently the caregiver received the more luxurious car and declined this one. As you can see, it is a Peugeot Estate car of the year 2002."

Sebastian already had his head inside the back end. He was nodding his head up and down indicating a yes, yes.

Jill slid into the driver's seat and said, "In the States we call these station wagons, and it is ideal for us and the children. I feel like Santa Claus has already appeared!" Her eyes glistened when she got back out and stood there admiring their new car. "Words cannot truly express how much we appreciate this gift." She began crying and Ellen handed her a tissue.

Sebastian shook his head in wonderment and when Jill got out of the car, he slid in and examined all of the buttons. Peter reached in and handed him the keys, which Sebastian inserted. The engine started immediately. Ellen thought to herself that it was like seeing two children with new toys.

Jill got in the passenger side and asked Sebastian if he would drive them back to the chateau and he nodded yes. Peter stuck his head in, "Here is the garage door opener and we will leave. It is now yours for you to stay as long as you want and to close up the house and gate. Take all the time you want to explore your new home.

Ellen and Peter got into their car to drive back to the chateau. "Whew! Peter, you do create magic and I love you for what you did."

"Sweetheart, it was the two of us who did it. Our children are going to be delirious with joy that they have playmates next door. With permission, I think I will install a gate between our two properties."

"That's a grand idea."

They were nearing their gate when they saw a police car talking to the gateman. Peter came to a stop and rolled down his window. Speaking in French, he told them who he was and the reply was that it was an urgent matter.

Ellen's heart plummeted and the color drained out of her face. Peter told the gateman to open the gates and he drove in first with the police car following him. Once they were in front of the chateau, Peter stopped the engine and got out. Ellen followed.

When the other vehicle stopped behind them, two police officers got out and the one not driving spoke. *"M.* and *Mme.* Douglass, we understand that you have in your employee a *Mlle.* Cerise Bertrand?"

Peter replied that he did. "Has something happened to *Mlle.* Bertrand?"

"*Oui.* It is our sad duty to say that *Mlle.* Bertrand has met with an unfortunate death." He did not wait for Peter or Ellen to ask questions as he went on to say, "*Mlle.* Bertrand was found late last night near the metro *Couronnes* in the *20th arrondissement* in Paris. We learned from her parents that she has been employed here and we find it necessary to inquire regarding anything you can tell us about her."

Ellen gasped, "Oh no!"

Peter's face paled and he asked the officers to follow them into the house. Peter led them into the formal living room. "I – my wife and I are shocked. We will tell you what we know. First, what is her condition?"

The first officer said that she was dead and apparently had been garroted. "Can you tell us when she was last here?"

Ellen replied, "It was yesterday afternoon around 5 p.m. She had completed the cleaning she had been assigned. Perhaps Marie, our cook can tell you more because Cerise is her niece." She looked at Peter and he said he would have Marie come in.

When Marie arrived she was already crying. She had learned by phone about Cerise from her sister.

Peter calmly told her why the police were here and could she tell them what she knew.

Marie's face was in shock with tears flowing down her face. She managed to stammer in French that Cerise had been employed as a house cleaner a year and there had never been a problem. "She, she had always been a shy girl, was quiet and never spoke of her life outside. She came and did her work, and she left. Perhaps Yvonne will know more, however she left for an appointment with *le dentist.*"

Peter interceded at this point. "When *Mlle.* Yvonne returns, we will have her call you."

The officer gave him his name and the telephone number of the police station.

After his departure, Ellen and Peter stared at one another with shock. Ellen spoke first, "My god! What more can happen? Do you think this is tied in with Sebastian's kidnapping?"

"It could be that, however I want to know more about her life. I want to know what she was doing near the *Couronnes*. I will tell Marie not to say anything to Sebastian or Jill when they return. I really don't want to ruin their happiness now."

"I agree. It is horrible she was garroted, meaning strangled. I am going to call Alain and see if he can find out more about this."

Peter leaned down and kissed her. "We have been through rough times before, and we can move through this."

ΩΩΩ

~ HY BRASIL ~
400 A.D.

DEPARTURE

Something unknown is an adventure to pursue.
~ *Anonymous*

Excitement permeated the Garenfeld. The journeys before Beltane were about to begin. Today, Lady Bertran and her entourage were setting forth on their journey throughout the realm. Bertran's cheeks were flush with excitement, which she tried not to show overtly. Her mission was very new for the realm and there had been much discussion as to the benefits of such a journey. The men for the most part were skeptical and some voiced their displeasure. The women were inwardly thrilled their plight was finally getting recognition, although there would be those who had their unworthiness ingrained so deep it was beyond their comprehension as to why the Magentheld even wanted to know.

The day before, in the quiet of the early morn, Rath, Matran, Frint and Hopenth, along with a few servants left without fanfare for their journey out of the realm. Their departure had almost gone unnoticed as the attention would be upon Bertran and her party. This had been planned. Brannon refused to participate in the departure of his wife, and he was furious.

Magdalena, along with Cyran was there to see the party off on their journey. The horses were already prancing with steam coming from their nostrils in the early morning coolness. The carriages were packed, and the women a bit teary-eyed as they said their farewells. Cyran, the Wise One, uttered a special blessing for their mission. The residents of the Garenfeld were gawking and laughing. At last, with drums rolling and the horns blaring, Lady Bertran with her entourage departed on the first leg of their journey.

Walking back to her quarters, Magdalena inwardly was relieved. By the time Brannon and Wexon made their first overt move, Bertran would be in the southern realm and out of harm's way. Quickening her pace, she looked forward to meeting with Oris. His perceptions were keen and she found him open and receptive to new ideas. He was aware of the treachery of Brannon before Magdalena first broached the subject to him. Already in place were spies of his own in Brannon's camp. He spent many hours keeping his army in shape. At his Hold, he had long ago constructed a large indoor training room where his men trained to keep themselves fit during the winter time. Some could be heard to grumble at the stiff pace he set for them. Oris joined them almost daily, and with his presence, deepened their loyalty to him and the Magentheld. In the evenings, he and his staff of officers poured over maps, plotted strategies and studied reports of the activities of the Skagerrak and Brannon's Army of the Left Flank.

Brannon remained in the Garenfeld and left the training of his men to his second-in-command, Thran. Brannon allowed his men to go home until the time to battle the Skagerraks and he did not foresee the long-term effect this would be as it weakened the loyalty of his army to him. Now it was almost time for Beltane and the weather warming.

Walking into the Council's chambers, Magdalena scanned with her eyes for energies and frequencies that were alien to her purposes. Wexon's powers would not be able to penetrate her chambers nor the chamber of the Council. Breathing an inward sigh of relief, she walked over to a cupboard and brought out a map of the realm. She was pouring over the map when there was a tap at the door. Oris had arrived.

"Come," she bade. After their initial greetings, she noted he was dressed in a midnight blue tunic with a peacock embroidered on the right shoulder. The effect was dazzling. She knew he was of a great lineage and this was the emblem of his House. His enemies attempted to deride such an emblem as vain and only seeking glory. However, Oris' prowess in the field had set to rest this rumor for the most part. She knew the peacock to be an emblem for *all knowing*. The tunic worn over grey breeches set off the deepened color of his skin enhanced by a shock of black hair worn in the manner of the times, which were long and caught at the back with a leather thong. There was gray showing at his temples and his green eyes were alert and lively. He was the first to speak.

"M 'Lady, it be reported Brannon has ordered several of his regiments to the hamlet of Skorn, which borders the Skagerraks and nae too far from my Hold. Methinks this bodes nae good, although on the surface it appears to be a bold move. The Skagerraks be mobilizing near Frawl, nae too distant from Skorn."

"What be the estimate of the Skagerraks strength Lord Oris?"

"If my reports be correct, it be roughly twenty-two thousand footmen and horsemen. The horsemen number twelve thousand troops and the footmen ten thousand. It appears to be a powerful force. I command eighteen thousand horsemen and eight thousand footmen. Normally we outnumber the Skagerraks in numbers alone, however, iffen Brannon has turned traitor, the numbers be changed drastically. The Skagerraks be known fer their brawn and nae fer their brains. Fer them to attempt an invasion of Hy Brasil, there be an inside influence."

Magdalena was quiet for a moment after Oris's report. She told him about Wexon and his entry into the events unfolding. "We 'ave nae proof, but it appears Sarenhild refused Wexon's offer, he took refuge in the Land of the Skagerrak. It be possible Wexon be the brains and the power behind all of this. If this be so, then we do 'ave a formidable foe."

At this moment, there was a discreet knock at the door. For a moment, it seemed Magdalena and Oris were frozen in time. Quickly sensing whom the intruder was, Magdalena relaxed and bade the door be opened. A smiling Callan entered the room carrying a large rolled parchment in her arms.

"M'Lady, I nae 'ave intruded if this had nae be of importance." As Callan was saying this, she deposited the roll on the part of the long table not covered by the map Magdalena had placed there. As she unrolled the parchment, Oris and Magdalena gasped in delight. "This be Brannon's map."

Magdalena asked Callan, "How did yew come by this? Will the disappearance of his map alert Brannon?"

"Tis naught to fear M'Lady. Tis but an exact copy secured during the sleeping tyme of Brannon and his people. It be made sure Wexon be elsewhere so there be naught to fear from him."

With a wide smile across his face, Oris quickly scanned the map. "Lady Callan, I dare nae ask of how yew came by this. I deem it best I nae be apprised fer the safety of those who procured this."

"Agreed," spoke Magdalena. With her knowingness, she knew Callan had either gone herself or used one of the advanced Druidesses. There were some who had picture memories, called sight retention.

The map revealed Brannon to be in collaboration with the Skagerrak. Oris sighed, "M'Lady, here in itself be enough evidence Brannon be a traitor. He needs to be removed."

Sitting herself down in a chair, Magdalena clasped her hands with both index fingers against her lips. Callan and Oris remained silent. Finally, she broke the silence after many moments of contemplation.

"Yere right, Lord Oris. However, 'erefore we do anything rash, we must consider all potentials and possibilities of Brannon's followers. To remove him does nae remove the sore he has created. It could possibly weaken our forces giving the Skagerraks the opportunity to move in while we fight amongst ourselves."

"M'Lady, I defer to yere wisdom. Perhaps if we give Brannon enough rope, he will hang himself."

Magdalena turned to Callan and asked her what her thoughts be on this matter. "I agree M'Lady. There be much more we need to know especially since Wexon entered the picture. There be an evil thread and must be pulled out in order fer the tapestry to reflect yere mission."

"Well spoken Callan. Will yew 'ave a copy of this map made fer Lord Oris?"

"Aye M'Lady." Replied Callan as she rolled the map up and left the room.

"M'Lady, I request permission to join my army as I sense there be mischief afoot."

"Permission granted. We shall be in touch and may the Isness of All protect yew and the wind be at yere back."

Giving Magdalena a deep bow, Oris left the room. For a moment, she was still and then with the map left the room to seek Callan. After she gave the map to Callan, she gave instructions to choose the scanners and give them the codes that she would give Oris. It was now the time to contemplate in her room what she saw in the future.

THE DAGGER

In defense of my kingdom, this I wield.
~ Anonymous

Magdalena sat in front of the fire in the fireplace contemplating the future. Strange visions came and she inwardly watched different scenes unfold. She again saw a vision of Oris in a deep dungeon in the Hold of Brannon followed by a scene of Wexon and Brannon laughing and drinking a toast. Still holding her vision, she saw a dagger and then it disappeared. When she emerged from her visions, she felt perplexed. Why did a dagger come into her visions?

She arose from her chair and walked to the window. The days were beginning to lengthen. She closed her eyes and sent a mental message to Cyran to meet her in the garden of roses. She put on her cape with its hood and left.

Cyran was already in the garden and he greeted her, "M'Lady, I deem yew be asking me questions. Let us walk."

She smiled. "Indeed." She commenced telling him of her visions with Oris being captured by Brannon.

Cyran replied "It be a potential, but nae be alarmed. Methinks there be something else be bothering yew."

"Aye, there be." She then described the dagger she saw in her vision. "I think I saw it as a little girl. In my vision, and its hilt be a black lion with a gold Serpent wrapped around its body. The same symbol represents this kingdom."

Cyran stopped and gave a sigh. "Aye, M'Lady. Tis the dagger of Scota. It be given to a Magentheld when Hy Brasil first came into being. Tis said the sky people gave it to Scota when she departed the land called *Aigyptos*." Her peoples brought it here.

"Where be it naow? I 'ave looked through the crowns, staffs and other memorabilia and I did nae find a dagger. What happened to it?"

"M'Lady, yew will find this difficult to understand. I learned Wexon coveted the dagger. Its possession determines who the ruler of this kingdom be."

"And?"

"M'Lady, I have taken it into the future fer safe keeping."

Magdalena was shocked. "Yew took the dagger into the future? How be yew do this?"

Cyran looked at her deeply 'erefore responding. "The ones of the star boats taught me all tyme happens at the same tyme. Meaning if one be trained one can move into a future or into a past."

She looked perplexed. "How, how be this done?"

"Methinks we best be sitting down. Let us go and sit on yonder bench and I be explaining."

Once they were seated, Cyran continued. "There be portals on this land to move into the future or the past. I searched yere lineage in the future. Knowing yew 'ave the blood of the Mary Magdalene and Sarah, I found a woman of this lineage and I found a portal. I carried the dagger with me in the future. Nay, I did nae hand it to her. I used the tools available in her tyme and sent it to her."

"I be aware of portals. Yere sure it be safe with her?"

"No thing be safe. There be always unknowns. I do nae deem it possible Wexon could find the portal I went through, however it be a possibility."

"How far into the future did yew travel?" she asked.

"It be in the twenty and thirteen ans from the year of our counting."

She did a quick calculation. "That be very far into the future."

"Have yew nae had travel out of yere body into the future?" he asked.

"Aye I 'ave and I did nae enjoy what I saw." she replied.

"What did yew see?"

"It be I thought of the events unfolding. I drifted into a sleep state and suddenly I felt a jerk and knew my essence be pulled from my body. I became alert and looked down and saw my sleeping body. I then saw what seemed to be a type of fold in the darkness and I be pulled into a pool of energy. A light moved into my awareness and the pull of the pool ceased.

"I observed my surroundings and they be strange surroundings. A hot sun be blazing on top of barren land. It be very different from the green of Hy Brasil. Great birds flew fast overhead spitting fire from their wings. The loud noise of these strange birds be very loud and disturbing. The birds be dropping eggs from the sky and exploded when they hit the ground. I heard screams and I, I saw hovels on the barren land were of the same color be the land. I then saw people running with blood streaming down their faces. Some appeared to be children.

"I could nae move and soon the birds left leaving behind a roaring fire with much screaming and wailing. A small figure ran towards me and I reached out to catch it 'erefore realizing the small figure could nae see me as it continued to run with clothes afire. I wondered what travesty this be."

She was silent as she remembered returning to her body with a start and shaking with sobs and fear. It be Callan who came and gathered her in her arms to comfort her.

The two of them sat in silence for a few moments. Finally Cyran spoke, "Tis a wonder yew be fearful of the experience. I 'ave seen such be this when I peer into the future. I 'ave often thought there could possibly be change when yere father named yew the Magentheld and I 'ave no regrets."

"Tell me about the dagger."

Cyran looked at her. "Tis well yew ask. The hilt of the dagger is a standing black lion with a gold serpent encircling the body of the lion. The word given to me be the meaning of *strength, loyalty, knowledge and eternal power*. Tis also said this be the dagger of Scota and she be the daughter of the great ruler of a land far away that be named Aigyptos.[5] This dagger carries the woman energy and naow it belongs to yew."

"Can yew bring the dagger back to me?"

"Tis not wise until the matter with Wexon be finished. Tis best it be in a safer place."

They became silent and Magdalena knew there be much to think about. "Thank yew Lord Cyran fer giving me this information. I will contemplate all be told. Go in peace and we will speak again."

---

[5] Ancient name for Egypt.

That evening, Magdalena asked Callan to dine with her in her quarters. They finished their meal and Mireen took the dishes away. Magdalena told her she would not need her fer the rest of the evening.

Callan was the first to speak after Mireen closed the door. "M'Lady yew did nae 'ave me dine with yew fer pleasure. There be something you want to tell me."

"Aye there be." She proceeded to share the information with Callan of what Cyran said and what he had done. "I do nae 'ave good feelings about this. I also 'ave a sad feeling that Cyran will nae be with us much longer."

Callan did not reply at once. Instead, she closed her eyes for several moments. "M'Lady, I foresee yere journey into the future to recover the dagger. I 'ave a sense Wexon followed Cyran and already knows of its whereabouts. It be possible Cyran will pass. It be a heavy mantle yew be wearing."

"Aye. Troubled I be. Callan, yew 'ave an ability to ferret out things. See if yew can locate the portal Cyran went through. Do nae go into it."

"M 'Lady, I will find it and hopefully before Wexon does."

Magdalena of Hy Brasil

THE STAR PEOPLE ~ AN ENCOUNTER

Knowledge is power ~ Francis Bacon

There was much to contemplate and she knew exactly where to go for her own solitude and contemplation. She quickly dressed in her riding clothes and went to the stables where one of the stable hands saddled her horse. She asked him his name and he managed to reply that it be Lark. "Lark, yew tell no one I be leaving fer a ride. Yew must remain at the stables until I return."

The young lad gulped and managed to say, "I be here yere Majesty Queen." He stood there until she be out of sight. *Garry be, me spoke with 'er ladyship*! He silently told himself.

Magdalena was dressed casually in her riding clothes and appeared to be a boy or a young man. She managed to pass the guardsmen and they waved her on. Once she was out of sight of the castle, she pushed the horse into a run using her knees. She knew she was heading for the small place where she encountered Oris; however, she was aware he was away. Thus, she would have time alone to ponder.

Once she turned off the main road, she slowly steered her horse to the small clearing. She tied the reins to a small low branch and sat down. She was now in her sacred space within when she felt a presence. Slowly she opened her eyes and saw a being standing near her. She knew this being to be a Star being. She could not recognize it either as a female or a male.

A hand was held up and in her mind, she heard the voice. "Gracious Queen do nae arise. I come to thee to say we of the Council be pleased with thy works. Lord Cyran already given thee the background fer the reason this country – this island be place fer humankind to move ahead with progress and evolution."

She nodded and spoke, "I be most pleased to meet yew and tis true Lord Cyran spoke of this being a place to experiment as I recall. I ask yew tell me what the meaning of experiment be."

The Star being continued to speak into her mind and nae using a voice. "Many, many ans back in tyme, this planet be pure and the beings innocent of the ways of anger war and mistrust. It be thought in the galaxy this be a place where beings could evolve into greatness. This be true fer many, many ans until the first anger appeared together with feeling jealousy. There be many failed experiments throughout the lands. The feeling of greed and power emerged. My people sought a place where we could begin anew to experiment and assist the Earth peoples to live in harmony and love and nae war. Yere's be the last experiment to be allowed. We be pleased with what yew be bringing about."

Magdalena was absorbing within her mind what she was hearing. She nodded in agreement. "The missing dagger. I be choosing a portal to go to a future to bring it back. This be important fer the experiment as yew named it."

Again, the being spoke in her mind. "Aye, it be. All lines of tyme happen at same tyme. Think on this. I leave naow. Grace be unto thee."

Before she could say anything, the being was gone. Within her, she felt an ache of the challenge given to her. She went within and reviewed what she had been told.

A forgotten memory came to her. She began remembering that while she was with the Druidesses there were at times when she was herding the goats and sheep in the high fields that she looked up and saw the sky boats. She asked about them and had been told they "be here fer untold ans. Their presence be of kindness."

Another memory came. She was almost fourteen when she woke up and saw a being standing by her bed. In her mind, it told her many things she would remember in the future and she be loved. She never told anyone about this. She thought it was only a dream.

The neigh of her horse brought her back to the present. She knew it was time to return to her responsibilities. There was much to contemplate and she knew to be alert to changes and a way to bring about the meaning of harmony and love. *Aye, t'was her mission.* First, she must contain Wexon and second, bring back the dagger. She knew it be a key to power.

She called her horse to her and climbed on. Slowly, she moved out of the sacred space and rode back to the Garenfeld in deep thought.

Magdalena of Hy Brasil

~ FRANCE ~
2013

Tragedy and Changes

Tragedy is a tool for the living to gain wisdom, not a guide by which to live. ~ Robert Kennedy

Once Sebastian and Jill returned from their new house, Peter had an open bottle of wine and was waiting for them. When they arrived glowing like kids who had experienced Christmas, Peter proposed a toast.

"To new beginnings," and the foursome clinked their glasses. Peter went on to say, we have been through some tough times together and we are still together. I want the two of you to remember that Ellen and I purchased the property next door because we love you and want you nearby. We have only given you what is rightfully yours with no strings attached."

Sebastian had tears running down his face. He wrote on his tablet, "*Mon Amies*, I think we each have been placed together for a greater purpose. All of you saved my life and I intend to live my life with purpose. I salute you and I love you." With a flourish, he signed his name on the new deed.

Jill reached over and touched his hand. "My beloved husband, I was meant to save your life," and she began giggling. She turned to Ellen and Peter. "After the two of you left to divert attention to the Magdalene scrolls we found, Sebastian and I began translating them. Or rather, he did and finally I got bored and seduced him.

Sebastian nodded his head in agreement. He wrote, "It was wonderful. It was the saving of my life. *Oui,* she was my seducer and my teacher."

Peter and Ellen were grinning from ear to ear and Peter replied, "I had already seduced Ellen before we left. Why do you think we were going on so many walks?" Sebastian grimaced from pain and Peter said, "Oops, I forgot about your jaw. Those were grand days even though we were playing a dangerous game."

Ellen nodded in agreement. "Yes, those were dangerous times for us, however if we had not pursued what we felt was right we would not be married or have our beautiful children."

Jill stood up with a big smile on her face. "I think it is time for Sebastian and me to call it a night. If I thought he could do it, I would seduce him tonight."

Sebastian wrote in big letters, "*OUI!*"

Several days later, after Sebastian, Jill and their children had moved into their new home, Jill called and asked if she could have Cerise to come and help her with the unpacking. When Ellen did not answer her, she asked, "Is something wrong?"

Ellen told her that there had been an accident and that she would walk over and tell her about it. When she arrived, she suggested that the two of them find a quiet place where they could talk. Jill suggested they go to the kitchen.

Once they were seated at the big round oak table, Jill asked, "What is this all about? Has something happened to Cerise?"

With tears in her eyes, Ellen nodded yes. She proceeded to tell her about the police visit while Sebastian and Jill were still walking through their new house, and that Cerise had been found in Paris dead. She had been garroted.

Jill brought her hand up to her mouth and almost screamed. "Oh my god! Did, did this have anything to do with Sebastian's kidnapping?"

"We really do not know at this time. My gut feeling is that somehow it is interwoven with the kidnapping and the police do not have clues at this time. We did not want to spoil the joy of having your new home, so Peter and I chose not to say anything."

"Did they question Yvonne or her family?"

"I am sure they did, however they are being tight-lipped about it. Alan is attempting to find out. He is having one of his detectives pass a picture around in the village and other places she might have spent some time. All we can do is sit back and call forth resolution."

"You are right. In the meantime, I need to hire someone to come and help me get this place settled. Do you think Marie can find someone? I certainly cannot depend on Sebastian to help us get settled."

"Of course I will ask Marie. In the meantime I have nothing pressing so let me help you for several hours."

"Oh Ellen, I accept. First, Sebastian and I need to go to Toulouse and pack up our belongings and furniture. Actually, we will sell or give away most of the furniture. I am asking that the children be left in your care while we are away."

"Of course we will take care of the children. They have never been a problem and they do get along with our children. Now, since that is settled when do you and Sebastian want to leave?"

"Possibly in three days. Sebastian has a doctor's appointment tomorrow and we will learn if he is strong enough to travel. I have a feeling that we will go with or without the doctor's permission. Oh Ellen! I am so excited! To think we have this beautiful new home along with a new car!"

"Well, you and Sebastian are certainly worth it and you both have earned it. Sometimes I wonder how we made it through getting the Magdalene scrolls translated and then the Sarah scrolls." Ellen gave a sigh. "I wonder who sent the dagger to me and why. It really is puzzling and why Sebastian had to be kidnapped."

Jill nodded in agreement. "Somehow, I feel there is a deeper meaning to all of this than we can understand at this time." She gave a slight shudder and said, "I find it too coincidental that Cerise was murdered. My gut feeling is that she was somehow involved with Sebastian's kidnappers."

"I have the same feeling. We have been in touch with her parents and they are devastated. The funeral will be tomorrow. Will you come with us?"

"Of course we will. I am including Sebastian because I know he would want to pay homage to her and her family. In the meantime, since you offered and the children are in school, let's tackle their rooms first."

The following day the foursome attended the funeral for Cerise with Jacques and Marie attending also. There were only a few in attendance and the parents were grateful that they had come. The service was brief with a funeral urn sitting on a stand holding her ashes. Cerise had been cremated due to her murder. *M.* Bertrand had asked them to come to their home now that the urn was placed in the *columbarium*, which was the cemetery building that housed the cremated remains.

The gathering in the home of the Bertrand's was primarily relatives with a few neighbors attending along with Peter, Ellen, Sebastian and Jill. *M.* Bertrand asked them to step outside and he shared what he had told the police. It seems Cerise had never been one to have a boyfriend. "As you know, she was not a pretty girl. She was quiet and had few friends. We do not know where she met him; however, I was told by someone who works with me that she had been seen with a man. When I asked her about it, she denied it. My informant described the man as being possibly Egyptian or Algerian." *M.* Bertrand sighed and went on to say it was hard to lose his youngest daughter. Peter thanked him for the information and after giving him their view of how loving she had been to their children, they departed.

On the way back to the chateau, they were quiet for a while. Ellen was the first to speak. "Yes, she was what one could say she was plain and unattractive, but I know there was goodness in her because she treated the children with love and kindness with their messes. She was also diligent in cleaning and doing whatever Marie wanted her to do."

Jill agreed with her and went on to say, "The fact that a co-worker of her father saw her with a man who appeared to be Egyptian or Algerian could be connected to the men who abducted Sebastian."

Sebastian nodded his head in agreement and wrote on his pad, "*Oui.* I have a feeling that this is all connected. I am devastated."

Peter agreed with they had said and told them he would connect with Alain when they arrived home.

Peter and Ellen together with Sebastian and Jill did not want to talk more about this sad event. The children had all been outside waiting for them. Peter and Ellen's children already knew about what had happened with Cerise.

Once Jill and Sebastian had gone, Magda came to Peter and Ellen. "I, I want to tell you that I knew something was going to happen to Cerise and I wasn't sure so I didn't tell you."

Peter sat her on his lap and hugged her. "Our dear sweet 'psychic', you could not have prevented it." He hugged her and kissed her forehead. "Never be afraid to share what you sense or feel. Your mother and me are so proud of you and love you."

Ellen had moved over and was sitting on the armchair. "Magda, I agree with your father and please say a prayer for Cerise wherever she is and her God will smile and say 'thank you.'"

ΩΩΩ

HY BRASIL ~
400 A.D.

WEXON

'Tis best to weigh the enemy more mighty than he seems. ~ William Shakespeare

The summer was the signal for activity all across Hy Brasil. The Druidesses sent into the countryside were posing as beggars, minstrels and bards in order to note the movements in Brannon's Hold as well as in other villages and places. News of changes, movements and attitudes were swiftly relayed to Callan who passed them on to Magdalena.

In a small hunting lodge not too far from the Hold of Brannon, smoke was coming out of the chimney. The lodge was occupied not by hunters, but Wexon and his cadre of seers. The great lodge in actuality was a smaller version of Brannon's Hold dwelling. Due to the density of the forest, there was little sun. A track led from the lodge to the main road leading to the Brannon's Hold. This suited Wexon's purpose of anonymity in the area. An old woman and man were the caretakers who served as preparers of the meals and keeping the lodge reasonably clean. When this adventure would be over, Wexon had no intention of leaving them behind to tell tales.

The old woman named Moreh and the old man named Prins were in the cooking room preparing the morning food for Wexon's outlaw Druids. Whispering, Moreh spoke to Prins, "They be up to nae good. There be strange doins here and I do nae like it. There be bad feeling comin' from them"

Prins nodded in agreement while he hastily looked around. He whispered into her ear, "Aye, tis foreboding. I 'ave to travel further afield fer game to feed this bunch of lackeys. I noticed the birds, game and deer nae longer come near this place. It use to be I put out crumbs and birds flocked here to eat. Since these uns appeared, they no longer come."

She nodded and whispered in his ear, "Aye. I be noticin' too. Naow why would Lord Brannon turn this place over to the likes of them?"

Shaking his head, Prins indicated he too be puzzled. While putting on his outside clothing, he spoke in his normal voice. "Game tis hard to come by this summer. I stacked the wood room and naow I go hunt meat fer the table."

After watching him leave, Moreh turned to her cooking with a heavy heart. She was almost afraid to think because she sensed they could read her thoughts. A shiver sped up her spine and she paused and closed her eyes. Silently, she asked the Great One fer protection fer Prins and fer herself. She soon heard the bell clang and she carried the ladened tray to the hall of dining. Upon entering, she noted the still empty place of Wexon. She noted he be gone for ten sunrises. When he returned, she surmised it be he just appeared.

Alfin, the apparent seer in charge motioned for them to be quiet while Moreh placed the hot steaming bowls and platters on the long table. His cold piercing eyes watched every move she made. The rest of the group sat immobilized until she returned to the cooking room.

As she closed the door, Moreh heard their bawd laughter and snickering and she felt her face become flushed. She had an urge to listen at the door, but stopped short because of her fear of being caught.

More than once, they had read her thoughts and she liked it not one bit. When she really wanted to think, she left the lodge and entered the separate bathhouse with its adjoining room for washing clothes.

Carrying his hunting equipment, Prins entered the woods. He walked for several hours fully aware he had not come across any tracks of animals or rodents. He thought it was strange, but then everything had changed since Wexon and his group took over the lodge. He turned towards the south and eventually came out to the road leading to Brannon's Hold. It was odd to see a lone walker this time of the year.

Holding his hand up in greeting, the stranger quickened his pace until he came abreast to Prins. Prins also held up his hand in greeting. For a brief moment, the two silently assessed each other. Satisfied, Prins asked, "And what be yere business in these parts?"

The shabbily dressed figure wore an old cap of a non-descript color. His face was covered with a bushy beard and his eyes were blue under brown bushy eyebrows. His mouth was framed with wide rosy lips and a smile lit up his countenance. The stranger replied "I be on my way to the Hold of Brannon to beg fer a bit of work." He went on to say his last place burned and soon after his employer was taken ill and died. It seemed a good idea to seek work from Lord Brannon.

Prins looked at the stranger long and hard. He thought the explanation appeared to be reasonable, and before he could form a question of his own, the stranger asked him from whence he comes.

Rarely did Prins have an opportunity to talk to another human other than his woman, and he thawed a bit and replied he was the hunting lodge keep for the Hold of Brannon.

"Ah, then methinks perhaps yew can put in a good word fer me with the Lord Brannon."

"Nay, nae I, Lord Brannon be off fighting methinks and his lodge be filled with strangers."

"Strangers yew say? Hmmm. Tis nae battle I deem involved. I likes me peace."

With a sigh, Prins agreed and suggested they pause in their travels and share a meal. Prins indicated he had plenty to share. The stranger was most agreeable and the two set off to find a secluded spot where they could not be seen from the road.

"Once settled, the stranger spoke, "Tis most rude of me. I 'ave not told yew me name. It be Berone."

Prins replied he be called Prins and his wife be known as Moreh." I 'ave little news of Brannon's Hold of late. I 'ave strangers Lord Brannon sent to the lodge. It be the hunting be little."

"Why be that friend Prins? I 'ave noticed multudious game along the road."

"Tis nae surprising. Methinks the presence of the strangers bode nae good at the lodge. I use to throw crusts out to birds and naow they nae longer come. Tis an evil thing I fear."

Usually Prins was a taciturn man, but the weeks of pent up thought and feelings welled up and he found the stranger Berone most agreeable. Somehow, it felt right so Prins opened up and poured forth his doubts and fears about the strangers at the lodge.

"I sympathize with yew. Strange doins'. Almost like evil craft." At the same moment, both Berone and Prins made the sign of protection. "It do smacks of myths of olde tell of sacrifices and spells caste."

"Aye, tis so. They appear and disappear and I find no trace of prints outside. Tis eerie. I find it more and more hard to leave Moreh. They read our minds and we speaks in whispers naow. At tymes I fear fer our lives."

Little did Prins know that the stranger he was speaking to was a Druid disguised as a beggar. Magdalena had enlisted the Druids as well as the Druidesses to ferret out information from the Hold of Brannon. Berone knew he had come upon a treasure trove of information. If only he could keep Prins from bolting, he would be a good pipeline as to the activities of Wexon. He felt sure he had stumbled upon the headquarters for Wexon and his seers.

"Friend, yew be indeed a troubled man and I hesitate to leave yew at this tyme. If there be a place I could stay, I be delaying my trip to the Hold."

Prins thought a moment and remembered a cave of sorts midway between the road and the lodge. It was not too far afield from the track leading from the lodge to the road. He gave this information to Berone.

With alacrity, Berone accepted and offered to help Prins with his hunting. At this moment, a magnificent stag appeared in the clearing and paused. Slowly, Prins held his bow and arrow up and shot the deer. Slowly it sunk to the ground.

Spellbound, Prins could only stare at the beautiful stag. It was as though the deer had offered itself. Shaking his head, he thought this was indeed a strange turn of events. Together, he and Berone gutted the deer and buried what could not be eaten or used.

Prins and Berone, each in his own way offered the spirit of the deer to the Great One.

Together, the two men carried the deer to the cave being careful to leave no traces along the way. Berone was most pleased with the cave and after careful inspection, told Prins it had not been used for some time. Leaving a piece of the deer for Berone, Prins set off for the lodge with a lighter heart. As he walked along through the forest, he knew he was having to cover his feelings of elation so the others would not realize there was someone else nearby. For all his trappings of being an old man, Prins was no fool. In this, the seers were sadly mistaken.

It was late afternoon when Prins arrived back at the lodge. He carried the deer to the small hut where the kills were dressed and quartered. He left it there while he went in search of Moreh. He found her in the cooking room.

When she saw him enter, she placed a finger to her lips and mouthed the word "Wexon." Prins gave a grunt. He knew Wexon had not been on the track this day; therefore, he must have arrived in his magical way. In a normal voice, he complained that "game be getting scarcer; but he met with fortune and downed a big stag."

Just as he finished his last sentence, Wexon came into the cooking room. Instinctively Prins withdrew into his mode of detachment he used for stalking game. Moreh, not knowing of the stranger Prins had met that day had nothing to hide. Both looked at Wexon with questioning looks.

"Olde woman. Olde man. Why nae the food ready? And what game did yew bag this day?" Wexon spoke with a slight mocking sound in his voice.

Biting back her resentment, Moreh told him she was ready to bring the food in when Prins only arrived.

Prins said, "Me lord Wexon, tis a magnificent stag I bagged this day. I beg yere indulgence fer this slight delay."

Giving a piercing look to each of them, Wexon turned and left the room. Moreh dished up a tureen of rabbit stew together with fresh bread. Prins carried the bowls and spoons. When they entered the dining area, they felt nine pair of eyes looking at them accusingly. Wexon broke the silence by announcing Prins brought new meat, a stag.

With a sign of relief, Moreh and Prins returned to the cooking room where she and Prins began eating their meal in silence while listening for the raucous clang of Wexon's bell. Upon hearing the bell, she went in and cleared the table. Moreh began cleaning the cooking ware and was surprised that Prins began helping her. She sensed there was a matter weighing on his mind. She knew she would be hearing of it in all good time.

After relieving themselves in the outside pit, Prins and Moreh wearily climbed into their hard bed next to the cooking room. Soon their rhythmic sound of Moreh's gentle snoring broke the night silence. Prins lay silently mulling over the day's events. He knew he had met up with a wise one and the beggar's clothes be only a mask. Perhaps there be help and hope after all. He knew this not the time to stir the imagination of Moreh, although she also knew to still the mind because she had accompanied him on many a hunt when Brannon and his parties were not here. Something within him urged him to keep the presence of the beggar to himself.

Berone sat very still while watching Prins depart. With his Kah of knowingness, he tuned into the spirits of the forest and of the cave. Satisfied that all was well, he asked permission to stay. A tingling feeling came and he knew he was accepted.

Using his digging tool, he dug a small pit in front of the cave. It took some time to amass stones for the lining of the pit along with sticks for a fire. Once he was satisfied, he had a good fire going when he scouted for more sticks to last the night. Once this had been completed, he cut a slab from the piece of venison Prins had given him and slowly roasted it over the fire. All the while, his senses were aware of movement in the forest. He was aware of the movement coming from the night creatures and he knew he had nothing to be alarmed over.

While he cooked the meat, he thought of Prins and his story. Berone knew he had a good friend and a source of information. He understood why Prins and his wife were fearful to eavesdrop on Wexon and his cadre of eight apprentices. He was glad Prins had given him their names and he committed them to memory.

Once he satisfied his hunger, he set about drying the reminder of the meat. He knew he 'had to use fire sparingly and while the meat was drying, he sat still and began using his far sight. He sensed Wexon's return. The river of thought flowed through him and he allowed his mind to expand. Yes, Wexon returned from the land of the Skagerraks and now was preparing to leave for the land of the Sarme to solicit support. Using his ability to be in two places at once, Berone transported his second body to the lodge.

A strong force field had been placed around the lodge and he stopped before he touched it. Wexon's intent was to have no unannounced visitors; however, there could be a weak spot and Berone scanned the force field to find the weakness. His Kah revealed to him a root cellar room with a passage into the cooking room and his Kah told him Wexon was unaware of this.

He moved into the cellar and went under the force field to enter the lodge. Wexon and his cadre were sitting around the great fireplace. They were focused on Wexon and what he was saying. For a brief moment, Wexon looked around as if sensing another presence and when he saw nothing, he continued.

"I leave on the morrow fer Sarme to gather support. Alfin be travel with me. Fer this trip we go in our own bodies and travel under the guise of travelling peddlers. It be tyme to establish our own religion of *Aowe*. The rest of yew travel as the new priests of *Aowe* and gather converts. Yew, Muern will go to the Hold of Oris. Yew, Sathal to the Hold of Kanen; Gorne to the Hold of Hyreck; Werdon to the Hold of Khern; Habin to Myliar; and Laeson to the Hold of Brannon. Yew, Cale will infiltrate the Hold of the Magentheld. Wherever yew travel, sow seeds of distrust and fear. These be our weapons."

Cale with a sneer in his voice remarked that "the Magentheld be in fer a few surprises." Wexon smiled and replied, "Do nae let the fact she be a woman fool yew. She be a dangerous adversary. Never underestimate her. We meet here at the next moon that be full."

Habin asked, "Be it we to dispose of our caretakers naow or wait?"

"Wait. I be giving them instructions they are nae to leave the premises unless to hunt. I want the game house filled by the tyme we return," replied Wexon.

Berone felt relieved Prins and Moreh were in no danger for the present time. He withdrew to his cave and reentered his body. Quickly he sent a thought to Cyran.

The hour before the sun began awakening, Cyran appeared before Berone who told him all that had transpired with full descriptions. After he finished telling his story, Cyran said, "Yew 'ave done well my friend Berone. Methinks it might be wise to 'ave Prins and his wife become 'sick' and be replaced with a couple who be told be Moreh's brother and his wife. These be a Druid and a Druidess. We 'ave until the fullness of the moon to set our plans into motion. I want yew to continue to the Hold of Brannon posing as a bard. Sing and tell tales of the Great One and the love all people. Yew in yere own way be a priest of sorts."

"Holy One, may I contact Prins and his wife and tell them of the plans yew 'ave outlined?"

"Indeed, it be most appropriate. Assure Prins and his woman they be generously recompensed and perhaps we can use their services elsewhere after her 'recovery.' I be sending word to yew where to send Prins and his 'sick' lady."

Before Berone could reply, Cyran vanished. It was not too surprising as it was typical of Cyran and the advanced Druids. Berone filled in his fire pit and began restoring the cave and its surroundings as close to their natural state as possible before leaving for the track to take him to the lodge.

He found a tall fir tree along the track where he had an excellent view of the lodge and the track. He climbed up into the branches and became attuned to his surroundings. The oaks and other non-evergreen trees were not full for cover. They now were swelling the nodes as their sap begins to rise. The sounds of the forest were silent this morn.

Smoke was puffing from the lodge chimney. One by one, Berone observed the cadre emerge and use the outside pits to relieve themselves. They appeared confident they had total privacy as none looked around. The sun was making its slow ascent into a clear blue sky and soon the group emerged from the lodge with their packs and began walking the track. When the group neared the tree holding Berone, he could hear the complaining of Gorne.

"I do nae understand why the horses could nae 'ave been brought to us at the lodge. This be most inconvenient to 'ave to walk out. It be degrading."

They were almost under Berone when Muern spoke, "Stop yere whining Gorne. Yew knew the instructions of Wexon 'erefore we came to the lodge. Naow shut up."

Berone felt the energy of the ill-humored group. He waited until there was no sound of their presence before he silently let himself down and made his way to the lodge.

Prins was chopping wood when Berone made his appearance. Prins was surprised to see him and he put his axe down to greet Berone with a questioning look in his eyes. Berone gave Prins a brief story of how he overheard the cadre now posing as priests of Wexon speaking about Prins and his wife and when they returned he and his wife would be slain.

Prins listened and his inner feeling knew this had been already planned. Berone went on to tell him if Prins and his wife left now, a place of safety would be found for them much more to their liking.

Grunting, Prins said, "Aye, I knew those scoundrels be up to nae good. Tis nae surprisin', and I suspect yew be much more than a beggar man. Aye, we come with yew."

With that, Prins entered the cooking room and spoke to Moreh. She came to the door and looked deeply at Berone and then nodded her head in agreement. "I cannae depart until I leave this place in order." She went back in and began completing her tasks in the cooking room.

Within the house, Prins and Moreh were packed and ready to depart. The fires were put out and

Berone was apprised of the departing of Wexon the night before.

Wending their way to the Hold of Oris, Berone and the couple spoke little and stopped only long enough to relieve themselves and to sleep. Once he was sure the couple were sleeping, he wave travelled to his Druid contact for an exchange of information. A decision had been made Prins and Moreh would be safe in the home of Orsad and his wife Leran. The farm they tilled was of good size and Leran would welcome help with the small brood of six children including two sets of twins.

At the same time, another couple arrived at Brannon's Hold and asked who was in charge of Brannon's property affairs. They said they had been told of Moreh's illness and the need for the couple to leave.

Suspecting nothing amiss, Rink interviewed the new couple who just happened to be asking for work. With a sigh of relief, he sent them to the lodge.

It 'was the season of planting and there was a greening of the land. For those who were aware, it was a time of wonderment. The song of the birds seemed to sing be louder, and the trees and bushes sang a song as the new growth swelled and broke forth in new leaves of green. The paths of the rivers and streams rushed merrily along their paths while carrying the melting snows. The long sleep was over.

🏠🏠🏠

Magdalena of Hy Brasil

~ FRANCE ~
2013

A Promise of Help

Help others achieve their dreams and you will achieve yours. ~ Les Brown

Sebastian and Jill were now settled into their new home. The death of Cerise still hovered in the back of their minds; however, the search for Sebastian's kidnappers was almost at a stalemate. Sebastian's recovery was moving at a rapid pace. He was now working at his computer and she had just returned from taking the children to school. While she was pouring herself a fresh cup of coffee, she smiled as she remembered the previous night. Sebastian wrote on the tablet that he was tired of not having any sex with her and he was demanding that this night they would make love in spite of his wired jaw.

She smiled broadly, remembering the tenderness of their coupling once again becoming so endearing and satisfying. *What a lover he has become! And to think he had been so shy and almost fearful when she first approached him.* Yes, he had thought he was dying and now he was alive and well except for the jaw. Sipping her coffee, she looked at her surroundings and felt so blessed. *Yes, this house was just right for them.* Thanksgiving was approaching and Jill had a sense that she and her family would spend the day with Ellen, Peter and family. She was delighted that Marie had found a Nanny called Isabelle along with a cook and housekeeper named Sabine.

At that moment, the phone rang and it was Ellen asking if she would go with her to Paris for the day. "I feel I have to have a change and it is time for the two of us to have a day out. Louise Bianchi called and invited us to lunch at the *Gaya Rive Gauche*. It is a fantastic place for fish and is on *rue de Bac* in the S*t-Germaine-de-Pres* area."

Jill loved the idea. "Yes! I need a change too. I love the house and the grounds, but I need a diversion now. What time?"

"I will pick you up in an hour. Can you be ready by then?"

"Indeed yes. I will notify Sebastian and let Isabelle and Sabine know to only make lunch for Sebastian. Oh this will be a great treat for me!"

Peter insisted she be chauffeured into Paris and at first, Ellen balked until he reminded her of Sebastian's' kidnapping. "I don't want anything to happen to you or Jill. Until this dagger event is resolved, please do what I ask."

Ellen sighed. "I feel rebellious inside and yet I know you are correct. I miss my freedom to drive myself."

"I know you do. Thank you my beloved and I will see you when you return."

While Charles, the chauffeur drove them into Paris, Jill asked if there was any more information regarding the two murders possibly connected to the dagger.

Ellen replied that Alain was keeping them informed and so far, there was no breakthrough. "I have a sense that there is something more than it being just a Dagger. My dreams are becoming chaotic and I see this beautiful woman off-and-on as though she is trying to give me a message."

"To me, I get the impression that there is someone from the past who wants to communicate with you."

"You are probably correct; however I don't know how to answer her." Ellen sighed. "I really don't know what to do about the dagger. It is like something – or a message is hidden in those symbols."

"I agree. Sebastian is researching and he is in his element. I am happy to say this because it is giving him more energy to heal."

"Thank god for that part of it! I really treasure our friendship."

Before they realized it, they were at the *Elysée Du Vernet* and Ellen told Charles, the chauffeur that she would call his cell phone when they were ready to leave. Peter's company employed Charles and his job was to run errands and to do odd jobs. He knew he was fortunate to have this position and took it seriously. Once he helped them out of the limousine, he moved the vehicle to the guest parking lot.

Louise was waiting for them at her reserved table and the three embraced before they sat down. As usual, Louise was dressed in a Sonia Rykiel creation that she favored. This was Jill's first time to dine at the *Elysée Du Vernet* and was enthralled with the domed ceiling. Ellen had already prepared her by telling her Gustav Eiffel, the creator of the Eiffel Tower, had created the ceiling. The grey-green stained glass ceiling was gorgeous. Once they were seated and their orders taken from the menu, Louise began asking questions about Sebastian. Jill gave the particulars and Louise gave a sigh, saying, "Blessed be the dear man. What a travesty! Alain has given me some of the information; however I want to hear it from the two of you."

Jill looked at Ellen. "I think that it is better if you share how this all happened."

Ellen paused to collect her thoughts. "I think I had best tell you how it all began." She then told the story of the dagger that had been sent to her. Louise shook her head in amazement and asked that she continue. By the time Ellen had completed the story including her dream of a woman from some ancient place, and before Louise could say anything, their orders were now delivered.

Louise suggested they eat and then she wanted to hear more. The conversation was light and Louise shared that her son Nicholas and daughter Amani were taking an interest in the Bianchi holdings with Alain tutoring them. "The four of us appear to be compatible and we are creating something that will benefit the world. Amani has fallen in love with one of Alain's *avocats* and it could be there will be a wedding and of course you will be invited."

Ellen suggested a toast with their wine to the budding romance of the couple. "I toast to their love and may it be a long, long happy relationship."

The three women clinked their glasses and Louise beamed. "Thank you. The two of you with your husbands and children are indeed to behold and I look forward to being a doting *grand-mère*." The serving persons removed their plates and brought them *du café*. "Now, I want to hear more about this dagger. What can I do to help?"

Ellen gave a rueful smile. "I really do not know. Alain is using his resources and the police are not having any results so far." She sighed and went on. "It is all so puzzling. So far we believe the culprits who kidnapped Sebastian were Egyptian and as far as the murder of Cerise, well it appears there are no leads."

Louise looked at her and said, "If I may be of assistance, please tell me. I will use all of my resources to work with Alain and we will see what we can do."

Jill now entered the conversation. "On behalf of Sebastian, I accept your help. Ellen and Peter along with Alain have been wonderful and we can use all the assistance we can use. Thank you."

Ellen smiled. "Yes, we are open to all assistance we can have. Perhaps with the two sources of your people and, also the police, we will begin to have answers. Thank you my dear friend. I also want answers as to why I was chosen to receive this dagger."

Louise looked at her watch and told them the luncheon had been delightful, however she had another appointment. "We will be in touch and I promise you that we will get action."

Once Ellen and Jill were in the limousine, they decided to go home instead of shopping as previously planned. Jill spoke first. "I am relieved we have more help. I know Alain is doing what he can, but I am not sure of what Louise can do."

"She has resources and combined with Alain's I have a sense that there is going to be a revelation before too long."

Jill nodded in agreement. "Perhaps you are right. The rest of the trip home was in silence with each of the women contemplating what had transpired with Louise.

ΩΩΩ

~ HY BRASIL ~
400. A.D.

CONTEMPLATION

What we plant in the soil of contemplation, we shall reap in the harvest of action.
~ Meister Eckhart

Magdalena lay in her bed contemplating the whereabouts of the dagger. She knew it was important for her to find it before Wexon. She was only getting wisps of images so she arose and went to the window to greet the day. The chill of spring was upon the land; however, she opened the shutters and breathed in the cold air while saying her morning greeting. Once she completed it, she stood and gazed upon the palette of nature. She noticed the leaves on the trees and it was as if nature painted a new picture of the landscape during the night. There was no favorite season because to her each one was unique and brought its own rewards. Schooled, as she was, the ways of nature never failed to intrigue her. She relished feeling the pulse of nature unfolding and enfolding. A soft tap on her entry door interrupted her thoughts and this brought her out of her reverie.

"Come," she bade while knowing it to be Mireen with her early morning meal. Carrying a steaming tray of hot tea and scones with butter and honey, Mireen placed them on the small round table near the window. She quickly shut the great window while scolding Magdalena for letting so much early morning air in. "M'Lady! Yew be catching the draught. Here, allow me to help yew with a heavier robe."

Magdalena allowed Mireen to fuss over her and she knew it was Mireen's way of showing love and concern.

"M'Lady, our High Lord Cyran, most Holy One, sent a message he awaits thee in the garden within the hour."

Magdalena finished her tea and scone while thinking the garden would be the safest place on the grounds for open conversation.

Cyran sat on a bench below a large willow tree whose leaves indicated a budding was taking place. He closed his eyes to contemplate what he desired to say to Magdalena. Then he spoke, "Greetings of the morn M' Lady Magentheld."

She laughed and replied, "Tis nae one can creep upon yew unawares. I 'ave received word yew wish to speak with me."

"Aye. Wexon and his priesthood be abroad with tongues wagging. We be blessed there be only a few of them. We 'ave bards and troubadours following with songs and tales to gladden each heart."

"Holy One, must it be done this way? Tis patience I am short on."

"Tis understandable M'Lady. The populace must be given a choice. There always be those tapping into fear. Tis most unfortunate fear often takes precedence over reason."

Magdalena nodded in agreement while she cast her eyes on a few crocuses. "There be much I 'ave to learn about living in what be called the past so the future be changed. And aye, I know my part be unfolding."

Cyran chuckled while he turned his eyes full of merriment on her. "Yew cannae make people do something to bring joy. When people be forced to change, it brings fear and oft tymes the other side of fear be other side be anger.

"Fer to create change, a people must be inspired – motivated fer an opening to allow a wellspring of creative mind to issue forth. We be dwelling on the plane of dualism. Therefore, there be always opposites. With a creative mind open, one can transcend the evil. With a creative mind, one can rise above the sorrow with an attitude of detachment. Emotions keep people embroiled in the swing of duality."

For a moment, Magdalena pondered this. When she spoke, each word was spoken slowly as though she was savoring each word Cyran said. "Then this be what brings on a Golden Age of when knowledge and the arts flourish. Could it be tis much akin to planting of a seed? An age needs the darkness of the negative to bring forth creative mind."

"Of course, M'Lady. Yew 'ave grasped well the concept. 'Owever, if darkness lasts overly long or the climate of mind becomes too destructive, the seers of this plane bring forth a seed of their own. Some may well call it divine intervention, and that be what yew be part of."

She laughed and bent over to smell and touch a budding plant filling its pattern of life, a new dream. "Divine intervention, indeed! I feel nae bit of divine in this moment. Wexon created a flock of priests culled from his psychics. The so-called *Aowe* be nothing more than a phantom fed by fear."

"Aye. If yew nae been called to become Magentheld, think of the potential fer darkness that be upon this land. Aye, yew know and I know well the falsity of *Aowe*, but the masses be very pliable. The poor souls 'ave drunk the sour wine of enchantment and naow become drugged by their senses. Yew must realize Magdalena, behind the masks of their personalities lurks a god waiting to be awakened. If we tell them within each is a forgotten god, we be branded as charlatans. An awakened god bids her tyme or his tyme by using patience and alertness. Tis all much akin to a game of chess."

"Thank yew dear Cyran. I be remembering."

"M'Lady, 'erefore we depart fer our separate duties, heed well the love of God, the Isness. Do nae keep Wexon in a holding pattern."

"Iffen I understand the love of God, yew be saying I am nae to hold in my mind a picture of Wexon and his known ways."

"Aye, tis that. Love him. Most people 'ave no idea of what love be. All interaction between people be nothing more than an exchange of energy. Most hold a belief love be lust or need. It be neither. Love be understanding, acceptance and allowing. It be free of all prejudices."

"I understand what yew 'ave said; however what he be doing to this kingdom cannae be accepted. I will love the god within him, but nae accept his outward expression. I be wary and always carry a big sword."

They stood up and bowed to each other. Magdalena and Cyran slowly walked through and out of the garden as a slight breeze rippled their cloaks. While walking towards the Garenfeld, she felt an inner urging to be alone out in nature. She paused a moment and sent a mental message to Callan regarding her intent and to cancel all appointments fer the day.

She pulled her dark cloak to her body and walked to the stables. Once there, she could see the work people were busy elsewhere. She swiftly saddled a great black steed. Now hooded and with her cloak masking her figure, she quickly led the horse out and through the grounds to the open gate. She barely nodded to the guardsmen standing watch and continued to walk until she felt it safe to mount the steed.

Once she was out of sight of the Garenfeld and watchful eyes, she put the horse to a full gallop. With the wind in her face, she let out a loud whoop and a shout of joy. It felt so freeing! Finally, she slowed the horse to a canter and turned off the main path to one barely discernible through the woods. She knew she was allowing her inner knowingness to lead her to a place of silence. When she arrived at a great oak tree with its budding of the leaves, she knew she had arrived at the right spot for contemplation. She alighted from the horse and, tethered the horse to a low branch. All the while she spoke to it and soothed its lathered brow.

She sat down beneath the great tree and made the sign of protection before proceeding to use the discipline of the breath taught to her by the Druidesses. Softly she spoke.

Beloved! Oh Holy One!
Isness of all!
Awaken me from enchantment so I may lead
*   these peoples.*
Come forth oh Mighty One!
Fill my mind with Awareness.
Fill my mind with Knowingness.
This I command.

She felt a deepening shift within. At this inner place, there be no time. There would be no space. There be only Isness.

A picture began forming in her mind. It was a web spreading out to eternity. The web began to dance. Potentials entered from thoughts of greed, hate, envy, jealousy and fear. The dance of the web became erratic with the potentials of wars and suppression. The overpowering feeling was one of sorrow. She remembered her time with the Druidesses and the years she lived with them. She was remembering the golden eagle flying around her when she went to the fields to herd the sheep and her being mesmerized. Other memories surfaced such as times seeing above the mists a great water with high waves. At times she could feel the mist swirling around her. She brought her focus to the place of observing and not participating.

Other potentials began touching the erratic dance and she noticed these were acts and thoughts of kindness and love with no judgments. Realization came and the dance became a beautiful rhythm as these thoughts neutralized the destructive thoughts. The love of the universe swelled within her and she rested in this feeling beyond any she had known before. Magdalena realized her mission to bring forth a harmonious flow of life in her people so there would always be a golden thread to be remembered in the future.

The soft nickering of the horse brought her back to the present moment. She brought her hands up together thanking the Isness for the teaching. Her awareness to the present caused her to pause as she again heard another horse nickering and the sound of it coming along the path. She stood up and her knowingness knew it to be a friend and not a foe.

Entering the small area came Oris on another black steed. He looked shocked to see her. "M'Lady Magentheld, I, I had no idea yew be here. I ask fer yere pardon fer this intrusion."

She stood there looking at him and a smile crossed her face. "Lord Oris, if I had known this be perhaps yere space, I would 'ave looked elsewhere."

"Nay, Nay M'Lady. I only come here occasionally to ponder and think. I, I be honored to find yew here."

"Tell me Lord Oris, do yew receive answers here?"

He smiled. "Indeed I do. There be moments when I 'ave needed to be alone and be among the trees."

"Do yew commune with the trees?"

He looked at her with a twinkle in his eye. "Aye I do since I be a wee lad."

"And what did the trees tell yew?"

"Ah, they gifted me with insight to understand the movement of the seasons, the trees, animals and people."

For a moment, she felt pulled into the depths of his green eyes and mesmerized. She brought herself back into the now. "Thank yew Lord Oris fer sharing this with me. I must be returning to the Garenfeld. I wish yew well."

Oris watched her astride her horse and moving out of the clearing. He realized his heart was beating fast. Oris sat down where she had been sitting feeling her energy. When he went within, he knew without a doubt he loved the Magentheld. He denied it in the beginning; however, when he watched her walking slowly down the Great Hall to where Sarenhild stood, he knew she was the woman he loved. He wrestled with this for days, and today he found her in the clearing. He knew he wanted to take her in his arms and kiss her and to mate with her. *T'will never do*, he told himself.

She noticed the sun to be past its highness when she mounted the steed, and began her trip back to the Garenfeld along with her responsibilities. Something awakened within her and she felt a deep feeling of attraction to Lord Oris. She felt unsettled not knowing it to be an awakening within her. As she moved her horse onto the road back to the Garenfeld, she contemplated the surge from her loins as well as from her heart when Oris looked deeply into her eyes while he was sharing his love for the trees. The thought came to her this must be the beginning when a man and a woman couple. She felt a blush rising in her face.

"Isness of All, this be all new for me – this attraction. Help me to understand." Within her came a reply, "Allow it to unfold."

She turned her attention to the challenges ahead with Wexon, the Skagerraks and Brannon. Once she arrived at the Garenfeld, she became aware of questioning looks of amazement from the guardsmen. She now rode in with her hood thrown back to reveal she was the Magentheld.

UNSETTLED FEELINGS

Feelings are not suppose to be logical ~ Anonymous

The reports coming in from the Druidesses and Druids indicated Brannon to be pushing forth to join the Skagerraks. Magdalena felt sick at heart even though she already perceived that he was going to do this. She felt his suppressed rage that she had been chosen the Magentheld. She was now sitting at the big conference table waiting for Oris and Lord Cyran to enter together with Callan. The map was in front of her. She closed her eyes and a picture formed in her mind of a battle to be fought in order for the present to be changed, and she knew it to be a benefit to her reign.

She looked at the map and the picture of a chessboard formed. She saw herself as the White Queen. The King – meaning Sarenhild – was dead. This left the Queen with the Knight being Oris the General and Cyran being the Bishop. The Rook represented the heavy infantry, or the horse soldiers followed by the Pawns who were the foot soldiers. At that moment, there was a knock on the door and Callan entered.

"M'Lady Magdalena, I do 'ave some news regarding Wexon. He be naow in the camp of the Skagerraks."

"I be nae surprised. I 'ave seen it to be this way. Does he 'ave his cadre with him?"

"Nay M'Lady. His cadre be attempting to stir the people with false information. Our Druidesses and Druids follow behind them and tell another story."

At this moment, Lord Cyran and General Oris entered. He looked at her and she felt for a brief moment of being swept into the depths of his eyes. Oris bowed. "M 'Lady, I be brief. My men be ready to move and do battle with the Skagerraks. I be saddened General Brannon be choosing to fight against us by joining the Skagerraks. Nay, I be angered."

Magdalena stood and offered he r hand to Oris who bent down touched his lips to the back of her hand. She felt a surge within her and withdrew her hand while asking him to be seated. "This will nae be long as I understand yere need to be on yere way. I 'ave faith in yew and we remaining behind will be attuned to what be happening. Our Druidesses and Druids be our messengers."

"I thank yew M 'Lady Magentheld. I leave Lord Cyran to relate to yew our conversation. I depart naow."

He bowed to Callan and Lord Cyran and left the room.

Magdalena looked at them and asked, "What naow?"

Lord Cyran spoke first. "M'Lady, this be a bloody battle. I 'ave trust in Oris. I 'ave already foreseen the outcome with the Skagerraks and Brannon defeated."

"I too 'ave foreseen this even though I 'ave visions of Brannon capturing Oris. I sense there be some way he be released unharmed. Let the three of us focus on the outcome to our benefit." She turned to Callan. "Do yew 'ave something yew wish to add?"

"Nay M'Lady and Lord Cyran. I too 'ave had the vision. The outcome be to our benefit."

Cyran nodded in agreement. "We observe and we wait fer the moment to strike. Tis Wexon I be concerned about." Knowing Callan already knew about the dagger, he went on to say. "Lady Callan has already informed me he found the Portal and went through it to the future tyme. I fear there be havoc in the realm of the recipient of the dagger I left with."

Magdalena replied, "I be nae surprised regarding the portal; however, I feel compassion fer the ones he possibly harmed. He be indeed, vicious in his ways. I will contemplate what options we 'ave. Lord Cyran I command yew nae go through a portal to retrieve the dagger. This be naow my responsibility."

"But, M'Lady, 'tis me who created this. I must be allowed to retrieve the dagger."

"Nay. I as the Magentheld command yew remain here." She turned to Callan, "What say yew?"

Callan, with her blue eyes turned to Cyran. "M' Lord Cyran, I agree with M 'Lady Magdalena. I be focusing on keeping Wexon in abeyance."

Cyran looked at the two women. "I cannae disobey M 'Lady Magentheld. 'erefore, I help to contain Wexon."

Magdalena smiled. "I thank yew and let us know the dagger be still in the care of the one yew entrusted the dagger. What be her name?"

Cyran leaned forward. "Her name be Ellen and she be of yere lineage. Possibly she could be yew in the future or an offspring of yew."

Magdalena felt a surge in her loins and she knew Cyran and possibly Callan already knew of her reactions to Oris. "Fer the tyme being, we focus on containing Wexon and his cadre." She stood up leaving them in order for her to ferret out her feelings.

Magdalena walked in the gardens and stopped at the rose bush named for her mother. She bent to smell the roses and then sat on the nearby bench. Within her mind, she called forth her mother and speaking silently,

"My mother, I remember well yere love fer me and I, I understand why yew chose to leave. What I miss naow be I 'ave nae mother to lead me into adulthood and to know the ways of love. I ask yew naow teach me the ways of love fer a man. 'Tis Oris who attracts me and I feel a surge in my heart, my mind and my loins. Be this love?"

A soft breeze came and surrounded her. She knew her mother was here. She sat still and felt the breeze caress her. Within her, she heard a voice. "Me daughter, thee I loved the most. Yew be of my loins and of yere father. Deep within yew be a wellspring of love fer this man Oris. He be yere mate. Allow it to unfold and be nae afraid to love. Cherish the moments yew 'ave with him. It be destined yew be mates."

Magdalena sat there contemplating what she heard from her mother. She began feeling the rush in her loins and knew there would be a time for them to couple. Within her there was a peace and an understanding.

FIRE AND LOVE

Love makes your soul crawl out from its hiding place.
~ Zora Neale Hurston

Slowly she opened her eyes. What was it she heard? Somewhere the drums were rolling and she knew Oris to be on the march with his army. She brought him into her focus and he appeared to be looking into her eyes as if he was also focusing on her. She contemplated their encounter in the woods the past few days and knew this was meant to be. In her training with the Druidesses, she had not been taught about love with a man. While she lay abed, she thought of Oris and what it would be like to kiss him and to couple with him. She felt an energy rise from her loins and knew it to be only a beginning.

She left her bed and went to the window to greet the day. The sun was shining and she felt deliriously happy. It was as if Mireen knew how to time her morning meal and there came a light tap on the door.

"Enter," she bade and Mireen came in with the tray. This morning there were berries and cream along with fresh baked bread. Just as she was finishing her meal, Callan knocked and at Magdalena's command entered.

"M 'Lady Magdalena, I bid yew a grand morn. I 'ave with me yere appointments fer the day."

"Come," bade Magdalena. She stood up and embraced her. "Ah yes, appointments." She sighed with a twinkle in her eye. "Be there problems I must deal with?"

"Nay. They be at rest fer the moment; 'owever, it came to me the lodge where Wexon and his cadre took over from Brannon. Perhaps since the couple who be the caretakers 'ave been sent to the Hold of Oris, I deem it be wise to fire the lodge in order to cleanse the energy Wexon left."

"Be I understanding you deem it wise to burn the lodge?"

"Aye, M 'Lady. The Druid couple be receiving bad vibrations and want to be sent away."

"Very well. Send them permission to burn the lodge and say the Magentheld ordained this. They need be returned to their own communes' fer further instructions."

"Be there anything else you need from me?"

"Aye Callan. Yew also knows about the Star people who land in the shrouded cove. Keep me informed of anything yew see or hear. I desire an audience with them. Lord Cyran said Hy Brasil be seeded by them as an experiment many ans ago."

"I will do so. I 'ave at tymes felt their presence and they appear to be benevolent. We 'ave had wars and conflicts and my premonitions is this war with the Skagerrak be possibly the last one fer a long tyme."

"I agree with yew. In my contemplations when I be becoming a Druidess, I began to know we be living in what one may call a good and bad world. It be likened to the game of chess, which Cyran said the Star people brought. Oh Callan, would it be we could create a world of moving into a new level where there be less bad and more creative ways to live in harmony and love..

"Aye. I agree with yew. I 'ave also wanted to see more energy placed on creating new ways to bring us out of the past and into a new future."

"I agree. Since I be the first woman Magentheld, it behooves me to create a new era to promotes the mind and brings forth new ways of seeing things. Callan let us both contemplate on what we can offer to our people to move them out of the past. I feel we be at a stalemate with this war."

"Aye, I be doing so and naow I must be off and leave yew to yere contemplations."

In the early afternoon, Magdalena asked Lord Cyran to meet with her in the garden at the pergola. She arrived first and sat on a bench in the pergola. She remembered when she had been a small girl her mother asked the wood makers to create this open air covering in the garden. When the sun would be hot in the summer, her mother used this place for her contemplation and to view the gardens. It was one of her joys. Magdalena also spent much time here. Now the summer heat was here, and she often came to this refuge. The roof was similar to a cone standing on pillars. The floor was of flat stones cooling to the feet and a small waterfall nearby. Thus, she could be cool and watch the bees as they took nectar from the flowers along with wee birds having long beaks taking the nectar with their wings moving fast.

Cyran appeared almost out of nowhere, and she sensed his presence. "G'day Lord Cyran. Thank yew fer coming."

His eyes twinkled and he took her hands and bowed towards her. "M 'Lady Magentheld I be honored to be here. I deem yew 'ave questions."

"Aye, I do. I want to know more about the Star people. Yew 'ave told me little about them. Does one enter through the mist around their base, or does one be surprised when they make an appearance?

"M 'Lady, they be almost unnoticed with their comings and goings. The mist be close to being a strong curtain nae one can enter. As yew know, the mists be away from the shores of Hy Brasil fer the fishermen to fish. Their landing place also be circled by mists. When they communicate, they appear here at a tyme we know nae when."

"What do they look like?"

"Likened unto us, but different. We communicate with mind only."

"Ah, thank yew. I deem they come unannounced."

"Aye, tis so. Yew know by the change of energy and the energy be strong."

"Lord Cyran, I 'ave met with one of the Star people."

"Aye, tis tyme yew met. How it be with yew?"

She smiled and said, "I be in a small clearing not far from the Garenfeld when this being appeared. There be no name. I be taught much about history of this planet and what my mission be. I deem yew know what the mission be."

"Aye, I do."

"I be told to instill in the peoples what love be and the turning away from hate and war. If I do nae succeed, it be the demise of our wee country."

"M 'Lady, yew be chosen ere fer yew be born. Yew 'ave a fire within to bring this into being. Twill be a hard journey."

"Thank yew. I naow share with yew I gave permission fer the lodge of Brannon to be burned. The message I received be the Druid couple felt the strong negative energy. I chose to cleanse it."

Cyran laughed and his eyes twinkled. "I deem this to be a thankful way to keep them from returning. I 'ave a sense Wexon returns to assess the damage. It be difficult to enter his mind. His be strong."

"I perceive you 'ave placed a strong field around him to keep him from going into the future."

"Aye. I 'ave done so and methinks yew 'ave also done this."

She smiled. "Perhaps. I see in the future he and I meet in a challenge. I liken this nae."

"M 'Lady, fear nae this man. Methinks he may undermine himself. Be as it may, I feel concern fer General Oris."

"This be my feeling also. As I 'ave told yew, I 'ave had visions of Oris being captured by Brannon."

"Aye, love him. I 'ave seen it and it be a beautiful love. Be not fearful to love. It tis yere destiny."

She looked at him and took a deep breath. "Does it show? I, I 'ave nae spoken with him about this."

Cyran laughed. "M'Lady, he also loves yew, only he does nae know what to do. Inside of him he is mad with passion for yew."

She looked at him with surprise. "I, I 'ad no idea." She looked away to the garden and within her she trembled with great emotion. "I, thank yew fer yere knowing. Yew already knew I be nae been trained in the art of love making."

"Aye. There be no training. It be beautiful and simple. Allow it to unfold."

Her eyes welled up with tears and she reached over to touch Cyran's arm. "I be truly blessed to 'ave yere counsel."

For a moment the two were silent. Magdalena was the first to speak. "Tis tyme to finish this war and retrieve the dagger.

"So be it, M'Lady ."

Magdalena sat there contemplating her conversation with Cyran. She smiled and knew what she would do.

⛨⛨⛨

Magdalena of Hy Brasil

~ France ~
2013

A Breakthrough

Always remember that the future comes one day at a time. ~ Dean Acheson

Ellen and Jill were in the solarium having their weekly coffee visit. They had agreed to meet once a week at Ellen's and the following week at Jill's to visit and share what was happening in their lives. Sebastian's jaw had healed and it was great that he was at last able to talk. He was continuing to have physical therapy. Jill was in the midst of sharing that Sebastian's dreams of his kidnapping were slowly diminishing.

Ellen was about to reply when the phone rang. "I think I had better take this call as Peter was discussing a potential trip to the U.S." She looked at the caller I.D. and noted it was from Alain. "Hello Alain. This is a pleasant surprise."

"Ah, my sister, I have good news for you. Louise was good as her word because we were able to get a copy of the face of the man who attempted to kill Sebastian on the bridge from the morgue files. With her contacts, copies of the photo were sent out and the man has been identified."

"Thank god!"

"I agree. The photo is being circulated and hopefully the men with him will be identified. There is a possibility that the man seen with Cerise Bertrand could be the one she was seen with."

"And, he could also be the one who killed her."

"*Oui*. There is also the possibility that one of these men also killed *Mme*. Gillet. I will call when I have more news. *Adieu*.

Ellen turned to Jill who had a question in her eyes. "As you could hear, that was Alain and the man who was about to kill Sebastian has been identified from a photo taken at the morgue and circulated through the contacts Louise has."

"Thank god that there is some action now. I, I just want this unfinished business to be completed."

"I agree. Are you going to tell Sebastian?"

"Probably. Perhaps when I find the moment is right. At the present, he is still recovering from his ordeal. We really do not talk about it. I have thought about him getting therapy for his trauma, but he can be stubborn and will possibly reject the idea."

"I can understand that. I have noticed that at times he appears to have a haunted look in his eyes."

"Yes. He won't talk about it, and I sense that the fact he killed a man is a deep wound. When he thinks he is alone, I have observed him weeping silently. "

"This might sound trite. I know forgiveness is the key and it begins within to first forgive our self and then forgive the other."

With tears in her eyes, Jill nodded in agreement. "I hold back from telling him what he could do and I have to allow him to heal his spirit. I will say this, he is taking long walks and he will sit out in nature for long periods when the children are in school. I refrain from joining him because I know this is his alone journey."

"Jill, I have a small booklet that has helped me through rough times. It is called, "*Journey of Discovery.*" It is written by someone whose signature is written as Anonymous and it is a gift from me."

"Oh my god! Yes, I will give to Sebastian and perhaps he will let me read it. I, I think I will go home now."

The two women stood and looked into each other's eyes. Jill was the first to speak. "I know we have been together in previous lives."

Ellen nodded. "I have always felt that we have. Now, it is time to wipe the tears away and to move ahead in this life. We are truly blessed."

ΩΩΩ

Journey of Discovery

The teacher who is indeed wise does not bid you to enter the house of his wisdom but rather leads you to the threshold of your mind. ~ Kahlil Gibran

That evening after Jill's visit with Ellen; she waited until the children were in bed before giving the *Book of Discovery* to Sebastian. Jill began by sharing with him her visit with Ellen and the phone call from Alain. Sebastian nodded, but made no comment. "Ellen asked me to give to you this small book that she said has helped her immensely. It is her gift to you."

    He looked surprised and took the book from her. "What is this? Why do I need to read about something such as this title, *Journey of Discovery*? I found you and I love you. You are my treasure."

    "Yes, I know and I accept. I think you might find this a little bit different. It is up to you to read it. I am only the delivery person."

    For the first time in some days, he managed a smile now that his jaw was healed. "I, I will read this for you *ma chère.*

    She stood up and came over to kiss him. "I am going to bed and yes, I love you. In fact, I don't know what I would do without you."

Sebastian sat there with the slim book in his hands. He turned it over in his hands and noticed the author was *Anonymous*. He opened it and the Dedication intrigued him:

Dedication: *To those who walk the path.*

He turned the page and read:

Hark unto those who trod the path of life. Life is a gift and is to be treasured. The following are only stepping-stones. The treasures herein abound for one to contemplate.

He turned to the next page.

Life is a journey of discovery. Beware of the pitfalls and judge not yourself. Contemplate this.

He realized that each page had a statement and the words *judge not yourself* stood out. He settled back in his chair and took a sip of wine from the glass he had not finished. He continued to read page by page while stopping to think about each message.

~ Hold not on to anger. It poisons the cells of the body.

~ Judge not the actions of others lest you be caught into a snare.

~ Give up prejudices, bigotry and hatred. The three actions take you away from your path of freedom.

~Release the past before it places a lock on your future.

~Old wounds – old hurts are to be shed like a dog shaking off water.

~ Take not a life unless it is to save your own.

He stopped reading and put the book down. *My god!* he thought. *This, this is for me. I suffer because I caused a death.* Tears welled up in his eyes and he brushed them away with the back of his hand. Taking a deep breath, he continued to read.

~ Be aware of fear. Fear can eat away your future. Fear imprisons your dreams. Move beyond into freedom.
~ Freedom is a choice. Use it or lose it.
~ Take not from another unless it be a gift.
~ Mock not that you know nothing about.
~ Tarry not into the past unless it gives you pleasant memories.
~ Memories can be keepsakes only if they reflect pleasure and joy.
~ Seek knowledge for it will serve you well.
~ Jealousy eats away your future and poisons the cells of the body.
~ Be not envious of another for you know not what lurks behind the mask.
~ To lie is to bear false witness against you.

~ To cheat another is to rob you from loving yourself.

~ Problems are only waiting for a solution.

~ Life is a labyrinth. When obstacles appear move through them by finding solutions.

~ To turn the other cheek is to remove the focus from problems and obstacles. Into Love.

~ To forgive is to remove the barnacles from the Soul.

~ Look beyond the surface of another and see the God within.

~ Nothing is impossible.

~ Failure is only an opportunity to move to the next step.

~ Laughter is the key to resolution.

~ He or She who injures you, forgive. Forgiveness unlocks the door

~ All people have God within them. Most do not know and look here and yon.

~Your Holy Spirit is your Fiduciary and has the power to act in situations for you when you give your trust, honesty and loyalty.

~Ask and you shall receive.

~ Kindness is an action of love. Use random acts of kindness to bring joy to another and have peace within your Soul.

~ Be an Observer and you will gain knowledge.

~ There are no failures. There is only the giving up.

~ Pursue that which makes you happy and fulfilled.

~ Never live for another. Live for yourself.

~Forgive your enemies and forgive yourself. Those who do not forgive move not on to the Path of Freedom.

~ Find a partner who shares your dream and whose dream you share. Be on the same path.

~ Compassion is loving another who is in the throes of challenges yet gives no advice or judges.

~ Gratitude and a Thank You have great rewards and eases your Soul.

~ Journey of Life is when you speak it, believe it and know it is real.

~ At night before you go to your slumber, review your day and that which is joy or disturbing. Forgive and sleep well.

~ Love is the Power that moves mountains. Find the frequency and live it fully.

> *~ True love is a frequency that can change all things.*
> *~ Love is the Key. Contemplate.*
> *~ Author Unknown ~*

Sebastian was immersed with these statements and he was jolted when Jill came in and spoke to him. "My darling, it is 3 a.m. and you need to be in bed."

He looked up startled. "Ah, *oui*. I am intrigued with this small book Ellen sent over. It has much in it to contemplate." He sighed. "You are correct. It is time I come to bed."

Hand-in-hand the two climbed the stairs to their bedroom. After he undressed and got into bed with her, they snuggled and the snuggling led to passion. "*Ma chérie, ma chérie*. I love you and I want to come into you now."

Jill opened herself to him and with gentleness, he entered. It was slow and loving in the beginning and when the passion became a fire, it was an act of ecstasy. Finally, he was spent and withdrew.

"Oh my god!" Jill moaned. "You, you were beyond words."

He lay there with his arms around her. "*Ma chère* you are the one who taught me." They both chuckled and drifted off to sleep.

The alarm rang and Jill managed to open one eye to see it was 7 a.m. She knew that she had to get up and see that the children were dressed and ready for school. *Oh yes,* she thought. It's *Ellen's turn this week to drive the children to school.*

Even though she wanted to wake up Sebastian, she did not have the heart. He was sleeping so peacefully and they had one of the best sex since his recovery. *Well*, she thought. *I know it will be greater as time goes by.* As she thought of their coupling in the wee hours of the morning, she felt a surge in her vagina. *God, I'm horny!*

Sebastian had slept late and when he woke up he went in search of Jill. "I thank you for the most beautiful union. We will do it again. *N'est-ce pas?*

She embraced him and lightly ran her hand over his face. "Sebastian, I accept." She stood back. "I will be going into the village with Ellen to pick up a few things. When you are ready to eat, let Sabine know."

He nodded and told her he would be contemplating what he read the previous night. After she left, he asked Sabine for coffee and croissants to be brought in the salon. He sat down and picked up the slim book. The title *Journey of Discovery* intrigued him as well as the statements on each page. He looked at the paper then the print and began feeling the paper. He realized this was done by a lithographic process and from his use of translating old documents sensed this had been printed in the early 1900's.

Sabine had left a pot of coffee and he poured a fresh cup and sipped it while contemplating the first page statements.

Hark unto those who trod the path of life.
Life is a Gift and is to be treasured.
The following are only stepping-stones.
The treasures herein abound for one to contemplate.

Within him, he felt a trembling as if he was awakening to something new. After taking another sip of coffee, he turned to the next statement.

Life is a journey of discovery.
Beware of the pitfalls and judge not yourself.

Contemplate this.

He re-read the statements repeatedly. When he felt he could almost memorize them, he asked himself what he had discovered about himself. He remembered when he first met Jill, Ellen and Peter whom he already knew. He was ill, in despair and ready to die. Translating the *Magdalene Scrolls* found by Jill and Ellen resurrected his desire to live. *Oui,* he thought. *This was a major discovery for me. And, and it was Jill who assisted him.* He chuckled, *Mon dieu, she seduced me and taught me about the sex process.* As he was thinking this, he felt an arousal of his penis. *What a lover she made of me!* He chuckled again. *She also taught me how to dance.* He continued to contemplate. *I am so blessed. I have a wife and two children. Perhaps I have not been a great father to the children. Perhaps I can change and be aware of the treasures I have.*

Sebastian realized he had just made a major discovery. Within him, he felt lightness.

When the children came home from school and Jill from her village shopping, Sebastian greeted them with open arms and a smile. Arthur asked him, "Papa are you healed?"

"*Oui*, I am healed." Aimee wrapped her arms around his legs.

"Now we go and find Sabine and see what treats she has made for you today."

Jill stood there with tears in her eyes and thought, *Oh, my god! This is a miracle.* As they turned to leave, she asked, "May I come too?"

Sebastian, Aimee and Arthur stopped and in unison replied, "But of course."

That night after the children were in bed, Sebastian shared with Jill what he was learning from the little book Ellen had given to him. "*Chère,* I invite you to join me in utilizing these messages."

Jill took the book he offered to her. With tears, she acknowledged her acceptance, leaned over, and kissed him. Together they read the Dedication: *To those who walk the path.* Sebastian read to her:

Hark unto those who trod the path of life. Life is a gift and meant to be treasured. The following are only stepping-stones. The treasures herein abound for one to contemplate.

He handed the book to her and asked her to read the second step.

Jill began reading:

Life is a journey of discovery. Beware of the pitfalls and judge not yourself. Contemplate this.

When she finished, she looked at him. "My beloved, we have been on our journey of discovery together since I first met you. Yes, we have had our pitfalls and let us live not to judge our self or each other."

He nodded in agreement. "I think we are to go to bed and blend ourselves as one."

With tears sparkling in her eyes, she took his hand and they walked upstairs to their bedroom.

For once, Jill felt that she no longer had to be the one to initiate their sexual copulation. It would be a together desire and sharing. Sebastian began by removing her clothes while nuzzling her neck. She was thoroughly aroused. She then began undressing him and she could already feel his erection. Together they lay on the bed.

Sebastian began caressing her body and kissing her breasts. She was thoroughly aroused and he began touching her clitoris. She gasped and asked him to enter her. Gently he thrust his penis into her and gently rubbed his member against her clitoris. She climaxed and with her arms around him she felt him reaching his climax. He lay on top of her and kissed her again and again with her responding.

"*Ma chère*, I think we have arrived."

She gave a light giggle. "I agree. This was the best I have experienced."

"*Moi aussi.*"

They lay together entwined and drifted off into a blissful sleep."

ΩΩ

A Shot in the Dark

The best weapon against an enemy is another enemy.
   `Friedrich Nietzsche

The previous evening had been a joyful dinner with Jill and Sebastian He was effusive in his appreciation of the book Ellen had given him. As Ellen lay in bed, she thought of the change in the two of them. She sighed thinking of how she found the book. She and Peter had been walking along the Seine next to Pont Neuf as an outing when she had the idea of checking out the old books in the stalls of *les bouquinistes*. Peter knew she loved old books. The one that caught her eyes was titled, *Journey of Discovery*. She and Peter were both intrigued with the small book.

They looked at each other and Peter said, "I think this is the book for Sebastian. I know he is still suffering from his kidnapping and injuries."

Ellen reached up and kissed him. "I had the same thought. Perhaps this is why we were led to walk along the *quay* and find this delightful stall. I feel the energy coming from this book is one of love and understanding. What a great find!"

She smiled when she had thought that perhaps she and Peter should read the short book before giving it to Sebastian. They found it so profound that she had copied the list from the book and now she and Peter were discovering their own journeys and to update them. She was doing her best to conquer her own fear.

The alarm went off and Peter rolled over and grabbed her. "I gotcha!" She laughed and settled in his arms. She told him about her own morning contemplation. He listened and he replied that he realized that fear was like a devil's pitchfork – ready to tear apart anyone's thoughts and presence.

Laying in his arms, she realized she felt safe. "Peter, I, I have a nagging feeling that we are - well, I sense that something ominous is going to happen."

He tightened his arms around her. "I have also had that feeling."

"Really? And you haven't shared it with me? Drat you Peter Douglass!"

He quickly kissed her in a way that left her almost breathless. "I'm not going to let you get by with this. Oh, no!" She quickly moved on top of him and began kissing him. This now became an arousal of Peter's penis and the quickening of her vagina.

When the two had completed their copulation, they lay back and snuggled. "Well Mr. Big Guy, you do have a way with me. I can only say I enjoyed it."

He kissed the top of her head. "That goes for me too. I think it is about time for the children to be up. I know Yvonne will have them dressed; however, I want to have breakfast with them."

Ellen quickly got out of bed and told him, "Me too, and I will beat you to the shower."

He laughed and allowed her to be first. He knew that with his long legs that he could outrun her.

Breakfast with the children was almost a daily event. Peter and Ellen enjoyed their company and listened to what they wanted to share. It had been a game to see who asked to speak first. Joseph put his hand up to be first. "Since this is October, what are we going to do for Halloween?

Peter answered him by saying, "First I think you should understand the origins of Halloween. It is said that the custom began in England some hundreds of years ago by the Celtic celebration of Samhain. The Celts believed that it was a day when the spirits rose from the dead and visited those who were living."

The three children were listening wide-eyed, and Joseph held up his hand to speak. "Is this where the ghosts come in?"

Peter replied that it possibly was. "It is alleged that the Celts left food by their doors to invite the good spirits and they also made masks to scare off the bad spirits."

"Wow! Then how did it get to France?" Joseph asked.

"Halloween has not been a traditional holiday in France. I am not sure; however, it is possible that American companies such as McDonald's, Coca Cola and Disney brought the idea over from the United States by introducing pumpkins and Halloween ideas with their publicity. Now it is gradually taking root here in France."

Joseph held up his hand again. "Do you think we can invite our friends here for Halloween and have a party?"

Magda held up her hand to speak. "Papa, I think Joseph has a great idea. We can invite our friends from school and we can ask them to come as ghosts and goblins. I want to make my own mask."

Ellen spoke up. "Why not Peter? I think it is a splendid idea."

Eleanor put her hand up. "Me too, me too."

Peter replied, "Okay. Here are the rules. First, you each make a list of whom you want to invite. Second, you give the list to your mother and then she will have you write invitations. Three, do not spread this about to your schoolmates until you have your list and your invitations. Agreed?"

Three pairs of hands went up with each saying "Yes."

Ellen told them that it was now time to go to school and she looked at Peter. "I think today is your day for driving."

He stood up and went over to her and kissed the top of her head. "It is a pleasure and we will pick up Arthur. Is there anything you want from the village?"

"Not at this moment. I think I will take a walk and be in nature."

Ellen loved the mystical feeling of the woods and the stream that ran through into the lake. She always found peace when she sat by the stream. Peter had a bench placed in a certain spot for her. She sat down and it was almost as though she could hear a melody of the water. She listened to the birds with their beautiful songs and the rustling of the leaves that were now falling. She closed her eyes and went into a deep silence asking what the next step regarding the dagger.

In her inward vision, she again saw the beautiful woman from somewhere in the past. She sensed that the dagger belonged to her. However, why was it given to her? She was also remembering that the woman looked similar to her mother. Was this someone from her lineage?

She had an ominous feeling that something more was going to happen. She remembered the statement from the book she gave to Sebastian. *Be aware of fear. It can eat away your future. Fear imprisons one's dreams. Move beyond into freedom.* She began to breathe out and in until she felt a sense of freedom. She told herself that she had to be detached and only then can she have her freedom.. She continued to sit and listen to the gurgling of the stream. She felt at peace within. What came to her was something like a short poem.

> *Bright flows the river.*
> *The river of life*
> *Bright flows the river,*
> *Shedding all of strife.*

She felt a letting go of worry and the ominous feeling. She knew she was ready to return to the chateau.

When she entered the chateau, Marie told her that *Mme.* Bianchi had left a message asking that Ellen return her call. Ellen thanked her and went into her office where she dialed Louise's phone number. She was surprised that Louise answered.

Louise said her reason for calling was to invite she and Peter along with Jill and Sebastian to join her and Alain for dinner this coming Saturday night at *Alain Ducasse au Plaza Athenee.* "I have a reservation for the six of us at 6 p.m. It's time we threesome get together and perhaps we can discuss ongoing events." Ellen knew what she meant.

"If you will give me the Gontard telephone number, I will call them."

Ellen replied, "I know Peter and I are delighted to have dinner with you." Ellen then gave her Jill and Sebastian's phone number.

After Louise severed the call, she sat there and wondered what this would portend since Louise indicated they would speak of ongoing events. She then dialed Peter's office direct line and when he answered, she told him about the invitation. "I told Louise we would accept."

Peter said he was delighted and if Sebastian and Jill accept the invitation, we can drive in together. "This will be interesting. Another aside, Nance received a phone call that her older sister just passed away. She will be leaving tonight for Cleveland, Ohio. Will you wire flowers?"

"Oh yes. It sad although we have known that Elsie has been ill for a long time. I have a pen and a pad. Be a sweetheart and give me the name and address where to order the flowers."

Peter gave the information to her. "I'll be home for an early play time with the children as I promised." He gave her a kiss over the phone and hung up.

Ellen remembered the time difference so she made a note to herself when to place the call and the order.

Friday night arrived and the two couples gathered at the chateau and had a glass of wine together before leaving. Peter was the designated driver. Arthur and Aimee were spending the night with Joseph, Magda and Eleanor who were thrilled. Yvonne had said that the five would be fine with her.

The trip into Paris was smooth and the talk was filled with lightness and laughter. Jill was inwardly happy that she and Sebastian were having an outing at a posh restaurant. When Peter drove up to the Plaza Athenee, a car valet helped the women and then gave Peter a ticket when he received the keys.

Alain and Louise entered behind them. With hugs all around, Peter said, "That was great timing. You must have synchronized this with the time it takes to come from our place."

Alain replied, "Perhaps. Would you prefer a drink in the bar first, or go in for dinner?"

Louise made the choice when she replied, "I think the restaurant would be best. The bar is not the place to talk."

The others agreed and the *Maître d'* greeted them and showed them to their reserved table. The *sommelier* came and offered them a bottle of champagne, which Louise accepted, and this was followed by a server who placed a menu at each place and gave them a spiel of what was recommended on the menu.

The three couples toasted to a splendid evening with their champagne, and then each perused the menu to make their choices. Jill and Sebastian silently were taken aback by the prices. Louise suggested that they have appetizers of the *Amuse-bouche* that was langoustine with caviar and lemon crème and the hot pasties filled with foie gras, spinach and mushrooms. She also suggested the Saddle of lamb with sautéed artichokes, Roasted poultry with chantelles or Lobster with Sea potatoes. Once their menu was selected, the *sommelier* came to the table and suggested the wine. Once the wine was poured, the appetizers came.

The talk was light with Alain and Louise sharing some of their trips and also about her children and Alain's son who was now in South America on holiday. When they had completed the meal and were drinking *Café au lait*, Alain began talking about the latest news regarding Sebastian's incarceration. The place where he had been taken had now been found and perhaps Sebastian did not remember his shoes because the kidnappers had left them there.

Sebastian almost choked on his café. *Merde!*

Jill offered him a glass of water and everyone began laughing. He shook his head and he also joined in the laughter. This was a major breakthrough for him to be able to laugh.

Alain continued. "It was not wise of them. The fingerprints found in the building are being processed to find a match. Also, there was a pair of men's socks near the shoes."

Again, there was laughter with Sebastian now joining in. He managed to speak. "*Ah non.* They can keep the socks."

Alain shared that the shoes and socks would be held as evidence when they caught the other two men. He glanced at Louise. She nodded and he said that the restaurant was closing and it was time to leave. The server brought the bill to Louise. "This is on me since I invited you. She looked at Sebastian. I want you to know that we will hunt the people down. Please be assured."

He nodded and stood up and walked over to her and kissed her on both cheeks. Everyone followed suit and thanked her profusely as well as Alain.

Their two cars were waiting for them and just as the car valet was opening the door to Peter, there was a loud gunshot aimed at Peter and another gunshot aimed at Alain's car and then a car sped away with screeching tires.

The car valet had fallen down and blood was streaming from his left shoulder. For an instant they were shocked and then the *le guardian* arrived and using his cell phone called the police and called for an ambulance. By now other people in the hotel began coming out as well as others from nearby. They were stunned and *le guardian* asked them to return to the lobby as the police were on their way. With murmuring, the people went back into the hotel; however, they looked through the glass.

Sebastian gripped Jill and his face lost its color. Alain was on his cell phone also calling in his people. "*Merde!* He or they must have been sitting down the street waiting for us to come out. How did they know where we would be?"

Peter wrapped his arms around Ellen and he suggested to Alain that perhaps one of the cars had an attached tracker device under the cars. Louise had been the first to reach the valet who had been shot and speaking to him in French. She stooped down. She was asking him if he had seen any suspicious persons nearby when he parked the car. The reply was that he had not.

Louise could hear the sirens coming and she suggested to Alain that they needed to have the two cars searched underneath to make certain there was no bomb. He replied that he would suggest that the police do it. She nodded and went over again to the car valet. He was biting back his tears from the pain and she took one of her handkerchiefs and rolled it up and asked him to open his mouth and bite down on it. Within minutes, an ambulance arrived along with the police.

Immediately the street was cordoned off. Photos were taken of the scene by police cameras. Before they arrived, both Peter and Alain had used their cell phone cameras to take photos. Police detective Reynaud was the first to arrive followed by *l'inspecteur* Fortier. They both recognized Sebastian and asked him if he was all right.

He replied, "*Oui, je suis bien.*"

Fortier sent two of his men in to ask for a lower floor room for privacy. He then sent the Gontards, the Douglass's along with Louise to wait for them inside. They nodded and left. Alain remained as he was on good terms with Fortier and Reynaud.

Once inside the lobby, the police asked everyone to remain and one of the officers began taking down names and asking for identification. Two officers followed by two *sténographe de la police* came in and were directed to two meeting rooms. Peter was selected for the first room with Louise in the second.

Questions were asked of Peter as to what occurred. Peter told him that the group had dined and were leaving to return to their homes. Two car valets had brought their two automobiles to the front. The injured valet had opened the driver's door and was handing him his keys when the shot hit the valet. The shooter apparently was in a car driven by someone else as it sped away. "Of course I was shocked. When the valet went down, *Mme* Bianchi was there and attended to the valet. I was also concerned for my wife and the rest of the party members. It happened so fast that I could not see the type of car as it sped by."

One by one Sebastian, Jill, Ellen and Louise were interviewed and their statements taken down. The last was Alain. He had already told Fortier and Reynaud what happened and he was there when the two vehicles were examined. What surprised him was that tracking devices had been placed under both cars. This surprised him because one vehicle was actually Louise's. He went on to say that, *M.* Gontard was standing in front of *M.* Douglass' vehicle and it was possible that the sniper was aiming at him.

After Peter gave his statement, he called the chateau and spoke with Jacques and gave him a brief statement and asked him to make sure the grounds were secured and that the children were safe. "*Oui, M.* Peter. I will make sure the security guards are alert."

Reporters were already attempting to get through the police barricade. It was now 3 a.m. and Louise had called her people to bring two cars to the back of the hotel to transport them home. The hotel would move the autos belonging to Peter and Louise to the parking garage. The threesome quickly moved through the hotel to a back door. The night manager was solicitous and had chairs brought for them to sit on.

No one wanted to speak at this time as they were all shaken. Louise whispered to Alain that when the shot rang out her cell phone rang and she was answering it. On impulse, she clicked on the camera and now had a shot of the car as it sped away.

Alain looked at her with shock and admiration. "That was indeed an inspiration. I should never be amazed at what you can do."

She smiled. "I chose not to surrender it to the police because I did not want them confiscating my phone. I sent you a copy and now it is up to you to share it with the police."

He shook his head and opened his cell phone. The picture of the car showed a black Renault of an unknown year. She had managed to get two photos and the second one showed the license plate on the rear. "*Merci.*" This is going to be sent out to all my contacts and that includes the police. After we leave the hotel, I will send a copy to Fortier and Reynaud saying that this was sent to me and that is a truth. Perhaps you should be the one to send it."

Louise smiled. "It will be a pleasure. They will not dare to confiscate the cell phone."

The two limousines ordered by Louise arrived each with a chauffeur. She gave orders for the Douglass' and Gontards to be driven to their homes and for *Avocat Delacroix* to be taken to his residence. She would be the last to be driven to her residence.

The trip back to the chateau and to Jill and Sebastian's home was silent for the most part. Peter suggested that they meet for lunch at 1 p.m. at the chalet. It was agreed. Sebastian spoke softly, *Je ne crains aucun mal.* "I will fear no evil."

The following morning, Peter and Ellen woke with a pounding on their door. Peter groaned. "I have an idea it is our beloved children." He answer, "Yes, who is it?"

"It's me, Magda. It is almost noon and we haven't heard anything from you. Are you all right?"

Peter smiled. "Indeed we are okay. We just had a late night. Have you had breakfast?"

"Yes and now it is lunchtime."

Ellen groaned. "Lunchtime?"

Peter told Magda to come in. Softly she opened the door and walked in. Peter was sitting up in bed and held his arms out. With an almost leap, she fell into his arms. "Papa, I have been scared about you and Mamma. I felt that something bad was happening to you."

He cuddled her and kissed the top of her head. "Magda, we had a wonderful dinner with Alain and Louise and then something happened."

"The something bad?"

"Yes, it was bad. All of us are okay. We were not hurt. Outside the hotel, someone drove by and shot the car valet. No, he did not die. He was shot in his arm or shoulder. I really do not remember which one."

Ellen was now wide-awake and Magda crawled over her father and hugged Ellen. "I was worried Mama."

Ellen now had tears in her eyes. "You have always been sensitive and knowing. As your father said, there was only the valet who was injured."

Peter reminded Ellen that Jill and Sebastian were coming over between 1 and 1:30. "While you two beautiful ladies cuddle and talk, I am going to take a shower."

"Mama, was it really awful?"

"Not really awful because no one was killed. It took a long time for the police to take statements from us and others who witnessed it."

"Was Oncle Sebastian scared? I know his kidnapping was bad and I was concerned."

Ellen held her in her arms and stroked her hair. "I was proud of Sebastian. Do you remember that book I gave to him?"

"The thin one with all those statements?"

"Yes. I think he is applying it to his life. What he said on the way home, is "*I will fear no evil.*" I think that all of us must remember this and not to fear any evil."

"I, I don't think I am afraid of evil after that time when Arthur and I were kidnapped. I know the Magdalene came and rescued us. I think I lost my fear then."

Ellen hugged her and kissed her cheek. "I think I hear your father shutting off the shower and now it is my turn. You can welcome Jill and Sebastian when they come. We will be discussing last's night's event and I am asking you to help Yvonne take care of the children."

"I will Momma. I love you and Papa so much." She hugged Ellen and left.

Peter walked in toweling his hair. "It's your turn my love. I will dress and go down to see if Sebastian and Jill are here or call if they are not."

The two embraced with Peter stroking her hair. I do not want you to worry. We've been through rough times before and this too will pass."

Ellen stood back and looked up at him. "You always say beautiful things and they come true. I'll be down as soon as I get dressed."

Peter pulled her close to him and tilted her chin up. They kissed with passion.

Magdalena of Hy Brasil

Peter had entered the breakfast room and noticed that Marie had kept the buffet ready for him and Ellen. Jill had called and said that she and Sebastian were fine and decided to bypass talking about what happened last evening. They wanted to spend time with the children and to share together the book Ellen had given Sebastian.

Peter felt relieved in one sense. His cell phone rang and it was from Alain. He was calling to let him and Ellen know that the young car valet was not injured seriously. Louise had called the hotel and asked that the young man be retained on salary until his arm was healed. The manager agreed.

Alain went on to say that, a photo had been taken the instant the car shot past them. When Peter asked who had the camera, Alain told him this was not to be dispersed to Ellen or the Gontards. "It was Louise. She had just answered her cell phone when the shot came and she cut off the phone and switched it onto the camera. When Peter asked if they had told the police, Alain, said that the photo had already been sent to them.

Peter chuckled. "It appears that Louise is as good with a cell camera as someone shooting a gun."

Alain laughed. "I think she was shocked that she could do it. I will be in touch. Keep your family safe. All of you are dear to me. Give my love to Ellen and the children."

Peter sat for a moment and made a decision to play with his children, take a walk with Ellen and let the previous evening be pushed aside. He was a fortunate man.

ΩΩΩ

HY BRASIL
400 A.D.

Kidnapped

The thing I feared has come upon me.
~ Job

Magdalena was completing her breakfast when Callan arrived. 'G'morn M'Lady. 'Tis indeed a fine morn. There be news from Hopenth."

"Ah, I 'ave waited fer news."

"Hopenth came to me during the night and said the ship arrived in the land of Gaul. A storm blew them off course and it be fortunate they made it to Gaul. He went on to say the group be a bit shocked as to their backward ways. I tell him this be a great learning fer them and to keep us informed.

"Fortunately, Bertran and her group be far away from the fight with the Skagerraks."

"Thank yew fer the information. I be relieved our group reached Gaul. Regarding Bertran, I want her and her party nae be hasty in their travels. Please urge the Druidess to keep them delayed and this gains more information regarding the women of Hy-Brasil."

"Aye, M'Lady. I 'ave nae received information regarding the Skagerraks this day. The last I heard Wexon be with them. Tis an ill-wind."

"I agree. There be something unsettling in me. I woke this morn with a foreboding."

"M 'Lady, tis well to sit and project our minds to the battle at hand."

Magdalena and Callan closed their eyes becoming quiet. Within, they each were scanning the battle with the Skagerraks. All was quiet until Magdalena gasped. "Oh gawd! Oris be taken!" She shuddered and opened her eyes.

Callan came out of her mind projection. "M 'Lady, I too see it be. It be nae the Skagerraks that took Lord Oris. T'was – "and before she could say, Magdalena screamed.

"It be Brannon! Oris be in Brannon's dungeon."

"Aye, M 'Lady. Tis so."

Magdalena stood up and her face was one of rage. "How dare he take my general! By taking Oris, he thinks the Skagerraks win and he be the Lord of the Realm. It nae happen!"

Callan also stood up. "M'Lady, I deem it important to remember our training be deep. We be given abilities when in trouble we use what we be taught."

"Bless yew Callan. Let us ponder this to create a plan."

The two sat down again closing their eyes to mind scan the possibilities. Finally, Magdalena broke the silence. "Callan, this night we, travel with our mind power to the dungeon of Brannon. It be in Brannon's Hold."

"Aye M 'Lady. As I deem it to be, we set the guards into a dream state."

"And I take a key to unlock his door. I saw Lord Oris chained to a wall and he be injured."

Callan nodded in agreement. "I be the one to take care of guards. Yew use a key to unlock his door and chains. I come and we two transport him."

"Callan methinks first we visit Brannon's stables to 'ave two horses ready. Oris rides with me and yew follow."

"M 'Lady, Druid Berone traveled to Brannon's hunting lodge. He told of a cave nearby." It be off the track and best we place him there to attend his wounds."

"I carry with me my healing bag. I liken yere idea. I be with Oris and yew return to the Garenfeld to bring a wagon to fetch him back."

"Aye, I do this."

"Callan, 'erefore nightfall send the message to Brannon he be to return to the Garenfeld posthaste. I deem him to go his Hold since he captured Oris."

"Aye. I be calling forth the message to the Druids who be near him."

"In the message, he be told General Oris be missing and we 'ave need fer General Brannon. This be my message. Tell Lord Cyran Brannon captured General Oris and to 'ave a nice cell waiting fer him when he arrives. Rath be in charge of guardsmen here and ask him to come see me. I want the Garenfeld guarded well."

"Aye, M'Lady. I return at the hour when all be asleep."

After Callan left, Magdalena met with Cyran in the garden. She told him of Oris' confinement in Brannon's dungeon. She went on to tell of her plans with Callan.

"M'Lady, perhaps someone who be nae the Magentheld journey with Callan."

She smiled. "Nae. It be the Magentheld who goes to her General in need. I deem yew be the alternate Magentheld until I return. Quiet this must be." She stood and bowed to Cyran and left.

He began walking and contemplating the newest event and it came to him all would be well. He smiled at the audacity of this young female.

Magdalena told Mireen she would not be in the Garenfeld fer several days for a mission needed to be accomplished. She made Mireen swear that she is to pretend the Magentheld be not feeling well. She wished to be alone.

      She then called Rath and gave him her plans. He was aghast she, the Magentheld dare such a journey. She swore him to secrecy and ordered him to drill his troops and to keep watch over the Garenfeld. He left shaking his head at the thought of her intent.

It was the hour of the changing of the high moon when she and Callan transported themselves to the Hold of Brannon. They quietly went to the stables and calmed the horses. They found two and put cloths over their hooves. They left them under a spell and moved on to the building housing the dungeons. There were two guards with a sputtering lantern. Callan placed them in a spell where they were not aware and could not move. She managed to take the ring of keys and gave them to Magdalena.

      Magdalena using her sixth sense found the door locked with Oris inside. She used the key and quietly entered. His wrists were in chains as well as his legs. He looked up when she began unlocking the chains.

      "M'Lady…" Magdalena placed a finger on his lips and he sat there in astonishment thinking that he was dreaming. Once the chains were loose, she gave him a draught that would keep him in an almost state of sleep.

      Callan came in and the two picked him up and sat him outside the door until the door was locked. Callan returned the keys to the guards who were still under a spell. Callan went for the horses and returned to assist Magdalena in carrying Oris outside to the horses.

They managed to lift Oris into a saddle and Magdalena climbed on behind him. Callan led the way. Soon they were out of sight of the Hold. The moon was now under cloud cover.

It seemed to be a long journey, as they could not travel fast with Oris being in the condition having been beaten and was almost falling off the horse. Using her knowingness, Callan led them off onto a track and following directions of Berone, they found the cave. All seemed to be well with the owls making their night sounds. Callan lit a torch and went inside the cave, and saw it was empty and taking a blanket she removed from the jailors, she made a pallet for Oris.

She and Magdalena managed to get him off the horse and into the cave. Magdalena brought a flask of water and cloth along with her medicals. She bathed his wounds while managing to keep her anger in check. Once Callan brought the food and water into the cave, she left to take the horses back almost to the Hold and let them roam free.

Magdalena sat down beside Oris and began using her medicals for healing. With the torch giving off enough light for her to see, she was appalled at the beating done to him. After she cleaned his wounds and had given him a powder to sleep, she thought about what she and. Callan had done. She looked down at him and knew she loved him. After using the healing treatment she had been taught, she lay down beside him and slept.

When she awakened, she sensed it to be early morning. She stood up and went to the opening of the cave. All seemed to be quiet and she found a spot to relieve herself. Once she was back in the cave, she created a nourishing gruel to give to him when he awakened.

It was mid afternoon when he awakened with a groan. She was sitting by him and reached over to touch one of his hands. He opened his eyes and looked shocked when he realized it was Magdalena, the Magentheld. She placed a finger over his lips and told him he was safe and to take some water. He managed to drink from the cup she held to his lips. He fell back asleep.

In her contemplation, she knew Callan to be on the way with the wagon. It would be the following day when it arrived. She managed to start a small fire and brought out from her bag some dried meat. She let it boil in a small kettle she had brought. When he awakened again, he looked at her in wonderment. She asked him if he needed to let go of his water and he indicated he did. She help him up and to walk to the cave opening. While he had slept, she found a sturdy stick outside the cave and handed it to him so he could walk a few steps.

Once he relieved himself, he returned to the cave. "M'Lady Magentheld, I find I be in a dream and yew be here."

"It be no dream. Callan and me-self brought yew here."

How be it yew could do this?

She smiled. "It be a Druidess way. Naow, I 'ave meat broth and I ask yew drink it to gain strength."

He nodded and sat down as she handed the gourd cup to him. He drank a little at a time and looked at her with wonderment. Once he finished, she took his wrists and using a balm, rubbed it in and then his ankles. He looked at her the entire time.

When she finished, she sat on her haunches and looked at him. There was a yearning in her for closeness. He lay back down on the pallet and soon slept. She lay beside him and thought of the future. Her loins ached for him and yet she knew this not the time. She slept.

He awakened in the early morning and felt her body next to him. He slowly looked at her and felt a surge in his manhood. *Nay*, he thought. *I dare not take her.* He slept again.

It was high noon when Magdalena heard a birdcall. She then heard the wagon on the track. She sent another birdcall back to Callan. Soon they would be here bringing a woven stretcher for Oris. With Callan were two Druids, one being Berone and the second Foren. They quickly entered the cave and by now, Oris was awake. He was surprised and he felt relief. With no words, they placed him on the stretcher and put him into a wagon. Oris looked at Magdalena, "M 'Lady I, I be honored to be treated in this manner."

She smiled. "General Oris, you be a worthy man. I be meeting yew in the Garenfeld. Yew be in good company naow." She watched the wagon driving away and soon on the road.

Callan finally spoke. "M'Lady I deem it wise to take ourselves back to the Garenfeld. All signs 'ave be erased."

Magdalena hugged her friend. "Aye, tis well we move ahead."

The two closed their eyes and using their mind tools, they were away in a flash and back in Magdalena's room.

THE RENDERING

We win justice quickest by rendering justice to the other party. ~ Mahatma Gandhi

Once back in the Garenfeld, Magdalena lost no time in sending out the call to arrest Brannon. She knew Bertran to be on her way back and she wanted to interview her regarding her relationship with Brannon. She also sent word to have a cell room cleaned and made ready for Brannon when he arrived. She requested the cell below the Garenfeld to be furnished with clean bedding and a pot for him to relieve himself. Once she knew he was there, a force field would be placed around his cell to prevent Wexon from retrieving Brannon. She knew it to be inevitable that she and Wexon would battle with their minds.

Oris now was recovering in the Garenfeld medical facilities and Magdalena requested that he be held there until he was completely healed. She dared not visit, as she knew her love for him to be too apparent.

It was several days after her return when word came that Brannon had been intercepted on his way to the Skagerraks. Word already had been passed in his army and his troops transferred to General Oris's army. Oris's second-in-command sent a small cadre of officers to take charge along with a company of soldiers. Brannon's army was to be re-trained before they would be sent into battle with the Skagerraks. Magdalena sent a message that Brannon's former army were to be treated kindly and blend in with General Oris' army. Those who rebelled would be confined until she makes a decision.

Brannon entered the Garenfeld on a horse with his wrists shackled by a small cadre of Oris's army. He was immediately taken to the lower retention cells under the Garenfeld where he was removed from his horse and taken to the cell prepared for him. He sneered at the jailors and swaggered inside the cell. Once inside, his demeanor changed. He was frightened, and he was not going to show it. He was relying on Wexon to get him out. Little did he know Magdalena placed a force field around the underground cells, including his. His shackles were removed from his wrist. He felt surprised he had not been chained.

His cell keepers were ordered not to speak to him or to give him anything to eat for two days. He was to contemplate.

Two days later Bertran arrived from her travels and brought to Magdalena. Bertran was frightened as she already learned what Brannon did. Magdalena met her in her outer chamber and requested Callan to be there as well as a scribe.

When Bertran entered the room, she curtsied. Magdalena greeted her kindly and asked her to sit. Magdalena began by asking about her travels around the country and Bertran expecting to be interrogated about Brannon, stammered and then began to tell of her travels. From time to time, Magdalena asked a question and the scribe wrote down all she said.

Once Bertran's statements were completed, Magdalena asked if she was happy with her relationship with Brannon.

Bertran looked down at her hands. "Nay M 'Lady. I be sent to Brannon by me father, as a payment fer what me father owed him. I be fifteen at the tyme. Naow I, er we 'ave three children being two girls and one boy."

"What be their ages?"

"M'Lady, Arria be ten ans, Galla eight ans and the boy Caius four ans."

Magdalena said nothing for several moments. "Be yew happy in yere marriage?"

Bertran, who was looking down at her hands, looked up. "Nay M 'Lady. Yew be kind when yew sent me out to seek ways of women. I thank yew."

Magdalena then spoke. "As yew 'ave heard, Brannon betrayed Hy-Brasil and as Magentheld, it be my duty to see he be punished. 'Erefore yew say anymore, I tell yew it be my decision to sever yere marriage to Brannon. Yew naow be the steward of his Hold and his wealth."

Bertran gasped in shock.. "Oh M'Lady Magentheld, I, I be loss fer words."

Magdalena smiled. "Naow Bertran, I will see yew be schooled in the ways of owning and taking care of the Hold. Yere children to be schooled in the ways of learning and reading. I be sending Druidesses to show yew and to teach yere children."

Bertran began crying. "Oh, M'Lady, yew, yew do me an honor. I beholden to yew."

"My dear Bertran, the ways of women be changing. On the morrow, I be holding court fer Brannon's betrayal. Yew 'ere nae to be watching the court proceedings unless yew desire to. Callan, who sits with us naow, will be taking charge of yere schooling and that of yere children. Callan and the Treasurer Kanen will assist yew in yere learning so that yew be a great steward."

"Naow an apartment be held here fer yew and yere children be brought here. Yew will stay until it be deemed yew be ready in charge of yere Hold. Until then, there be Druids and Druidesses taking care of yere Hold."

Bertran was sobbing by now. "M'Lady Magentheld, yew do me much honor and I promise I will nae fail."

Magdalena stood. "Callan will naow take charge." She thanked the scribe and asked to see her later in the day.

Once she was outside the room, she smiled thinking to herself; *Bertran will be a kind steward and a wise woman.*

Magdalena called a court for Brannon's trial with her being the judge and the jury. The word went out to the lords and ladies of the realm to attend if they so desired. Oris was healed and asked to be in attendance. The morning arrived and Brannon was brought to the Great Hall. He had to walk in shackles the length of the Hall in front of those attending.

This morning she dressed in a dark blue gown with the chain of the judgment around her neck. She wore the crown of Hy-Brasil. She walked down the stairs with her guardsmen and entered after the lords and ladies were seated. With her soft eyes, she could see fear on some of the faces. Others looked in anticipation.

Once she was seated, Lord Cyran called all to order and asked the prisoner Brannon be brought forward.

Brannon's wrists were shackled and he was escorted by two guardsmen. Magdalena could see he was shocked with the Hall filled with people. His face became reddened and he looked ahead at Magdalena with hatred.

Bertran was sitting at the front and he ignored her. He stared ahead at Magdalena. The guardsmen halted him just before the dais. Brannon looked up at her again with hatred and anger.

Magdalena spoke. "Brannon, yew 'ave betrayed this country and its people of this country. Yew kidnapped General Oris and beat him badly 'erefore placing him in shackles in yere dungeon at yere Hold. Do yew ave anything to say?"

He nodded his head 'nay'.

She looked at a scroll in her hand and unrolled it. "Yew be charged with betrayal, conduct unbecoming a General and treason by working with the Skagerraks." There was a gasp from the people attending. Magdalena went on to say, "I 'ave severed yere marriage with Lady Bertran and the children be given in her keep."

He looked shocked and said nothing.

"Yere Hold is naow belonging to Lady Bertran with all yere monies and properties. I strip yew naow of yere military rights. I give yew two choices; yew be incarcerated fer the rest of yere life or yew be let adrift to fend fer yereself amongst poorest of the land."

He was shocked. Magdalena could see his emotions were now in turmoil. "What be yere choice Brannon?"

"Neither," he answered. "Kill me naow if yew dare." There was a gasp from the assembled.

Magdalena looked at the energy field around him. What she saw was volatile and from this she made her decision. "Very well Brannon, as the Queen and Magentheld of Hy Brasil, I order yew to be hanged. The hanging be tomorrow early morn. May yere soul gives yew rest." She then nodded to the guardsmen to take him away." She stood up and announced," This court be now recessed."

After she walked down the long aisle looking neither right nor left, the people came out of their shock and began talking almost at once. Callan removed Bertran out through a door behind the dais. Bertran began crying. "Tis over. Praise God, tis over." It was now Callan's jobs to have the Druidesses teach her and then take Bertran back to her Hold. Thus a new teaching and a new way opening new doors for Bertran and her children.

Magdalena, once she came back into her quarters, allowed Mireen to take off the crown and help her into a day garment. She sighed. "Mireen, this be nae a g'day fer me. I be saddened."

"M 'Lady, yew did what be right. Fret nae."

At that moment, Callan knocked on the door. "Come."

She entered and looked at Magdalena for a moment. "M'Lady, what yew did be necessary and he be the one to choose his death."

Magdalena nodded she agreed. "I want his hanging to be quick and early the morrow 'erefore the cock crows. I want his body be placed where it be named the pauper's place. He be indeed a pauper naow. Let there be present only the hangman and those who assist him. If he chooses Cyran to be there with him, let it be asked."

Callan left to give the news to Cyran and then to give the orders to the hangman. It had been many a year before anyone was hanged in the Garenfeld.

Elsewhere in the realm, Wexon received the message that Brannon was to be hanged. He sneered thinking Brannon to be a weakling and of no use to him now. He realized he needed to be quiet and plot the demise of Magdalena. He knew he must recover the dagger, but where? He knew Cyran had taken it into the future and he found the location, but could not break into it. The imbeciles he chose failed miserably. Aye, he had much to contemplate.

THE HANGING

Pale Death beats equally at the poor man's gate and at the palaces of kings.
~ Horace

Magdalena was up and dressed before the cock crowed. She paced around her room with a ladened heart. Never, she thought would she be condemning a man to death. She began weeping for Brannon and asking his god to love him and take him into his bosom. She asked her god for forgiveness. There was a knock at her door and she knew it be Callan. "Come."

Callan had not slept well either. "M'Lady Magdalena, sorrow nae fer this death."

Magdalena fell into her arms and wept. "Tis a sorrowful day a Magentheld puts a man to death."

"Aye. It tis. Remember he could 'ave destroyed Hy Brasil and pushed us back into the days of olde. I fear his shadow will plague yew fer even as he died, he may nae leave."

"Yere right. He may play havoc such as those be named mean spirits. Be it wise to seek the voice of Cyran. Bless yew Callan. Yew do know what I need."

"Methinks he be alert and come to yew after the hanging. As it be naow, I be on my way to take Bertran to be with her children. They 'ave been with a sister who knows no love fer Brannon. I 'ave communed with Lady Alinor and she be sending three Druidesses to Bertran."

"Callan I do nae know what I would do without yew. Go in peace."

After Callan left, she sat in contemplation. She realized by hanging Brannon she had set his spirit free. If his spirit was to be mean, there could be havoc. She gave a shudder and knew the Hangman completed his job. She closed her eyes and blessed him on his next journey. At this moment, Mireen knocked on her door.

"Come."

She brought in the breakfast and behind her was Cyran. Magdalena stood up and greeted him. "Thank yew Cyran fer coming."

"Indeed M 'Lady. I knew yew be deep in remorse. I be with Brannon and I observed his energy field. I placed a spell in him and asked his spirit to guide him to a resting place of wounded souls."

She choked back her tears and asked him to breakfast with her. Mireen set the table for two and once they were seated, she left. Cyran looked at her. "Tis a blessing he be sent to the other side."

"But Cyran, will he come as a shadow and plague me?"

"Tis unlikely as I placed a spell in him as he be leaving and communed with his spirit. I deem it be accepted by his spirit."

Magdalena nodded. "Since General Oris has his health back, I be sending him to be with his army. He 'as much to do."

Cyran stroked his beard. "Aye, M'Lady. He be well. A company of his soldiers 'ave arrived and will be with him. Tis said they leave this next day."

She again nodded. "I 'ave asked him to meet with yew and me in the morning at the hour called eight."

He thanked her and the two talked of creating a larger circle in addition with the generals, the Keeper of the Treasury, Arms Keeper, and the Trainer of the Guardsmen. "I thank yew fer the break-fast and naow I be about my business."

Magdalena stood up and thanked him in return. He left and she stood there wondering what to do. She thought of the small glen where she went to contemplate. Quickly she dressed in her riding clothes and found her way to the stables without anyone seeing her. A stable boy was there and she asked him to saddle her horse. She swore him to secrecy.

When she rode out of the Garenfeld, she created a shield of invisibility around her so none of the guards saw her. Once she was out of sight, she loosened the horse's rein and let it run. It knew where to go and once she was in the glen, she tied the rein to a small tree limb and moved to her favorite tree to sit against it and commune with her Spirit. The deeper she went within, the calmer she became. She felt a love and a peace within her being. Her awareness to the present began and she heard a horse give a soft nicker.

She opened her eyes upon hearing a movement. She knew within her knowing who was coming.. Oris appeared in the glen and stopped when he saw her. "M 'Lady, be I disturbing yew, I leave naow."

Her heart began beating rapidly and she managed to stand. "G'day Lord Oris. I be most happy yew came." For a moment, it seemed as if there was no time. They looked into each other's eyes and he began walking towards her. When they met, she moved towards him and touched his face. "I, I be most happy yew be well. I, I, wanted yew to come."

"M'Lady, I, I..." and within a moment they were embracing and she lifted her face up for the kiss.

He bent down and tenderly kissed her and as the passion grew, the kiss became intense. Finally, they broke the kiss and looked at each other.

She placed her hand over his mouth when he was about to speak. "Nay Oris, do nae be ashamed. When we be in the cave I wanted yew."

Holding her, he looked deep into her eyes. "I also wanted yew and I dared nae. I, I," and he kissed her again with passion. Oh god he wanted her!

She pulled him down on the ground and whispered, "Take me."

He be shocked. "Yew be ready? Yew really want I enter yew?"

"Aye." She began undressing him.

He looked at her with wonder as she did and then he began undressing her. Together they lay on the softness of the earth and she whispered, "Show me what I must do."

Startled, he looked at her. "This be yere first tyme?"

"Aye. I want yew."

Slowly, he began caressing her breasts, kissing each nipple and then kissing her mouth, her face and her neck. She moaned with delight and began kissing his shoulder, his body and he responded by touching her privates. "Be yew sure yew want me to enter yew?"

With him on his knees over her, she said, "Enter me naow. I want yew."

Slowly he entered his manhood into her and began to move in a gentle way and he broke the shield that guarded the entrance within. She gasped and held on to him. He did not ejaculate until he had triggered her clitoris. She moaned with joy and when she arrived at her peak, he allowed himself to ejaculate.

They lay arm in arm and he asked her if he hurt her. "Nay," she answered. I 'ave wanted this every since I met yew. Yew 'ave given me a gift."

He kissed her again and held her closer to him. "I, I be honored and I admit I wanted yew when I first saw yew enter the great Hall and be declared the new Magentheld. I be going in the morn. Fear nae fer me. I worry I be leaving with yew bearing a child."

"Oris, fear nae. I knew we couple and I took care I be barren until yew return. Later we make babes." She noticed the sun at high mid-day. "Be it tyme I return to my duties. I ask yew come to my quarters this night and be with me."

"I be honored and I be there after the eating hour. Best I be with my companions who ride with me in the morrow."

They began donning their clothes. He brushed the twigs and leaves from her hair tenderly. "I will tarry here until yew be gone."

She nodded and they embraced with the last kiss.

She was glowing. She took a track off the main road and came to the nearby river. She looked into the water and made sure she would be presentable and placed the cap she had worn back on her head. She cared not what others thought most of the time, but thought of her encounter with Oris. She created an aura of sadness around her most would feel. In one way, it would be real because Oris be leaving on the morrow.

Somehow, Magdalena fulfilled her appointments. Callan had not returned and Regan was there to assist her. After the last appointment, she told Regan she wanted to be alone for the day and evening.

Magdalena ordered her dinner to be brought to her. She did not want to dine with anyone this evening. Mireen drew her bath and placed her nightclothes on her bed. She removed the dinner Magdalena barely touched. Mireen thought it all due to the hanging.

It was several hours later when she heard a light tapping on her door. She opened it and knew it to be Oris. He came in and she closed the door locking it. They stood there gazing into each other's eyes. "Magdalena, I love yew and I want to enter yew."

She smiled and replied, "I also love yew and I want yew to enter me."

She helped him undress and then he undressed her nightclothes. They stood there naked for a moment and then he picked her up and placed her on the bed. He lay down beside her and began kissing and caressing her body and their passion grew. She responded and caressed various parts of his body. With her legs wrapped around his body, she moaned, "Naow." He entered with his member. She shuddered with joy and then lay still in his arms. How many times did he enter her? It was early morn when he kissed her saying he must be on his way. She got up and washed his body clean. He allowed this, and said, "Careful M 'Lady or I will enter again."

She began laughing and then began kissing him all over. "Yew will know I be with yew and yew will return to me."

She showed him the hidden door leading to the lower part of the palace. Once again, they kissed and embraced and then he was gone.

Magdalena walked to the window and looked out at the early morning sky announcing the day's arrival. She went over in her thoughts of the day and night with Oris and she shivered with happiness. It was the first time she had felt happiness in many years. She thought. *Aye, he returns safely and I know within me he be my life mate.*

⛩⛩⛩

Magdalena of Hy Brasil

France
2013

Sebastian's Breakthrough

The power of intuitive understanding will protect you from harm until the end of your days.
~ Lao Tzu

The week following the shooting at the Plaza Athenee had been one of contemplation and more interrogations by the police. The vehicle Louise had taken a photo of was found and the fingerprints erased. Alain and Louise were using their contacts and were hopeful that the culprits would be found. There had to be a second man in the auto with one driving while the other shot the valet. They felt that another someone was paying them a large sum of money.

Today Peter had gone to his office. Having purchased the property next to the chateau had its benefits. One of his projects was creating an advanced quantum computer as well as other inventions. All he had to do was walk to his business complex, which was a renovated chateau housing his offices. The carriage house was also renovated to house most of the employees and there was another building where most of the inventions were created and tested.

When he arrived, he found Nance already at her desk. "Welcome back. I regret your sister died and thought you would take more time."

She smiled. "I couldn't stay away. It didn't take too long to settle her estate and I do not regret her passing as she had been ill for a long time." She took a tissue and blew her nose. "Darn it, I keep thinking that if she had only changed her attitudes and beliefs that she would still be alive. Why do people hang on to their old worn-out beliefs?"

"Well Nance, as I see it, they create a rut in their brains and it's like an old record that plays over and over. While you were away Ellen and I made a copy of an old book we gave to Sebastian and it is helping us to look at what is occurring now and to find peace within us."

"This sounds interesting. What is it about?."

Ellen and I were walking among the bookstalls along the Seine and stopped at this one bookstall. She picked up this old book and it had some interesting statements, or as some would call them verses. The title of the old book is "A Journey of Discovery."

"This sound interesting."

Each statement is meant for whoever is reading it to ponder the meaning beyond the meaning. As an example, *Be aware of fear. Fear can eat away your future. Fear imprisons your dreams. Move beyond into freedom.*

She shook her head. "God knows you and Ellen have had many occasions to have fear and yet, the two of you seem to move on to something greater. Yes, I would like a copy of these statements."

Peter smiled. "We are in sync with each other."

She nodded. "Are there any more leads on Sebastian's kidnappers?"

He chuckled. "Nance, while you were away, we were thrown into another piece of the puzzle." He then recounted the shooting of the valet at the hotel."

She looked at him wide-eyed. "That was meant for you Peter."

"Perhaps. This is why we are staying close to home as well as Sebastian and Jill."

"Have you learned anymore about the dagger?"

"Sebastian is doing what he can to make a breakthrough. Why not come over for dinner tonight? I will call Ellen and I know she will be pleased."

"I would love to. I have missed being here. Now to get on with doing what I am paid to do here."

That evening, Nance came for dinner and the children were delighted and loved her dearly. She had brought gifts for each one. Joseph received a video of *The Hobbit* and he was ecstatic. Magda's gift was a necklace with a gold fairy, which she loved. Eleanor was delighted with her butterfly doll. After they thanked Nance with hugs, they could hardly wait for dinner to be over so they could watch *The Hobbit* in their children's' area.

Nance watched them leave the room and shook her head. "They are growing so fast. I have to hand it to you two that you are doing something right. I want to hear more about what has been happening since I have been away. I am always amazed how the two of handle and bounce back with your unexpected, uh gifts."

Both Peter and Ellen laughed and before either could reply, the phone rang. Peter answered it and began listening to the caller. "That's great! My god! You have to come over and tell Ellen. Nance is here and we will open a new bottle of wine." He turned to Ellen and Nance, "It was Sebastian. He has broken the code on the dagger."

"Oh my gawd! At last a breakthrough!. He's coming over here now?"

"Oh yes. He and Jill are both coming. They are both excited. I am going to open another bottle of wine so we can toast to this great event."

Nance asked, "What are we drinking now? I find it delicious."

While he was opening the new bottle of the same wine so it could decant, he replied, "This is from the Bordeaux Region and it is *Chateau Belair Monage St. Emillion 2008*. I thought you would enjoy this."

It was not too long before Sebastian and Jill arrived with both smiling from ear to ear.

After hugs, kisses with Nance, they sat down. Sebastian had the photos of the dagger with him that he used to interpret the symbols. He was glowing and excited. He placed the photos on the coffee table and began explaining what the symbols on the blade indicated.

Jill sat back as she had already listened to Sebastian's explanation to her.

Sebastian began by explaining that in his research he learned that the dagger was in all probability from the Egyptian 18th Dynasty. At first, he thought it might be Akhenaton's, but it did not seem right. The handle of the dagger appeared to be more feminine than masculine. "I began researching all of the female Pharaohs as well as those who were the daughters. He was not sure until he was able to decipher the hieroglyphics on the blade itself."

He took the first photo and gave it to Ellen to pass around. "This one is deciphered as "Wise be the Serpent." He then took the second photo and after she looked at the first, he handed her the second photo. "The other side of the blade means "Truth Conquers."

"Oh my gawd! I, I now understand the symbology. The serpent, or the snake means knowledge and this is why the Bible is so misunderstood about the Garden of Eden. Eve offered Adam knowledge because she was the evolution of the Adam."

Ellen received a round of applause for her understanding. Sebastian then said that there was one word etched into the blade that did not make sense and that was the word "Scota." I have searched the Egyptian hieroglyphs and other symbols of that period and cannot find the meaning."

For a moment, the group was quiet. Ellen was the first to speak. "It seems that I have heard that name before. It eludes me now; however, I will search the web for it tomorrow. Let's have another toast."

Peter led the toast. "To a forever ending story. May the dagger be returned to its rightful owner. *Santé!*"

ΩΩΩ

SCOTA REVEALED

Knowledge is power. ~ Francis Bacon

Ellen and Peter had discussed the dagger after Nance, Sebastian and Jill left and they were intrigued by the word "Scota" on the blade. Peter said, "I can understand the "Truth conquers" and "Wise Be the Serpent," however I want to know what *Scota* means."

"I agree with you. You know how I love to research, so in the morning I will surf the net and see what I can find. For now, I think it is time for bed."

After breakfast was over and the children sent off to school, Ellen went into her office with a carafe of coffee and turned her computer on. She typed in 'Scota' and came up with several entries. The first one was a book by English author Ralph Ellis with the title *Scota Egyptian Queen of the Scots. Wow!* She thought. She also knew she had to have the book. Another interesting article titled *Claims Irish Have Egyptian Ancestry.* This article was a review on a new book, *Kingdom of the Ark* by Egyptologist Lorraine Evans. In this review it was written "The invaders were led by Princess Scota, the daughter of a pharaoh who fled her native land."

Ellen continued on-line and ordered the two books. She was excited and could barely contain herself from calling Peter or Jill. *So, Scota is a name of an Egyptian daughter of an Egyptian pharaoh. Nevertheless, how did she get to Scotland or Ireland?*

The more she contemplated this information along with having an ancient dagger in her possession; she reviewed her past history with the *Magdalene Scrolls* along with the *Sarah Scrolls. Why me?* She asked herself.

At lunch she shared her Internet finds with Peter. "Well sweetheart, I will say this that life with you is never boring."

"Peter!" She started laughing. "I think that perhaps you are correct; however, I really want a reason – a solution as to why I am the recipients of these ancient scrolls and the dagger."

"Why don't you ask your mother about your lineage? It just might shed some light."

"I think you are right. Somehow, I have avoided researching my ancestry."

"Afraid of what you might find?"

"Perhaps. Thanks for mentioning my mother. I think I will call her now. She should be awake and up since there is an eight hour time difference."

"I am anticipating some great news when I come home this evening." He stood and leaned over kissing her with passion.

"Oh gawd, you do stir up my passion. I'll hold it until you come home."

Ellen placed a call to her mother, and she answered after a few rings. "Hello Mother."

"Ellen! How wonderful to hear from you. Jim and I were only talking about you last night. How are the children?

Ellen then proceeded to tell her of the latest update on the three children as well as Sebastian.

"Besides, wanting to connect with you, I also want to ask you about something."

"What is it you want to know?"

"Do have an ancestry chart?"

"An ancestry chart? What for?"

"I am getting a urge to find out about our background."

Her mother began laughing. "I have not thought of researching for our background; however, I do recall an aunt who did some research. I think I have a copy of it somewhere. As you already know, my maiden name was Wood and a Wood family immigrated to Ohio from Canada. Oh dear, I will just have to find Aunt Tess' papers and I will fax them to you."

"Thank you Mother."

They continue talking and updating each other on recent events. After Ellen hung up, she decided to go for a walk. She had much to contemplate and knew the woods were a comforting place for her. The fall leaves were dropping and she smiled as she walked. She realized that it was nature's ritual of birth, death and renewal. *This is very much like the cycle of we humans. We enter this world as a new born baby, grow into adulthood, become aged and pass on to recycle ourselves again.*

She came to her favorite spot and sat on the bench that had been placed there. She felt a soft breeze caress her and she smiled. She began thinking of lineages. Something tugged at her mind. *Oh yes,* she thought. She remembered the article about the hereditary maternal DNA carried by the mitochondria.

The article was attributed to Rebecca Cann of the University of Hawaii and with her two male co-worker surprised the British Journal *Nature* in 1987.

. I remember the mitochondria is passed from mother to daughter and any mitochondria in the male sperm dies and is not passed to the daughters or the sons. She continued with what she was remembering. *So, if a man and a woman only have sons, then the woman's mitochondria's carrying the lineage dies out. It is the woman's mitochondria DNA that is passed to daughters and that...*She paused. *Oh gawd! Those lineage charts that most people think the male carries the bloodline is a bunch of dis-information. This, this means that it is the female who carries the bloodline! No wonder the ancient Egyptians knew this! This is why a male Pharaoh married a daughter or a sister and from that union it was necessary to carry on the bloodline.*

If what Sebastian told us is true, the dagger belonged to a female and the word Scota could possibly be a female name. She stood up and began walking back to the chateau. She now was on a mission to search the Internet to find what she could about Scota.

Once back at the chateau, Ellen went to her computer and began searching the word Scota. She was amazed at what she learned. She found that an old manuscript written by William Bower, Abbot of Inchcolm Abbey from 1440 had added to one written by John of Fordun's *Chronica Gentis Scotorum in* 1385 based on ancient manuscripts. The more she searched for additional information, the more she realized that the name of Scota was important and she printed out this information as she felt it was something she wanted to re-read and share with Peter, Sebastian and Jill.

That evening, she, Peter along with Sebastian and Jill sat down in the family room after all the children had been put to bed. She began with what she had found on the Internet.

Ellen began by saying, "I went on the Internet today and found a trove of information regarding the name Scota. Stay with me as I share what I found. According to an ancient manuscript attributed to William Bower, Abbot of Inchcolm Abbey in 1440, Scota was a name attributed to Akhenaton and Nefertiti's eldest daughter Meritaten. There is a possibility that during the last days of Akhenaton's reign the plagues began in Egypt. There is also a possibility that Akhenaton was also Moses and he led his people out of Egypt to Canaan. As an aside, he and his people did not wander for 40 years in the desert.

"History is not always accurate; however, Scota (Meritaten) married a Greek or Scythian prince with the name of Gaythelos or Geytholos and in some writings he also was named Mil. It is possible that Meritaten was co-regent or married to Akhenaton as Queen Nefertiti seemed to have disappeared. It could have been due to the plagues as they lost several daughters also.

"According to my research, Meritaten began using the name Scota and its meaning is *ruler of the people*. She and Gaythelos gathered the people who did not go with Akhenaton towards Canaan and with Egyptian ships set sail to the west on the Mediterranean. It is said they first went to Iberia on the Ebro River, and this is where Gaythelos took up the name Mil. The people in Iberia did not take kindly to them, so they set sail again."

Sebastian had sat listening intently. "*Mon dieu*, this is indeed amazing. I am most appreciative of your research. Please continue."

"There is a possibility they again began sailing and perhaps landed in the Canary Islands. This would have taken them through the Straits of Gibraltar. Why I say this is that an Egyptologist Dr. Joann Fletcher alleged that when Spanish adventurers arrived in the mid fourteenth century that they found caves with bodies embalmed. Perhaps Scota and her people did stop here; however this is not the end of their journey.

"Scota and Mil (Gaythelos) together with their fleet and people sailed on and landed in the land we now call Ireland. As an aside, Eusebias the historian wrote that she had married a Scythian, a prince of the Gaels." She stopped and asked for a glass of wine, which Peter gladly poured for her. He filled the glasses of Sebastian and Jill also.

"I say, let's toast to our beautiful researcher. To Ellen and all she is sharing."

Ellen smiled and gave a chuckle, "Peter, I thank you. I was beginning to think I was too long-winded."

"M' love not at all. Please continue."

"According to the research, Scota and Mil had two sons named Eremon and Eber. There was a war between the local people, possibly the Tuatha de Danaan. Possibly Mil had died before they reached Ireland. There are indications that Scota was a mighty warrior and was killed in a battle and her people won. Eremon and Eber are said to have divided Ireland into two parts.

"It is alleged that Scota's grave is south of Tralee town in County Kerry. It is known as Glenn Scoithin. Now, it is possible that son Eber's name was altered to Hiber and Gaythelos also known as Mil was given the name of Gael or Gaelic. Therefore Hiber became Hibernia and Scota became Scotia when some of her people went to Scotland and settled. Thus, the Scota name became Scotland. That is all I have found so far.

Jill shook her head. "My god Ellen! You have done some awesome research. What I want to know is where the dagger has been all these hundreds of years."

Ellen laughed. "That is the sixty-four dollar question."

Sebastian chuckled. "I understand your English from an old television program. I also want to know where it has been. *Voila,* my research has ended and I do not regret all that happened. I am much wiser now and I thank you."

Peter looked at Ellen. "I can say one thing; there is never a dull moment with this beautiful woman. I want to know that whomever this dagger belongs that he or she comes and gets it. I think it is time for it to be with its rightful owner."

Jill smiled. "Well said Peter. I think we are ready to move on and I hope to god that it is something pleasant."

Sebastian nodded. "*Moi aussi.*"

Ellen laughed and added, "I am more than happy to have this ended; however it won't end until the culprits who killed, Cerise, *Mdme*. Gillet, kidnapped Sebastian and attempted to shoot Peter are brought to justice. It was a sobering moment for all of them. Peter cleared his throat. "I agree with you and we will persevere. Now I think this session is over until the next one."

Jill laughed. "Let us focus on a pleasant session of the four of us."

ΩΩΩ

HY BRAZIL
400 A.D.

CYRAN'S REVENGE

No trait is more justified than revenge in the right time and place.
~ Meir Kahane

With the hanging of Brannon, Cyran told Magdalena he was taking a journey to discover what Wexon and his cadre was creating. He sensed that there could be trouble. Magdalena agreed and told him to do whatever he deemed necessary. He bowed to her and left. Little did she know what he was planning.

Cyran knew action needed to be done. He already knew Wexon and his cadre were on their way back to the Garenfeld area after hearing of the hanging of Brannon. He went to his secret place where he put together herbs for remedies. He began gathering the dried herbs necessary for this one draught. Knowing Magdalena would be curious as to what he was planning, he placed a field around his plan and himself.

    He used a nice jug of aged red wine and began placing the various herbs in it. He let it sit for two days and when he thought it had ripened, he passed the mixture through a cloth and poured the wine back into the jug. He knew it to be poison. He began creating an antidote. Once he was satisfied it was ready, he set out to the hamlet of Burfeld by bi-locating.

    The only inn was the Red Fox. Cyran entered the section for eating and drinking. His plan was to arrive when there would not be others there except the

Innkeeper. He sat down at one of the long plank tables and beckoned the Innkeeper to come over. Cyran told him he had some special wine for friends soon to arrive. He gave the man some coins for not buying the inns' wine. The man looked at the coins and knew it to be generous. Cyran told him when the group arrived this would be the time to give them a tankard of this special wine. In the meantime, Cyran ordered a tankard of the inns' wine.

It was not long when Wexon and his cadre came into the inn. They looked shocked to see Cyran sitting at the long table. Wexon asked, "Well, Old Druid what be yew doin' here?"

Cyran looked at him and replied, "Me be here as I be thirsty. I be on my way to General Oris' encampment. Iffen yew be thirsty, sit with me."

Wexon looked skeptical, but his Druids began sitting down at the table and Wexon followed. "Yew payin' Old Druid?"

"I just might be." He lifted his finger and the innkeeper brought over the jug of wine Cyran had brought.

Each one began drinking the wine, including Cyran. Wexon looked undecided; however he began to drink. "So yew be on yere way to Oris. The Skagerraks will win as Oris be nae much of a general."

Cyran did not respond to Wexon. He lifted a finger again and the innkeeper brought over the jug of wine and filled all the tankards. What no one had realized was that Cyran had slipped an antidote in his tankard. He pretended to be getting drunk. "Wexon, yew be thinkin' yew can out-do me. I can drink another tankard and out do yew."

The innkeeper brought over the jug and filled the tankards and they all began drinking the third tankard. Again, Cyran managed to put an antidote in his tankard.

Before the druids realized they were getting drunk, Wexon looked at Cyran with a question in his eyes and he fell onto the table. The others also began leaning on the table top. When Cyran was sure they had enough, he called the innkeeper over. "It seems these men be taken a dose of poison. I want yew to bury them deep and nary a word to anyone."

The innkeeper nodded his head he would when Cyran handed him a bag of silver. "I see 'em in here 'erefore and they be mean. Good riddance I say. I thankee Lord Cyran and go in peace."

CYRAN'S REVELATIONS

There is the joy in pursuing truth which nearly counteracts the deed done.
~ Anonymous

Magdalena thrust her attention into managing the realm of Hy Brazil. It was only at night when she allowed her thoughts to divine where Oris was and how he was fairing. She knew as the Magentheld her first commitment had to be the people of the realm. She had been delighted with the report that Bertran had managed to send to her through Callan. As she read it, she realized the women were definitely not equal to the rights of the men. She knew she had to make changes gradually. However, since she now was the lawgiver, she could begin revising the laws of the realm. While she was contemplating this, Callan knocked on the door. Magdalene bade her to come in.

Magdalena knew Callan to be her most trusted ally. "Good morn and what be it you 'ave to share with me this morn?"

"M'Lady, I felt yew calling me to come."

"Aye. With the hanging of Brannon and the settling in with Bertran, we 'ave missed our conversations. I read the document Bertran gave to yew and I deem it advisable I create new laws in the favor of the women."

Callan nodded. "I 'ave seen yew do this and I be thinkin' yew want I assist yew in creating the change in the law of the realm."

Magdalena laughed. "We do make a fine pair. Using what Bertran learned on her journey, I be asking yew to create the laws needing be changed."

"Tis me pleasure M'Lady. What else need be done?"

"On the Council there only be men. Brannon is naow gone. There be no General fer the left flank. I deem it advisable Oris be the only General. A document proclaiming he be the only General be made giving him all the rights and privileges of the only General. In this document, I deem it be he promotes the best and most trusted officers to high ranks. Let there be two documents giving Oris this power. One he keeps. The second, he signs and it be returned to me."

Callan smiled. "I be doin' this naow."

"When I sign this, I want yew to take these documents to Oris and bring back the sign copy for me."

"This I do."

After Callan left, Magdalena closed her eyes and sent a message to Cyran to meet her in the garden. She knew something happened in the realm. She searched with her mind for Wexon and his cadre and knew he be no longer in the realm. This troubled her.

Cyran sat in the gazebo waiting for the arrival of Magdalena. He knew he be telling her of what happened in Burfeld.

When she arrived, he stood up bowing to her and allowed her to speak first. They sat on the bench and Magdalena shared with him her sense Wexon and his cadre be no longer in the realm.

He nodded. "Tis true M'Lady Magentheld. Wexon and his Druids be on their way back to give yew trouble and stopped at an inn in Burfeld. They be thirsty and drank some bad wine. They be gone to perhaps join Brannon."

Magdalena looked at him and said nothing for a moment. "Does this mean Lord Cyran yew foresaw this and perhaps this be something yew assisted with?"

Cyran looked at her with his deep blue eyes. "M'Lady they be gone to another realm. Tis best it be laid to rest."

She looked away and sat while contemplating this. In her mind, she knew Cyran killed them. She felt no compassion fer the wayward Druids. She wondered if they would be coming back to haunt her.

"Nay M'Lady. They be nae haunting yew."

Within her, Magdalena felt a sense of relief. "I ask yew Lord Cyran to tell me more about the dagger of Scota."

"It came here many ans ago when Scota's people arrived. Scota and her mate be in their graves some ans 'erefore the Sky people brought her people to Hy Brazil. The dagger be with them. This be the purpose of the emblem yew see of the black lion and the serpent. The black lion be fer strength and power. The serpent be fer knowledge. This dagger be given to the Magentheld ruling many ans ago. This be the symbol the Magentheld rules wisely."

"Then since I be the Magentheld, it be my duty to move into the future and bring back the dagger."

"Nay M'Lady. Tis nae be wise."

She smiled. "Yew telling me it nae be wise? How wise be it when yew sent it there. Tell me who be holding the dagger."

Cyran looked at her and could see her resolve. "Her name be Ellen. She be many ans in the future. She be of the lineage of the Magdalene who graced this place in the past. Wexon followed when I moved through the portal. He wreaked havoc to regain the dagger."

"Then it be my duty to bring it back. With Wexon nae longer in the body, I have nae thing to fear."

Cyran knew it best he allow her to go through the portal. He sighed. "M'Lady since yew deem it be yere right as the Magentheld to go, I give yew naow what it be yew must do." He then gave her instructions and also what to expect. He gave her also the frequency of the lady called Ellen.

She thanked him and replied that she would contemplate all he had shared with her.

The rest of the day she spent with Callan revising laws giving women equal protection and freedom. She knew the men to would protest. Callan had already prepared a proclamation and they discussed the timing to announce it to the people.

"M'Lady, I deem it yew desire to fetch the dagger from the future."

"Aye, I do. I be seeking signs fer the right tyming. Naow, I must first be mindful of this war with the Skagerraks. I sense it be nae long."

"Aye, I agree with yew. I 'ave created additions to yere Council."

"Callan, yew be indeed a marvel. I can see yew 'ave a list. The Council be too short of members. We 'ave had two Generals, the Keeper of the Treasury, the Arms Keeper, Trainer of the Guardsmen and the Historian. Naow, tell me what yew 'ave added."

Callan smiled and said, "Fer our talks, I 'ave listed fer the Council members leaders of Schools, Trades, Women issues, Music, Crafts and General of the Realm since Brannon be nae longer here."

Magdalena nodded in agreement. "I deem it to add, healing. There be need to take care of well being of all peoples. Naow tis the challenge to choose who be in charge of each that yew 'ave well researched. I deem it to be wise to 'ave Bertran be the member of the Women's Issues. Her background fits her well."

I agree M'Lady. I deem it to be wise to have General Oris as the Council member and he be in charge of the right flank and the left flank."

Magdalena nodded in agreement. "We do nae need two generals who oppose one another. Oris it will be. Create his duties and under his charge be lesser generals and officers."

Thus began a major change in the realm of Hy Brasil.

THE SKAGERRAK WAR

Mankind must put an end to war before war puts an end to mankind.
~ John F. Kennedy

The battle with the Skagerraks continued with Oris' army pushing them back to the sea. Oris met with his officers to plan a new attack. "It be imperative we push the Skagerrak more to the east and into the ocean." His officers nodded in agreement. "The plan be to polish the shields our men use to where they shine."

One of his officers asked, "What be the purpose of this?"

Oris smiled. "We begin marching towards the east when the sun be in front of us. By shining our shields into their faces, our army slows them down and our attack be forceful. They think they be wise to 'ave the East to their backs.

The officers began smiling. One spoke, "Naow I begin to get it. We blind them with the sun reflectin' onto our shields."

Oris smiled. "We be dazzlin' them and we begin our march at the breakin' of the day. We meet them when the sun be high enough to shine on the shields. I order yew to practice this with our soldiers."

Each morning the men began training and polishing their shields. During the period of training, Oris also ordered the horses to have small polished shields on their foreheads. Oris was pleased with the results and asked the Druid Falco to give him a time best for the march. Falco replied, "I be scanning the potentials fer the best tymes".

Gradually, the army began marching towards the Skagerraks. The leaders of the Skagerraks were at a loss as to where Wexon and his cadre were as they were their spies. It was not known that Wexon and his group had passed this plane.

General Ketil of the Skagerraks had sent his scouts out to see what they could learn. Only one came back and he reported Oris' army be training the troops. He was unable to get too close. Ketil sensed perhaps he should take his troops and fall back towards the east. Little did he realize he would be falling into a trap.. Within a few days he and his men could hear Oris' army. Ketil ordered his men to spread out in a long line and be ready for the battle.

The battle began with the reflection of the sun on the shields of Oris' army moving towards the Skagerrak troops. Oris's army swung their swords, threw their two-edge axes, and gradually pushed the Skagerraks back towards the ocean front. The Skagerrak lost many men and the battlefield was bloody. Finally General Ketil ordered all his men to make for their ships.

Oris watched this from afar and called forth his troops to continue pushing. He ordered the archers to use pitch and set them afire when he could see the ships were beginning to move out. The archers had a long reach and with the firing of arrows some of the ships caught on fire. The mist closed in and no longer could the Skagerraks and their ships to be seen. Oris ordered many of his troops to scout the beach fronts to see if any of the Skagerraks or debris from their ships was washed up on the shores.

Oris told his second-in-command to remain for the week to give the men time to scour the beaches and to rest. He moved through the ranks and spoke of his pride for what they accomplished. The wounded were to be cared for and the few who died, to be carried back for an honorable burial. All were to be accounted for. Oris already knew the Druids had sent messages back to the Magentheld.

With a few of his men, he began his journey back to Magdalena, the Magentheld. He smiled knowing he would be having a private meeting with her.

Magdalena smiled when Callan brought word the Skagerraks had been routed and sent out to sea. In her own way, she already knew of the outcome. Within her there was a trembling of excitement to be in his arms once more.

Magdalena of Hy Brasil

FRANCE

2013

Ancestry and Scota

Character is better than ancestry, and personal conduct is of more importance than the highest. ~
~Thomas John Barnardo

Ellen's mother faxed Ellen the information regarding the Wood family. She sat down to read what her aunt had accumulated and her eyes widened. *Oh my 'gawd!* She thought as she continued reading.

RESEARCH ON THE WOODS FAMILY –
By Tess Woods

In researching our family lineage, I found it difficult to trace our family until I found an old diary in my grandmother's attic. The pages were brittle and old. They had been in an old hand-made box that fit the size of the paper. The faint date written in ink was dated 1830 and signed with the name of Mary Elizabeth. It has been difficult to read as the ink is faded.

Tis with the Grace of God that I write this. My brothers and sisters have all been separated and given to different families. I can no longer hold back what I know about the family. There be seven of us children and each of us given to different families. Tis known by few that our father

Magdalena of Hy Brasil

be Prince Edward Augusts, Duke of Kent. He be a son of King George of England. Mercy be on us. Our mother be Therese Bernadine Julie de Montgenet. They be married in the grand cathedral in Montreal. I was baptized in the cathedral I am told. Some of us were sent to families named Green. One brother and me went to the Rees. I remember one went to the family named Wood. My true father the Duke was sent back to England. Our mother went with him. The children could not go. I learned my father the Duke died in the year of our Lord 1820. Our mother died the year of our Lord 1830.

    I began searching for my brothers and my sisters. I found Robert Wood. We went to Montreal and learned of our baptisms. We been told to tell no one. The crown wants no word that we be the children of the Prince Edward and our mother Julie de Montgenet.

    Given this year 1830
Mary Elizabeth Rees also named Mary Elizabeth daughter of Edward Auustus, House of Hanover.

Ellen sat there stunned. She continued to read the fax sent by her mother who wrote, "I am sure this is a surprise. Whether we are descendents of Prince Edward and Therese Montgenet is only a possibility. I do not know about you; however, I do not want to pursue this. I went on Internet and learned that Prince Edward married a Victoria Mary Louisa of Saxe-Coburg-Saalfeld. Two years before he died. They had one child who later became Queen Victoria. . The rest is old history.

Love, Mother"

Ellen re-read the fax over several times. *I agree with Mother,* she thought. *Oh, wait until I share this with Peter.*

Ellen knew the information her mother sent her was not something she wanted to pursue. Her favorite time for contemplation was a walk in the woods. The fall leaves were changing and she loved the smell of them as they fell.

While she walked, she thought of the possibility of being of the lineage of royalty. She gave a slight chuckle when she contemplated it. *I am happy right where I am and with the man in my life. I have no desire to pursue my lineage. It really isn't important. I am well pleased with my husband, our children, Jill, Sebastian, their children and my brother. Perhaps I will give him the information.* She knew it was time to return to the chateau.

When Peter came home for lunch, he brought her a package that had been brought in the mail. She knew it was a book she had ordered and it could wait. She began sharing what her mother had sent her as a fax.

Peter grinned. "Oh my lovely wife, there is a faint possibility you are descendents of royalty."

They both began laughing. "Well, I did as you said and asked my mother. I feel more at peace now. What I really want to know is about Scota and I think the book I just ordered will give me some clues."

He watched as she opened the carton. "Ah, more of your research. Perhaps I should bring you on board to research my scientific operations."

She laughed. "Oh no because science is your passion and I have my own kind of research." She opened the book titled, *Kingdom of the Ark* with subtitle, *The startling story of how the ancient British race is descended from the Pharaohs by* Author Lorraine Evans. She looked at it and then handed it over to Peter.

"What? You are going to allow me to be the first to open it?" He read the first inside of the cover flap. "Kingdom of the Ark is the tale of a lost princess. A member of the Egyptian royal family and daughter of the 'heretic pharaoh', Akhenaton, and his wife, Nefertiti, Princess Scota fled her homeland, persecuted and friendless and landed on the shores of Britain." He stopped and looked at Ellen. "Is this fiction?"

She laughed. "No. The author is a student of Ancient History and Egyptology. I will share with you what I learn."

"Well my love, I am going back to the office and will leave you your reading." He stood up and pulled her up to him. He touched her chin saying, "You are the greatest thing that has ever happened in my life. Life with you gets better and better." He gave her a long, lingering kiss and left.

Ellen smiled as she watched him leave the room while thinking; *He's the best thing that has happened in my life too.* She was happy that the children were in school and she had a few hours to read the book.

Ellen began reading and some of it she already knew from researching the Internet. *Hmm, Lorraine Evans is quite a researcher,* she thought. *There is a possibility that Scota was another name for Akhenaton's oldest daughter named Meritaten. And, from what I am reading it was later a possibility that she became her father's wife.* Ellen began taking notes as she was reading.

<u>Ellen's Notes:</u>

*Good source of information: Book *Scotichronicon – The Chronicles of Scottish History* – 1435.A.D. written by William Bower, Abbot of Inchcolm Abbey who finished the book begun by John of Fordun. Wrote of an ancient time before the Romans arrived in South Britain.

He must have had some kind of manuscript or information about Scota. Her time was the time of Pharaoh Akhenaton in Egypt. Could this have been information left by the Romans? Or, was it information handed down by the Druids? She began writing down what she was learning.

*Scota was daughter of Akhenaton. She was the first daughter. Mother was Nefertiti.

*Apparently there was an exodus from Egypt possibly by plagues. Akhenaton took much of his people to the East to Canaan.

*Scota aka Meritaten could possibly have become the Pharaoh's wife when mother faded out of history possibly due to death. Scota is said to have married a Greek prince named Gaythelos, Gaythelos or Geytholos could have been from Scythia. She and Gaythelos along with a large contingent of people set sail from Egypt and sailed to the west. From the Bower manuscript, "It is however stated elsewhere that many Egyptians fled in terror far from Egypt and their native land not just in fear of men, but in fear of the gods. Seeing the fearful plagues and portents with which they had been inflicted, they did not dare stay any longer. It is said that some crossed over to Greece."

*Supposedly they arrived at the Ebro River in Iberia (Spain) and it is unknown how long they stayed there. However, they built a community and towers that stand today. Then the group sailed possibly to the Canary Islands as mummified remains were found in a cave there. It also appears they sailed to the Western side of Spain. Next, they sailed on to what could be the southern part of England and then on to what is now called Ireland.

*When in Iberia, Gaythelos or Geythelos's name changed to Mil. Could this have been when her name was changed from Meritaten? But, do not think so because of the name on the dagger.

*According to Evans research, Eusebius alleged that she married a Scythian, a prince of the Gaeis. Gaeis?

*Sometime in Spain/Iberia Scota and Geytholos had children – boys. Possibly girls but not mentioned. Perhaps not all sailed on to what is now called Ireland. This is where the real evidence is. The Irish Book of Leinster, a 11th century manuscript of the Historia Brittionum gives some information. Scota was a Scythian name meaning *ruler of the people*.

*There were at least two sons named Eremon and Eber and later names changed to Eremhon and Emher.

*From the *Annals of the Four Masters*, Evans wrote about Scota and Mils arriving in Ireland. *"Hmm. I think I will go on-line and check out the Annals of the Four Masters.* Ellen found the information she was seeking. *The Annals of the Four Masters* was an electronic text.

The fleet of the sone of Milidh came to Ireland at the end of this year, to take it from the Tuatha De Dananns; and they fought the battle of Sliabh Mis with them on the third day after landing. In this battle fell Scota, the daughter of Pharaoh, wife of Milidh; and the grave of Scota is to be seen between Sliabh Mis and the sea.

Another segment:

This was the year in which Eremhon and Emher assumed the joint sovereignty of Ireland, and divided Ireland into two parts between them. It was in it, moreover, that these acts following were done by Eremhon and Emher, with their chieftains: Rath Beothaigh, over the Eoir Argat Ros, and Rath Oinn in Crich Cualann, were erected by Eremhon. The causeway of Inbher more, in the territory of Ui Eineachglais Cualann, was made by Amergin. The erection of Dun Nair, in Sliabh Modhairn, by Gosten; Dun Deilginnsi, in the territory of Cualann, by Sedgha; Dun Sobhairce, in Murbholg Dal Riada, by Sobhairce; and Dun Edair by Suirghe. By Eremhon and his chieftains these were erected. Rath Uamhain, in Leinster, by Emhear; Rath Arda Suird by Etan, son of Uige; Carraig Fethaighe by Un, son of Uige;

A dispute arose at the end of this year, between Eremhon and Emhear, about the three celebrated hills, Druim Clasaigh, in Crich Maine; Druim Beathaigh, in Maenmhagh; and Druim Finghin, in Munster. In consequence of which a battle was fought between them, on the brink of Bri Damh, at Tochar Eter Da Mhagh; and this is called the battle of Geisill. The battle was gained upon Emhear, and he fell therein. There fell also three distinguished chieftains of the people of Eremhon in the same battle; Goisten, Setgha, and Suirghe, were their names. After this Eremhon assumed the sovereignty.

The first year of the reign of Eremhon over Ireland; and the second year after the arrival of the sons of Milidh, Eremhon divided Ireland. He gave the province of Ulster to Emhear, son of Ir; Munster to the four sons of Emhear Finn; the province of Connaught to Un and Eadan; and the province of Leinster to Crimhthann Sciathbhel of the Damnonians.

Ellen sat back and thought about what she had read. *According to this Irish account, Scota had been real and she was buried in Ireland. Surely she must have had a part greater than what is given here. When did members of her 'tribe' go to Scotland? They must have been powerful. Why was Scotland given its name from Scota? She must have been truly loved to be remembered.*

Ellen continued to go through the lengthy *Annals* and was unable to find what Evans wrote in her book, where she states that in the *Annals* that forty-eight couples with servants arrived in Ireland from northern Spain.

She continued reading and learned that in England ancient Egyptian beads and boats had been excavated and some were now in museums. *So, Egyptians were in England also. I would think that they were traders and were not totally confined to the Mediterranean area. But how did her dagger come to me? What connection do we have?* She sighed and shut down her computer and the book. She knew that a walk in the forest would help her think.

As she walking in the forest, she felt a peace and serenity within her. She felt like they were caressing her. She stopped a moment because she had a vision that the woman who had come to her in her dreams would arrive here in the forest. She felt a tingling in her body and the thought came that no harm would come from her. Whoever the woman was, she felt a tremendous feeling of love.

That evening Peter and Ellen walked over to have dinner with Jill and Sebastian. Peter had suggested that she take the book and let Jill read it. "I will read it later. In the meantime I will use your information."

"Well, that is generous and Jill can translate it for Sebastian. It may or may not help him in his translations."

"I agree my beautiful wife. Let's stop and take a look at the moon. It appears to be a harvest moon."

They paused and looked at it. "Peter, perhaps in some way we are getting to the end of this. I walked in the forest and had a vision of the woman in my dream. Perhaps the dagger belongs to her."

He nodded his head in agreement. "Do you think she will come in person from ancient times?"

Ellen laughed. "Oh gawd! Now that would be an exceptional meeting."

ΩΩΩ

Dinner with Alain

The closing of a door can bring blessed privacy and comfort - the opening, terror. Conversely, the closing of a door can be a sad and final thing - the opening a wonderfully joyous moment. ~ Andy Rooney

The week after their dinner with Jill and Sebastian, who were delighted with the book she had given them to read, Ellen received a phone call from Alain asking that she and Peter have dinner with him and Louise at his apartment the following evening. She asked him if this was for pleasure or did he have something to share. He laughed and told her that it would be a splendid dinner and evening.

Ellen mulled this over in her mind. Somehow she felt something brewing in the wind as her grandmother use to say. She and Peter had almost no social life and it was their choice after what they had experienced with the Magdalene Scrolls followed by the Sarah Scrolls. There were times when they had occasions to be social with Peter's employees and his clients. She loved her cocoon as she labeled it. She thought about it and realized that at the present time she wanted to spin her own thread of laughter and joy with the children, Peter, Jill and Sebastian. She never felt isolated.

Ellen had chosen to wear one of her finer dresses and Peter whistled when he viewed her with her hair styled, wearing jewelry and a gorgeous dress. "I think I will take you out more often. You do look delicious and I am always amazed at how fortunate I am to have you."

"Well, my handsome prince I see you have dressed up too. We do make a fine couple. I checked with the children and they are happy to be entertained with *Alice in Wonderland.* Yvonne will see that they are bathed and put to bed."

While they were driving into Paris, Ellen's memories of when she first met Alain and learned that he was actually her half-brother, came to her. "Peter, memories of when we first came to Alain's penthouse have me chuckling over how we managed in Paris. In retrospect it was a great time."

He smiled. "Oh yes, I remember well those days. I remember the shock after you had gone into another room in his office suite and returned with a shocked look on your face. I was beginning to get riled up and hit him if he had molested you."

Ellen let out a whoop of laughter. "I was in shock when he told me my mother had an affair with his father when she lived in Paris and he was the result of their amorous affair."

"I appreciate all that he has done for us. I consider him the brother I never had."

The traffic was light for the evening. They arrived at the building where Alain had his law offices and his penthouse. Actually, he owned the entire building. The garage attendant recognized them and allowed them to drive in. Ellen noticed that Louise had already arrived as her limousine was there with the chauffeur waiting in the garage. There were two elevators, one available to all floors except for the penthouse. This was a separate elevator and apparently the attendant had already notified that they had arrived. The elevator was open and they stepped in and swiftly rose up to the penthouse. When the door open, Alain's long-time butler/valet and chef was there to greet us. He told them that *M.* Alain and *Mme.* Louise were in the salon.

Ellen noticed there were some changes in the salon; however, Alain favorite colors of blue and silver were kept. After the warm greetings were over, Alain suggested they have some hor d'ouvres and champagne as this was an evening to celebrate. Ellen asked, "And what are we toasting to if we are celebrating?"

Alain smiled. "My sister, good news and I will give Louse the honor to share what has occurred."

Louise smiled and I give a toast. "To honor those who were murdered and kidnapped! It is completed. *Salut!*"

Ellen and Peter lifted their glasses and Ellen almost had tears in her eyes. "You mean that the murderers have been apprehended for the deaths of Cerise and *Mme.* Gillet?"

Alain stood back and smiled while Louise continued. "*Oui.* There were three men of Egyptian heritage. Two are now in custody and the third one is the one who died in the Seine River. There have been rumors of these men seeking an ancient dagger for an odd man who spoke in an odd language. We have no idea who the man is or where he came from."

Peter said, "At least the deaths of Cerise and Mme. Gillet are avenged as well as the kidnapping of Sebastian."

Louise nodded in agreement. "As you know, I am always willing to avenge those who are harmed by others. Alain tells me that you have discovered a name on the dagger."

Ellen replied, "I am most grateful and I still do not know why the dagger came to me. I have researched the name Scota and without many details, I have learned that Scota was a daughter of a Pharaoh, in fact the Pharaoh Akhenaton."

"Really?" Louise interposed.

"Yes. During the plagues that happened during the time of Akhenaton, he left or disappeared and the daughter Meritaten whose name became Scota married a prince of Greece or Scythia and together with a fleet of ships went first to Spain and over the years made their way to Ireland. Soon after they reached Ireland, they were in a battle and she was killed. She is buried there now."

Both Louise and Alain were shocked. Alain spoke, "This is astounding! What are you going to do with the dagger now?"

Ellen smiled. "At the moment I do not have a clue. I have an idea that the owner of it will make contact with me. How? I do not know."

Alain nodded. "I have a sense that it will be a surprise visit similar to the one when you received the Sarah scrolls."

They all laughed at his statement. Louise shook her head. "This mystery is one of the most interesting events I have ever been a part of. Let us have another toast, "To the rightful owner of the Scota dagger."

After the toast, Ellen spoke. "I sincerely hope the owner comes soon. There are other options I want to do."

Alain smiled. "Such as?"

"Perhaps write a book."

Peter reached over and touched her hand. "I think I have a title."

She looked at him, "And, what is it?"

"The Game of Life and How to Live It."

ΩΩΩ

HY BRASIL

400 A. D.

A SECOND ENCOUNTER

I don't believe in accidents. There are only encounters in history. There are no accidents.
~ Pablo Picasso

When Magdalena woke up, she went to her window and to do her morning greetings. It came to her that she would have an encounter with one of the Star People and it would be at the place where she went to contemplate. At this moment, Mireen knocked on the door and Magdalena bade her to enter.

"G'day M'Lady. Tis a grand morn."

Magdalena smiled. "Indeed it tis."

Mireen busied herself placing the breakfast on the small table and then began tidying the bed.

Magdalena began eating her breakfast and sent a mental message to Callan to cancel the appointments for the morning. She then asked Mireen to bring her riding clothes as she felt like being alone so she could ponder.

Once she was on her horse and cantering out of the Garenfeld, she gave her horse its rein. When she arrived at the small glen in the forest, she went to her place where she often sat and contemplated. It was not too long before one of the Star people stood in front of her. She stood up bowing and it was returned to her. The person spoke to her through its mind. She felt it might have been a woman.

"Greetings, Gracious Queen. Grace be unto thee. I come with tidings of yere kingdom be cleansed of the vermin who desired to take over this kingdom and bring it down. The Game be ended. Yere newest strategy to bring forth new groups using talents be most pleasing. As these groups become more pliable in what they be creating, they be receiving in their minds thoughts and ideas to expand their creations."

Magdalena nodded and asked, "Please tell me about the dagger of Scota taken to the future?"

There was a pause as if the Star Being was contemplating this. "Thy dagger be safe at the present. Lord Cyran made a wise choice. From another land named Erin, came a group of beings forced from their land. These beings be called the Tuatha De Dannan. A daughter of an Aigyptos Pharaoh set sail with a large fleet of ships and her people to find a land to be theirs. This great woman knew there be many plagues. She be wanting to take her peoples to safety.

"She and her husbandment bore children. She be given a title named Scota. She be a grand lady. Arriving after some ans to Erin, a great battle between her people and the Tuatha De Dannan fer the land brought forth her death. The Tuatha De Dannan took her dagger as their prize together with some of her women and men left Erin. Scota's warriors be too strong fer the Tuatha. They be led here to Hy Brasil where my people began teaching them. Yew be of this lineage as well as other great beings."

"Will yew tell me more of my lineage?'

The Star Being again contemplated and then began speaking into Magdalena's mind. "Yere bloodline comes from a great line. From the land of

Aigyptos and the land of Aethiopia[6] yew be of great royalty passed down from woman to woman. Yere mother Golornia passed the seed of greatness on to yew."

Before she could say anything, the Star One was gone. She sat down to contemplate what she heard. She knew there was more to this about her bloodline. She stood up and knew with determination she needed a talk with Lord Cyran. In her contemplation she remembered living on the mountain with the Druidesses and began remembering the times she was able to see above the mists and view the great sea. Sometimes it was blue and other gray. There were also the times when she could watch the Star Boats leaving with mists around them. She also remembered when the winds began blowing strong off the seas. She remembered inhaling the beautiful smells. She smiled and thought, *Aye, I miss the mountain and seeing far past Hy Brasil.* She sighed and stood up.

She whistled and her horse came to her. There was much churning in her head. She was looking forward to the return of Oris soon and also enlarging the Council with new people who would be eager to expand their knowledge for others to know. She already had given Callan the message to organize the Council with new members.

Soon she would be at the Garenfeld and as she rode in, she would be saluted. The stable boy was there

---

[6] Egypt and Ethiopia

waiting for her and she thanked him by giving him a small coin. "M' Lady Queen, I thank yew."

She smiled at him and went to her quarters where she changed clothes. Mireen was there and offered her a cup of tea she kept warm, and which she drank. With her mind, she asked Cyran to meet her in the garden.

He was waiting there when she arrived. "Greetings M' Lady. I deem it be possible yew met with a Star being."

She laughed. "Lord Cyran yew be indeed a reader of the mind. I be asking yew to meet here as I want to know more about my bloodline. Yew 'ave a deep wealth of knowing."

He sat there with his eyes closed. Magdalena observed him knowing he was going back in time. He began speaking. "Yew be of a long lineage of great beings who ruled the lands of Aigyptos and the land of Aethiopia many ans in the past. There be great schools of learning to expand the mind and to know the god within. There be two great beings of these schools. They be sent to land of Canaan to teach peoples. These two mated. They 'ave a son and a daughter. The husbandment went into the multitude to give great teachings. Tis said he be hung on a cross and lived to go elsewhere. The mother called the Magdalene, in the dark of the night takes her children to Aigyptos."

"From Aigyptos, the Magdalene sails with her children and close kin to the land naow called Gaul. The boy be sent with the father of her husbandment to Brittionum. The Magdalene be a great teacher and she takes her daughter Sarah with her to teach in all of Gaul. She also sailed to Brittionum and Erin to teach. The daughter Sarah be a teacher and spawns one son. He be a Druid. She spawns three daughters. Yew be of this bloodline through yere mother."

Cyran stopped and opened his eyes and waited for Magdalena to speak.

She sat quietly to contemplate the information he spoke. "I thank yew Lord Cyran. I spoke with a Star person and be told of Scota from Aigyptos. Be my bloodline also the bloodline of Scota?"

"Aye. Scota perish in war in Erin. Women of her bloodline be captured by the Tuatha and the beings departed Erin and came to Hy Brasil with help of the Star boat peoples. The bloodline continues in yew."

"I be naow almost ready to move through to portal to retrieve Scota's dagger. 'Ere I do, I 'ave threads of the future to weave into a secure Hy Brasil."

"'Tis well you 'ave this to do. The portal be ready when yew speak."

While Magdalena was walking to her quarters, she had a vision of Oris being on his way back. Her heart leaped with joy and she quickened her step. She met Callan who was walking to Magdalena's quarters and asked if there would be a moment for her to speak. They went into the room where Magdalena officiated. "Naow Callan, yew be filled with joy it appears."

"Aye M'Lady. I 'ave here names of both women and men to be the heads of the guilds being created. There be a guild fer women's status; one fer ironworks; one fer music; one fer spinning; one fer sheep; one fer cattle; one fer glassmaking; one fer pottery; one fer writing; one fer schooling. I suggest each to travel throughout the realm selecting from many villages and those livin' outside to begin their own guild. There also be a merchant's guild fer each village.

Magdalena smiled. "Yew 'ave indeed be astute in yere search. I suggest yew 'ave a guild fer the birthin' women and one for medicines. To be on the Council, each head of a guild will meet with me in a fortnight. This be a test as to their abilities to be observant and a plan fer the future."

"M'Lady, perhaps we include Druids and Druidesses as teachers."

"Aye, this pleases me. Yew know I depend greatly on yere resources. I bless and thank yew fer being here."

Callan smiled. "Tis a joy. I be naow to secure Regan to be here iffen it pleases yew."

"Do call forth Regan to assist yew. She be welcomed. I ask a room be given to her."

Callan stood up and bowed. "It be done straight away."

This evening Magdalene chose to dine in her quarters. There was a knowingness that Oris was near and it would not be long until he came through the secret passage. Her loins ached fer him. After Mireen cleared the foodstuffs away, she bathed and dressed in her night cloth. With a sigh she went to the window and noted the clouds scudding across the sky. At times the moon peaked through. With her acute hearing, she listened to the night birds and then she turned. The secret door opened and there be Oris. With a gasp, she and he met in the center of the room and kissed. He began kissed her face, her neck saying "I 'ave missed yew. I want to take yew to bed."

She laughed joyously. "I 'ave also missed yew. Aye, take me to bed."

Their lovemaking was long. She felt every part of her body quiver when he kissed it. He mounted her and slowly enters her. He did not rush. He moved his member in deeper and she wrapped her legs around him. He allowed her to first come to her fulfillment and then he continued and completed his fulfillment.

They slept for a short while and then mated again and again. Early dawn began breaking and she awakened. She looked at him and noticed a small scar on his chin. She felt every part of her body vibrating from their lovemaking. She went into the room for bathing and cleansed herself. When she came out he was out of the bed and kissed her. "M'Lady, I give unto thee my love, my treasure."

Looking into his eyes, she knew he was telling truth. "Oris yew already knows my love fer yew and I ask yew to be my husbandment."

Oris looked surprised and stepped back. "M' Lady! I, I had hoped to marry thee. I knew nae to approach yew."

She nodded, "It be my choice to wed thee and to 'ave yere children. I want yew to be at my side and to counsel me in my reign as Magentheld of this realm."

He took her hand kissing it and then kissed her. "I, I 'ave a fear in me I nae be good enough fer yew."

She placed her fingers on his lips. "I want nae other than yew as my husbandment."

"Aye, M'Lady Magdalena. I accept. I returned to yew to give yew my report. I return to my armies in three days tyme."

She nodded in agreement. "I care nae what be thought of yew here in my quarters. I be the Magentheld and there be nae more secrets."

He smiled and kissed her again. "Tis done."

Magdalena walked over to a long round pipe-like object and she spoke into it. She told Mireen to bring breakfast for two as General Oris was having breakfast with her. He looked surprised and asked what the object be. She told him of some years ago the Star beings shared information and this object be named a calling tube be given long ago to a Magentheld.

Oris shook his head in amazement. Magdalena put a long robe on and walked to the window. She turned, asking him to come to the window. There be an early morning rain and naow there be a rainbow. He turned to her, "M'Lady, this be an omen our union be blessed. He bent over to kiss her when Mireen knocked on the door.

"Come," Magdalena called.

Mireen came in and smiled when she saw Oris here. She quickly set the tray of food on the small table. Magdalena smiled and spoke to her. "Mireen, this be in confidence. General Oris to be here often. He be my betrothed."

Mireen place her hands on her mouth and her eyes became large. "Oh, M'Lady, I be, well I be most pleased."

Magdalena told her this was sacred information to be shared with no one. Mireen nodded and gave a giggle. "I nae speak of this to others. I be yere trusted servant." She curtsied and left the room.

Oris and Magdalena began laughing. "Nae, know she be quiet until I tell her to let the news go out. I deem it be announced soon of our betrothal."

He smiled and nodded in agreement. "I, I be filled with happiness."

The two sat down at the small table and began eating their morning meal. Oris looked at her and she knew he 'had questions.

"Me beloved, yew be wondering what position yew be taking with me as the Magentheld. I 'ave thought beyond our marriage."

He stopped eating and looked into her eyes. "This be the tyme to hear yere words."

"I, as the Magentheld deem yew to be the Lord and General of the realm of Hy Brasil. I be sharing with yew my decisions; my choices. I be listening to yere responses. Yew be nae lesser than me as my mate. There be tymes when we be at odds. We discuss. We share. We come to a joint decision."

He smiled. "I deem it be we parlay and meet with fair and just decisions."

"Yew be correct. I 'ave contemplated this and yew be a strong man. It nae be I want a weak man. This be why I love yew."

He nodded. "Me mind quivers when I think of yew. Me thinks I want to couple with yew again." All thoughts of completing the meal disappeared and he led her to the bed where again, they coupled.

🏛🏛🏛

THE ANNOUNCEMENT

Therefore shall a man leave his father and mother, and shall cleave unto his wife: and they shall be one flesh. ~ Author Unknown

The three days Magdalena and Oris were together passed swiftly before he left to be with his army. They agreed there would be an immediate announcement of their betrothal with messengers sent to Oris's mother, sisters, brothers and the Druidess and Druid communes. A royal decree was to be sent to all the villages in the realm with the wedding to take place within two months. Lord Cyran and Lady Alinor were to officiate the marriage.

The word spread quickly and there was much talk with some wondering if General Oris was to be the new Magentheld and others claiming Queen Magdalena to be the Magentheld. Oris' officers and men cheered when they heard of the betrothal. He grinned and invited them to attend the wedding with a select few guarding the beaches so there would be no invasions.

Immediately festivities were being formatted. Magdalena and Oris chose to have the wedding in the large open space behind the Garenfeld. They agreed the Great Hall for the lords and ladies was not the place to marry. They desired to be with the people.

Lady Elinor arrived to assist in the festivities and brought with her a large group of Druidesses to assist the already overwhelmed servants, Callan and Regan were in charge of the festivities by Magdalena's

Decree. The auspices of the chosen day were chosen by Cyran so there would be clear weather.

Lady Elinor helped Magdalena to choose a dress her mother had worn to many festivities. The dresses were kept in a special room where Mireen made sure they were kept clean. Magdalena looked at the numerous dresses and when she spied the light purple dress, she knew this to be the dress. The sleeves came to the elbow with gold lace attached almost to the wrists. The front of the neck had an insert of the gold lace and around the neck a narrow band of the gold lace with pearls sewn on it. The skirt was bouffant. There would be no veil.

Magdalena chose her crown to wear and a king's crown for Oris. It was a decision for Oris to be with his army for one month. He was to return the month before the wedding. There was much to contemplate and she worried. She knew she must go to the future and bring back Scota's dagger. This had nagged at her mind for a long time. She knew this to be the time to go into the future. She called Callan and Lord Cyran to come to her chambers.

The two arrived within minutes to the sitting room where Magdalena now received her staff and others. She no longer chose to have her bed quarters open to others. This was only hers and Oris' with Mireen taking care of its cleaning and bringing meals upon request.

She spoke. "I 'ave seen me future and I deem it to be the tyme fer me to go and bring back Scota's dagger. Nae longer be I to wait. Lord Cyran, I command yew to teach me where I be to go and what I be aware of."

Cyran cleared his throat. "Aye, I 'ave known yew must go. I naow tell yew what yew can expect. It nae take long to leave this portal and come to the portal where a lovely woman lives and be holding yere Scota's dagger." He turned to Callan. Lady Druidess, I charge yew to remember what I be tellin'. She nodded her agreement and he continued.

"Yew be comin' into a forest on her land. Her name be Ellen and she be of yere bloodline. There be much disturbance when Wexon followed me through the portal. He hid deep. He found men of Aegyptus and with coinage paid them to find Scota's dagger. There be trouble with the men he paid. There be murder. There be injury. See Ellen as yew be. Yew both be alike. Fear nae trouble. Blessings be upon yew. He turned to Callan. We two be here fer her."

Callan nodded she agreed.

Magdalena spent the evening focusing on the coordinates Cyran told her to use. Early in the morning she met with Cyran and Callan. The three began walking to the area of the portal shielded by a copse of laurel not too far from the Garenfeld. Cyran stopped and pointed to the energy field of the portal. She nodded and walked to the portal. Within moments she was gone. Callan brought her hand up to her mouth while choking back her fears and tears.

Cyran spoke to her. "Lady Callan, we must be wise and nae fearful. Tis her journey."

⛩⛩⛩

Magdalena of Hy Brasil

~ FRANCE ~
2013

Scota's Dagger

The light at the end of the tunnel. ~ Anonymous

When Ellen woke up, she felt lightness within her. She stretched and smiled. She could hear Peter singing in the shower. She knew she was blessed and she began giving thanks for everyone in her life and the abundance she had. She got up and went to the window and looked out seeing a beautiful late fall day. Perhaps there had been a frost. Halloween was only a few days away and the children were clamoring for their costumes, which were almost done.

When Peter came out of the shower, he walked into the bedroom naked. She smiled. "Well, Big Guy, you are indeed a sight for sore eyes. If you didn't have an early morning appointment, I would take you back to bed."

He walked over to her and looked down. "Well, my beloved it just might happen and even though I am having an erection, I will postpone this until tonight." He bent down and kissed her.

At that moment, Joseph knocked on the door. "Eleanor has taken my mask and won't give it back to me."

Peter shook his head. "You deal with it. I think it is time for me to get dressed."

Ellen opened the door and stepped outside into the hall. Eleanor was running up and down the stairs with Joseph's Halloween mask. She told her daughter to give the mask back to Joseph. "You know better than to tease like that. Perhaps you are looking for a time-out."

Eleanor shook her head no and walked over to Joseph and dropped the mask on the floor. Ellen looked at her and told her, "There will be no story today. You are to stay in your room and I am telling Yvonne to have you practice your letters and numbers. Young lady, there will be no more of this."

Eleanor's eyes welled up in tears. Ellen told Joseph to get his school backpack and be ready to be picked up for school. She turned back to Eleanor and told her that teasing was not to be tolerated in this household. Eleanor turned away and went into her room.

Ellen walked down the stairs to the breakfast room. Marie already had fed the children and Peter. She smiled at Ellen. "Mlle. Eleanor in trouble?"

Ellen laughed. "Not really. She loves to irritate her brother and her sister and hopefully she will grow out of it."

Marie went back to the kitchen and Ellen drank her coffee along with a croissant and scrambled eggs. She sighed. *I think I will take a long walk in the forest this morning.* She went into the kitchen and told Marie where she was going and went outside.

The air was brisk and more leaves were falling. She loved the crispness of the morning and as she walked, she stopped from time to time to listen to the birds and to scuffle leaves with her feet. A flight of geese were flying overhead and it was a reminder to later go to the lake and feed the birds. She came to a bend in the path and came face-to-face with a woman who looked familiar.

"Who, who are you? What are you doing here and how did you get here?"

Magdalena stopped and looked at Ellen. "Me be Magdalena the Magentheld of Hy Brasil. I come fer me dagger."

"How do you know I have your dagger?"

Magdalena looked straight into her eyes, seeing a sense of reflection of her. "High Druid Lord Cyran brought it through the portal fer safe keeping. He say it be yew."

Ellen felt weak in the knees. She managed to say that the two of them should sit on a bench near them and talk. She noted Magdalena had beautiful red hair now in one long braid and her eyes were green. Her skin had a darkness to it. Something similar to the color of a dark tan.

Magdalena nodded. Within her, she felt no fear. In her being, she knew this woman could be her in the future. She observed Ellen's features. Although her hair was not the color of hers, it was dark brown with a red shine to it. Her eyes were blue and when she looked into them, she was seeing Golornia.

Ellen spoke first. "I am happy to meet you Magdalena. Yes, I have Scota's dagger and it is well hidden. First, please tell me why some people were killed for this dagger."

Magdalena looked deeply into Ellen's eyes and knew she was a great being. She began to tell the story of the dagger brought by Cyran and Wexon following him through the portal. "It be Wexon paid Aegyptus to find dagger. The dagger of Scota be a symbol fer a Magentheld to hold the country together. I be the first woman Magentheld. Wexon wanted to be the Magentheld. He be an outcast Druid. He chose a path of destruction."

"Magdalena, I, I found evidence of Scota in Erin and she is buried there. Tell me how the dagger came to Hy Brasil, and where is Hy Brasil?"

"M'Lady, her peoples brought it when she passed. These be the Tuatha. These beings bring women belonging to Scota's people."

"Will Wexon follow you to this place?"

"Nay. He be dead."

Ellen then proceeded to tell the story of how the dagger came in her possession and the murders and the abduction of Sebastian.

Magdalena reached over and touched Ellen's hand. "M'Lady, this be sad fer me." Ellen placed her other hand over Magdalena's.

"Please walk with me to my home and I will give you the dagger. It belongs to you"

Magdalena was intrigued with the trees, the lake and the grounds once they were out of the woods. She smiled when they came into view of the chateau. "This be yere home. I feel warmth."

Ellen looked at her and smiled. She took Magdalena through the front door and into her office. Magdalena was in awe of what her eyes were seeing. She watched Ellen spin some round things moving them back and forth. Her eyes widened when she saw it open and Ellen bringing out the box holding the dagger.

Ellen handed the dagger to her and there were tears in her eyes. "I am happy to return this to you. I ask that you tell me where Hy Brasil is."

Magdalena's eyes glistened. "Yew be a great woman. Be I honored to know yew. Hy Brasil be a place in a big body of water. It be on the west side of what yew named Erin. We 'ave mists be around our land. We 'ave mountains. When I be a young girl, I be sent to the Druidesses fer learning. At tymes, I be seeing over the mists. I tell yew this. I be wedded to my love when I go back through the portal. Naow I be leavin' and go back into the portal. Naow I can be wed to my General Oris."

      The two women walked to the portal where Magdalena had entered in the forest. They stood there and looked deeply into each other's eyes. Tears were in their eyes. After an embrace, Magdalena stepped into the portal and in the blink of an eye was gone. Ellen turned and went to the bench and sat down while she cried. She was crying for joy and for relief.

$$\Omega\Omega\Omega$$

All's Well That Ends Well

Whate'er the course, the end is the renown ~
Shakespeare

After Magdalena departed, Ellen sat in her office contemplating the exchange of information. *I must write this down before I forget. Oh I wish Peter were here, but he is having that conference of engineers today.* With a sigh, she began writing notes of her encounter and just as she finished, Peter knocked on the door and entered.

Ellen jumped up and went into his arms. This tall man bent down and kissed the top of her head. "What is this all about? Somehow, I think you know something I do not."

She stood back while still in his arms and looked up, "Peter, I have had the most marvelous adventure today. I have so much to tell you."

"First, I need a kiss from you before we talk." The kiss was indeed a long one. "Now, let's sit down and you tell me about your grand adventure."

Ellen began telling him of her walk in the forest and the woman who appeared seemingly out of nowhere. "She, she was the woman I have seen in my dreams beginning when she was a little girl."

Peter looked perplexed. "How did she get here?"

"She said through a portal from a place in the past. She called it Hy Brasil." Before Peter could reply, she continued. "I went on-line and looked up the name and there are a few sites that have given information. Apparently this is an island to the west of Ireland; however, some label it as a myth because it is surrounded by mists."

Peter shook his head in amazement. "Before you continue, Sebastian and Jill need to know about this."

"I have already invited them here for dinner. And, for your information I gave her the dagger. It belongs to her."

"Thank god! What are we going to do about the portal?"

"She said it would be closed when she arrives back to her time."

That evening after dinner and the children had been sent to bed, Jill, Sebastian, Peter and Ellen went to the family room to talk and have an after dinner coffee. The weather had turned cold so a fire was blazing in the fireplace. Jill was the first to speak. "Somehow I think you have something to tell us. I have known you long enough to know something new is going on. Care to tell us?"

Ellen began laughing. "I have long known I cannot keep a secret from you. This is about Scota's dagger."

Sebastian perked up. "You have new information?"

She nodded. "Yes, I do and it is wonderful. I have already shared this with Peter and it is only fair that I share it with you." Ellen began.

"This afternoon I went for a walk in the forest and as I came to the bend of the path, a woman was standing there."

Jill put her hand over her mouth and then sputtered, "You don't mean that some woman came and brought you another surprise!"

They all laughed. Ellen went on. "We looked at each other. Actually she is beautiful. I have had several dreams about her and I think I have already told of this. She asked if my name is Ellen and I said yes. She said that she had come for Scota's dagger. I asked who she was and how she came to be in the forest. She told me she had come through a portal and that her name is Magdalena and she is the Magentheld of a place called Hy Brasil." She paused to let this sink in.

Sebastian asked, "What is meant by portal?"

"I looked this up and a portal is a vortex of energy and is at times called a time warp meaning a distortion in time. Through a portal, from my perspective means that someone from another age or time can find a portal or a vortex of energy and move from one era to another and this is what Magdalena found."

Jill asked, "Is this how the Sarah documents were brought here? As I recall, it was an other-worldly man that appeared to you in the forest with a portmanteau filled with documents."

Ellen nodded. "Yes, I believe it is so. I had no idea there could be a vortex of energy in the forest."

Peter had already heard Ellen tell of her encounter and he was sitting back and enjoying the re-telling of it.

Ellen continued. "The country of Hy Brasil is historically a mystery island off the coast of western Ireland. As I remember, she told me it is in a large body of water and to the west of Erin as she called Ireland. She spoke in olde English. She is beautiful with long red hair that was braided as one braid. Her eyes are green and her skin is dark tan. She was dressed in what I would call a medieval pair of tight pants and a top something like a man's suit of those times. The color was a dark blue with gold trim.. She wore what I would call suede boots up to the mid-calf."

Sebastian asked, "How did the dagger come here?"

"According to Magdalena, the High Druid Cyran had scanned timelines and discovered a bloodline in this timeline and it happens to be me. He is the one who came through the portal and managed in some way to make it a parcel and have it sent to me."

Jill said, "Now we know how it got here. But why was someone trying to steal it and kidnapped Sebastian?"

"According to Magdalena, a renegade Druid with a name something like Wesson, found the portal and followed the High Druid. In some way, he managed to hire some men and it sounds like they were Egyptian. She told me that the renegade Druid was now dead. So, we do not have to worry about him!"

Jill almost shouted "Thank god!"

"One thing I have not told is that she is the Queen or as she called it Magentheld of Hy Brasil and that many years ago, the Tuatha were forced to leave Erin or Ireland and took with them some of the women from Scota's people. Along with the women, the Tuatha carried Scota's dagger and it is to signify that the ruler of Hy Brasil is of the lineage of Scota and entitled to be the Magentheld, or king – or queen."

Sebastian asked, "I will have to contemplate what is called time jumping. There is much I have to contemplate,. Druids, a queen, moving from one time to a future time."

Jill nodded in agreement. "It makes sense in a way. I will have to adjust my thinking about a queen from the ancient past coming through a portal to retrieve her dagger."

Ellen laughed. "I have been thinking of something I can do now that the dagger is no longer in my care. In one way it moved us out of complacency, or at least my complacency.

Peter reached for her hand. "Oh, I think we can find something exciting to help you."

Ellen looked at him. "No Peter. No more children. Three is enough"

Jill looked at her. "Why don't you write a book about this? You love to do research and perhaps it will be fiction."

They all began laughing. Sebastian spoke once the laughter was over. "I do not care that I was kidnapped now that I am recovered. I think it will be pleasant to have a normal life."

Jill looked at him. "I will say one thing, life has been a roller coaster since the four of us met and married." She sighed. "I would have loved to have seen her."

Ellen replied, "She reminded me of my mother when she was younger."

Sebastian stood up. "This has been a beautiful ending. Now my beautiful Jill, it is time to depart. I sense there are greater things coming our way.

$$\Omega\Omega\Omega$$

HY BRASIL
400 A.D.

THE RETURN OF THE DAGGER

A good action is never lost; it is a treasure laid up and guarded for the doer's need.
~ Edwin Markham

When Magdalena returned to Hy Brasil, it was early evening. Waiting near the portal were Cyran and Callan. She moved quickly to the two and by the aura around her, they knew she brought the dagger back with her. Cyran and Callan bowed to her.

Cyran spoke first, "M 'Lady Magentheld, yew indeed 'ave expanded yere reaches on behalf of Hy Brasil. I welcome yew."

Callan smiled."Aye ,yew 'ave indeed accomplished much. I bid to hear how yew accomplished this feat."

Magdalena's aura sparkled and she smiled. "I bid the two of yew welcome. Aye, I return with the dagger. I be indeed the true Magentheld. Let us move to my quarters where I be tellin' yew me journey."

Once the three were in Magdalena's receiving room, she asked Mireen to bring wine, bread, cheese and meat. She did not say much until the meal was brought and Mireen left. "I be surprised how quickly I be leavin' Hy Brasil and within moments be I in the future. It be so different. The energy be faster. I be in a forest as Lord Cyran told me. It be soon the woman named Ellen be walking and we met to our surprise."

"She reminded me of Golornia and I be wondering. We talked and aye, she agreed to return Scota's dagger. We walked to her home and it be beautiful. The dagger be in a closet and I watched as she turned something round one way and then back to another way to open a small door. She naow tell me I be in a place, a country named France. This woman named Ellen tell me in ancient tyme it be called Gaul.

"I tell her about Wexon following Lord Cyran. Wexon be a craven Druid. Ellen say to me Wexon gave monies to men to kidnap her friend. These men killed two men and two females thinkin' they be getting the dagger.

Cyran had a drawn look on his face. "Tis I who created all these deeds. I ask yere forgiveness M 'Lady."

Magdalena looked at him with compassion. "I hold naught against yew. Yew did what yew deemed to be in the interests of Hy Brasil. Iffen Wexon had nae discovered yere portal, the killings of those people in the future be never happening. Perhaps it meant to be. Let us nae be sorrowful. The deed be done. We naow rejoice fer the wedding.

Callan had sat listening to all that be said. Her eyes glistened with unshed tears. She was happy Magdalena was back. "M'Lady, naow yew returned, tomorrow be a day of planning. Let there be no sadness. Lord Cyran iffen yew had nae done what you did; it could 'ave ended in a far worse way."

Then they laughed. Magdalena held the dagger of Scota for them to see. "I be wearin' this at me wedding."

Cyran sat back to allow Callan to give the latest news. "M'Lady, yew be gone fer such a short tyme. The wedding plans be the same as when yew departed to the future

He nodded and bowed his head to Magdalena. "I thank yew M'Lady Magentheld and naow I be off and leave yew to yere rest."

After Cyran departed, Callan said she also be leaving to tend to matters concerning the wedding. "M 'Lady, yew be gone fer a short tyme. I be amazed."

Magdalena laughed. "Callan, it be liken I go through a door and poof! I be there. My mind be at rest with Scota's dagger naow be here. I be pondering this manner of traveling. Naow, what be happening with the wedding?"

The following morning, Magdalena had an urge to visit the river where she arrived when she came to the Garenfeld. She told Callan where she was going' and once her horse was saddled, she felt a sense of freedom. On her way she observed the houses, the barns, fields of plenty along with cattle and sheep. She was not dressed as the Magentheld and no one took notice of her.

She arrived at the place where the boat had come to shore. She alighted from her horse and tethered her to a nearby tree. There was a large rock and she went to sit upon it and allowing the peace and the flow of the river to surround her, Ah, a fish jumped up out of the water and then went back in. She smiled and thought it was welcoming her. Her thoughts touched on her journey to the Druidesses, and she chose not to dwell on it. Today was the present day. Her thoughts spread to the realm of Hy Brasil and she realized she had never been to the coasts where the mists were thick surrounding Hy Brasil. She remembered only at times when she would be in the meadows and seeing large waters above the mists. Now she wanted more.

She reached down and picked up some pebbles and one by one she cast them into the river watching the ripples move out in circles. She came to a conclusion that once she and Oris were married they would travel the realm gathering information and to meet the peoples. They will know that she and Oris would rule as one rule and to be seen. *Aye,* she thought. *We be learnin' about our peoples.* She felt a leap of joy within her and she now was ready to return.

THE WEDDING

Love is often the fruit of marriage. ~ Moliere

The day of the wedding arrived. Many people of the realm were arriving. The wedding was taking place in a large meadow for the people to watch. This would be a first time a wedding of this size would be open to the people. Table planks were in one area with soldiers guarding the feast until after the ceremony. Numerous benches had been made for the people to sit or stand on. Only close relatives and friends were given places near the ceremony. A large contingent of Druidesses and Druids were present as friends. Oris' close officers were given spaces along with their wives. There were music, jesters, acrobats and a clear day.

  Magdalena felt excitement within her being. Callan, Lady Alinor, and Mireen were assisting in dressing her in her mother's gown of light purple and gold. Once the dress was on, Lady Alinor began combing and brushing her hair. The red hair fell softly on Magdalena's shoulders. A sash of gold was placed around her waist and in this she tucked the Dagger of Scota. It was Mireen who placed the crown on her head and stepped back with tears in her eyes.

  Magdalena was now ready to walk down the stairs where an open carriage was waiting for her. Oris had left earlier to be with his family. They would be arriving before Magdalena..

  The carriage was festooned with garlands of early fall flowers and leaves. Callan and Lady Alinor rode in the carriage with her. When the carriage moved out of the Garenfeld, Magdalena gasped at the number of people lining the road to the meadow. There were cheers and laughter. She waved and blew them kisses all the while her heart was beating rapidly.

When the carriage arrived at the meadow, a path had been cleared and finally Magdalena had arrived. Slowly she walked the path towards Oris with her eyes only on him. The people were cheering and she stopped in front of Cyran and looked at Oris, she handed her scepter to Callan and then took the hand of Oris. Lord Cyran stepped forward and handed Magdalena a king's crown to Magdalena. Magdalena turned to Oris and asked him to kneel down.

"M'Lord Oris, as the Magentheld of Hy Brasil, I choose yew to be my husbandment. Together we rule Hy Brasil with yew being my beloved consort. She placed the crown on his head and then he stood up and held her hands.

"M'Lady Magentheld, yew be my wife as Magdalena and what you ask me to do as the Magentheld, I will do."

Cyran together with Lady Alinor stepped forward in front of the couple with Cyran giving a blessing.

With truth there be love,
With love there be honor,
With honor there be peace
With peace there be blessing,
With blessing, there be yere soul,
With yere soul there be yere god.
Love that which yew be as a gift to yere husbandment.
Love that which be as a gift to yere wife.
Yew naow be joined.

A Ram's horn blew and drums began beating sending messages out to the realm that the Magentheld and Lord Oris now were wed. Magdalena and Oris began walking through the throngs of people who chose to here for the wedding. Many people had tears of joy streaming down their faces. The feasting had begun and now Magdalena and Oris began walking back to their tables filled with family and guests.

She and Oris then began walking among the large crowd who were straining to touch the couple. Oris' soldiers were their buffer to hold the people back so they would not crush the Magentheld and her beloved Consort.

She and Oris both knew that they would travel around the realm and bring forth a new Hy Brasil.

Thus, began a new era for Hy Brasil.

Acknowledgements

I want to thank Jo Dean from Australia who urged me to write another Magdalene book. It has taken me several years, but I did it.

In addition, I also want to acknowledgement those who have helped me when I had stumbling blocks. Thank you my long-time beautiful friends Karolyn and Robert Hoffman, who have supported me since I published the first *Secrets of the Magdalene Scrolls*. I appreciate all who have helped me - Barbara Callahan, Peter Mooeyman., and Johan Poole

Last, but not least I want to acknowledge my son Kenneth Brown as he is the cover creator for all my books except for *A Christmas Awakening* and *What the Blank Do We Know About the Bible*.

I also want to acknowledge a teacher I have studied under for 27 years. He is called *Ramtha the Enlightened One* and I have attended his *Ramtha School of Enlightenment. An Academy of the Mind*. This is why I enjoy researching many topics for as Sir Francis Bacon said, *"Knowledge Is Power.*

Authors' Notes

In ancient times, Hy Brasil was known as a magical island located to the west of Ireland. Pliny the Elder, a historian and one who roamed the seas and oceans (23-79 A.D.) wrote that the Tuatha De Dannan left their homeland of Ireland after being defeated by the Milesians and went to the island named Hy Brasil. It is considered folklore. But is it?

In 1635, a Captain Rich and his crew spotted the island off the west coast of Ireland where they saw a harbor and headlands before it disappeared in the mist.

In 1644, a Boullaye Le Gouz is alleged to have become as close as one mile from the island and recorded he only saw trees and cattle.

In 1668, Morough Ley is alleged to have been kidnapped and taken to the island. He returned two days later to his home in Seapoint, County Galway. He was given a medical book by his captors written in Latin and Irish. He had been instructed not to open the book for seven years. He complied and at the end of seven years he received the gift of healing and began practicing surgery without being training in medicine. At that time he was thought to be a charlatan who had a good story. The book is known as The *Book of Hy Brasil* and is now held by the library of the Royal Irish Academy in Dublin.

In 1674 there was a Scottish sea captain with the name Nisbet who claimed he had landed on Hy Brasil. He alleged it was inhabited by gigantic black rabbits, a magician in a castle. He was unable to produce any evidence of what he had seen.

From the website of Top Secret Writers:

"One of the earliest known reference of the island stems from Irish myths. Supposedly the island was roughly 200 miles off of the coast of Ireland in the Atlantic Ocean.

It was said to be shrouded in mist, making it invisible to passing sailors. The mist lifts for only one day every seven years.

From there, the legends expound in every direction. In some renditions of the legend, the island is the home of the Gods of Irish lore. In other retellings, Hy-Brasil is inhabited not by gods, but rather by priests or monks.

These monks were rumored to hold a vast and ancient knowledge which allowed them to create an advanced civilization where the inhabitants led a luxurious and near effortless way of life.

No matter which version of the ancient Hy-Brasil story is retold, the two main components that remain the same are the rough location and the element that it was a paradise.

More recently, many individuals have associated the Hy-Brasil legend with Ufology. Some UFO researchers contend that the island was *not* the home of Celtic gods, but instead an alien outpost."

I want to acknowledge two authors whose books helped me to understand the potentials and possibilities of Egyptian presence in Ireland, Scotland and England where artifacts have been found. Even though Scota is buried in Ireland, the country of Scotland was named for her. For those who want to research, the two primary authors I used were Lorraine Evans and Ralph Ellis.

Why did I write this novel? Hy Brasil intrigued me and I have been requested by several readers to write a third book of the Mary Magdalene books: *Secrets of the Magdalene Scrolls* and *Mary Magdalene, Her Legacy*.

There is always a possibility that lineages do bleed through. I chose the name Magdalena because my deceased brother James B. Carter M.D. was an avid ancestry researcher. I learned from him that in 1640 in our lineage, a John Carter married a Magdalena Moore and in another ancestry chart she was given the name Magdalene. There is also in our lineage distant cousins named Moore. Five years ago a daughter was born to my oldest granddaughter and I was surprised when I learned that this baby had been named Magdalena.

I make no claim to being of the lineage of Mary Magdalene; however, it is interesting to note the two names of Magdalena and Magdalene are in my lineage. My maiden name was Carter.

Regarding the origin of the *Book Journey of Discovery* in the chapter titled, *A Journey of Discovery*, I will admit that I created this small book as being found in one of the book stalls along the Seine River in Paris. It came from what I know and learned through this journey of life.

I became interested in Michael Bradley's book *Grail Knights of North America*. His research is well worth the read. His research on Edward, Duke of Kent and later King Edward gives a story of Edward's marriage to "Julia" de Mongenet, Baroness de Mongenet, Baronne de Fortisson. They had five children and when Edward was commanded to return to England and marry a Princess, Edward and Julia sent their five children to a Woods family and the girls to a family named Green. I chose to use the name "Woods" for this book because there is a possibility this is true.

Sometimes we writers do have unpleasant episodes and it is time for me to share one of mine. In 2004 I wrote the 1st Edition of *Secrets of the Magdalena Scrolls*. I was so proud of my book and after it was published, I met another author who said she was also writing a book. It was a few months later that I began reading her book. I was shocked that she had plagiarized the story-line of my book. This author's book was published in 2005. It has taken me eight years to retire my anger and no, I will not give out her name. Yes, I went to an attorney and was told I had a good chance of bringing this to trial and it would cost me at the minimum of $50,000.00. I knew I could not come up with this amount, so I have let this simmer in the recess of my mind.

In that author's book, there are twelve issues that parallel my book. As I read her book, it was as though her characters were mirroring my characters and their routes and travels were almost the same as mine.

I have now come to the conclusion that perhaps I should be grateful that she liked my book enough to include much of it in hers. I am at last at peace. So, if you come across another book that seems to be similar to *Secrets of the Magdalene Scrolls*, smile and bless the author as she needs it.

Bettye Johnson's BIOGRAPHY

Moving from the cotton fields in Texas to the embassies of Paris and Tokyo, Bettye Johnson has a woven tapestry of experiences. Born in 1929, she has experienced the Great Depression along with an environment of bigotry, prejudice and with her many moves became a free thinker. She became employed in the Foreign Service of the U.S. State Department where she worked in the Paris embassy and later the embassy in Tokyo as a code clerk. This position was one of encoding and decoding highly classified messages. Johnson received a fascinating non-academic education from these two tours of duty.

Bettye left the Foreign Service to further her experiences by becoming the wife of a career military man, mother of three sons, a government employee, Federal Women's Program Coordinator for 5 government district offices, program director of a holistic health center, minister of Divine Science, and now an author.

Bettye Johnson is an award-winning author of *Secrets of the Magdalene Scrolls*, an Independent Publishers Book Award Winner 2006 and *Mary Magdalene, Her Legacy*, an Independent Publishers Book Award Winner 2008. Johnson's latest book, *An Uncommon Education, a Memoir* that she tells about her life as a code clerk working *in the American Embassy in Paris for three years.* Her other books are *A Christmas Awakening, Awakening the Genie Within, What the Black Do We Know About the Bible.* The Italian edition of *Secrets of the Magdalene Scrolls* is *Segreti Rivelati Nei Rotoli Di Maria Maddalena.*

I have always been a writer in one form or another. When I was 8 years old and in the third grade, I received a toy typewriter for Christmas. I loved turning the wheel to create words and this was a beginning for me.

Bettye's books are available on Amazon.com as well as
www.bettyejohnson.com
http:magdalenescrolls.com
You can follow Bettye on:
Facebook and Twitter

Will there be another Magdalene book? Not as it is seen in the moment.

With love and hugs to all of you readers,

Bettye Johnson
November 2013

Magdalena of Hy Brasil

A POSTSCRIPT

In September 2013, Bettye received an award from the National Association of Professional Women and named "Woman of the Year ~ 2013/2014" for her category of self-published author.

Thank you NAPW.

Magdalena of Hy Brasil

Magdalena of Hy Brasil

Magdalena of Hy Brasil

CPSIA information can be obtained at www.ICGtesting.com
Printed in the USA
LVOW09s1951171114

414122LV00021B/1245/P

9 781492 393764